DARK
POWERS

DARK POWERS

RAYMOND HAIGH

ROBERT HALE · LONDON

© Raymond Haigh 2015
First published in Great Britain 2015

ISBN 978-0-7198-1757-1

Robert Hale Limited
Clerkenwell House
Clerkenwell Green
London EC1R 0HT

www.halebooks.com

2 4 6 8 10 9 7 5 3 1

Typeset in Janson
Printed in Great Britain by Berforts Information Press Ltd

CHAPTER ONE

DARNEL HALL WAS ISOLATED, hidden within neglected grounds, enclosed by high walls. Its grimy stonework had succumbed to a powdery decay and the once grand interior was stained by patches of dampness. Faded curtains, drawn against prying eyes, were shutting out the golden blaze of a July sunset, and shabby, time-worn furniture lurked amongst shadows in dark, high-ceilinged rooms. On a long table, in a portrait-lined salon, the remains of a cold buffet – gnawed chicken legs, sliced meats, half-eaten rolls, wilting salad – were strewn amongst beer cans, empty wine bottles, paper plates and plastic knives and forks. Behind the closed door of one of the smaller bedrooms, Annushka Dvoskin was being fondled by Vincent Fairchild. His moist kisses and clumsy gropings were beginning to irritate her.

'Promise me, Anna, please promise me.' Vincent breathed the words into her ear.

'Promise you what?' She tried to make herself more comfortable on the sagging mattress.

'You know –' He kissed her neck '– what I asked you before the others arrived.'

She felt his hand creeping up between her legs and squeezed them together to halt its progress. 'No, Vincent!'

'You won't promise me?'

'No, take your hand away, and no, I won't promise you.'

He turned his attention to her breast, chafing the nipple

between his finger and thumb. 'Why won't you promise me?' he demanded petulantly.

'That hurts, Vincent.'

'Sorry.' He made another attempt to kiss her mouth.

Annushka turned her face away and wet lips slid across her cheek. She let out an exasperated sigh. 'Because we all agreed, at the beginning, at the very first party, that we'd avoid attachments and just enjoy ourselves. It spoils things when people become emotionally involved with one another.'

'But I simply can't bear it when I see you going into bedrooms with Farnbeck and Barksdale. I absolutely loathe it.'

'Try to be a little less uptight about things, Vincent, or it's not going to be fun anymore. You may as well stop coming.'

'I bet you wouldn't say that to Farnbeck.' Vincent's tone had become sarcastic. 'I mean, he's a viscount, isn't he? Son of an earl, a member of the bloody aristocracy. Girls seem to get off on that. You wouldn't mind being exclusively involved with him.'

He began to press angry, frustrated kisses on her throat and breasts while his hand made another assault on her thighs.

Annushka sighed. Vincent was being so terribly, terribly boring. Tall, dark haired, handsome in a half-formed way, he was the youthful image of his father. Similarity ended with appearances. When it came to sex he was painfully inept whilst his father was so very accomplished. The Right Honourable Alexander Fairchild had given her the sweetest tenderest kiss when she'd first met him at her friend's wedding, but it wasn't until they'd met for the second time, at that ball, last summer, when everyone was out on the terrace ooing and ahhing at the fireworks, that he'd made her realize what this sex thing was all about. Before Alexander it had always seemed rather meaningless, a part of socializing, something one did after abandoning the pastimes of childhood.

Vincent's father had awakened her to its delights. He hadn't rushed things, he'd been calm and relaxed, not the least bit concerned that they might be discovered on the billiard table. And although he'd been so very gentle, he'd been ... mmm ... not masterful, no ... more like confident and assured, accomplished in the art. He'd murmured such sweet things to her in that deep velvety voice of his, caressing her with words as well as his hands, making her feel protected and secure. And he'd smelt so wonderfully clean and fragrant, not stale and sweaty. Compared to Alexander, the young men and boys she'd encountered were mere beginners in the game of love. If only they could meet more often; if only they could be together always.

A sudden discomfort roused her from her reverie: Vincent's hand had made its way to the top of her thighs. What possessed him to think that his clumsy fumblings could give her any pleasure? She sighed out her exasperation. Better get it over with. Just let him do it. It wouldn't take long. If she didn't, he'd only start throwing the toys out of his pram. Was it just public schoolboys, or was it all boys? So impatient, so insensitive, so utterly inept.

Annushka lifted her haunches and hooked her thumbs under the elastic of her knickers. It was then that she caught the faint sound of voices and laughter approaching along the passageway, heard a distressed girl crying, 'You pig, Julian Barksdale! Give me that phone!' The laughter grew louder as the crowd passed the bedroom door. Rising above it all, a male voice of somewhat affected refinement was saying, 'It's only a memento, Nicole. Something for me to treasure through those long lonely nights when I'm back at Oxford.'

'Give it to me.' The voice was tearfully insistent. 'Give me that phone.'

More jeers and laughter drowned out the girl's pleadings, then the commotion began to fade as the girl and her tormenters jostled on towards the landing and the stairs.

Annushka pushed Vincent away and propped herself up on her elbows. 'What was that all about?'

'Some of the boys have been creeping around, taking pictures and videos of people having sex. They've been doing it for most of the evening. They were doing it at the last party.'

Alarmed, she swung her legs from the bed, picked up her short black skirt and wriggled into it. 'Have you been doing it, Vincent?' She slid her feet into black patent leather shoes, then pulled a crimson sweater over her head.

'Not had a chance, have I? I grabbed this room for us, then waited ages while you were with Benson. I told you I was going to find a room. Couldn't you have stayed with me, let me be first for once?'

Ignoring him, she snatched up her bag, then, on an after-thought, took his phone and car keys from amongst a pile of coins on the bedside table.

'Dammit, Anna, we've not finished. We've not even started. I waited ages, and now you're dashing off. Come back to bed. Don't take any notice of those silly buggers. Come back . . .'

She opened the door and looked towards the landing. Young men in various stages of undress, some completely naked, were jostling around a naked girl. One of them was holding a mobile phone above his head. Distressed and agitated, she was leaping up, breasts bouncing as she tried to snatch it from him. Annushka turned and peered into the gloom at the other end of the passage-way. A dark-haired girl was leaning out of a doorway, exposing a naked hip and shoulder.

'What's all the shouting about?' the girl asked.

'They've been taking pictures and videos.'

'What sort of pictures?

'Intimate pictures. Couples having sex. Is anyone in the room with you?'

'He's gone to the bathroom.'

'Get dressed,' Annushka urged. 'Take his mobile, then come and help me find as many phones as we can. I don't want snigger-ing boys watching videos of me.'

Annushka darted into the adjoining bedroom. A naked girl, her long hair dyed blue, was sitting on a rumpled bed sharing a joint with a girl in black satin underwear. Annushka searched jackets and trousers strewn on the floor, found two phones, then turned to leave.

'Looking for something?' The blue-haired girl's voice was slurred. She giggled, then passed the badly made spliff to her friend. The girl in black underwear dragged on it, grinned sleepily, then passed it back.

Deciding it was best not to spread the word, Annushka said, 'Car keys. We're going to put them in a bowl, then we're each going to choose a set, find fresh partners, liven things up a bit.' She noticed a mobile phone on a dressing table, crossed threadbare carpet and snatched it up. The two girls were giggly and relaxed, their dulled senses hardly able to grasp, much less remember, that a tall blonde girl in a short skirt had taken something.

'Don't forget to tell us when you start the draw,' the girl in black underwear called after her. 'And make sure you leave a Rolls or a Jag for me,' cried the other. They collapsed in a fit of giggles.

As she emerged into the passageway, Annushka almost bumped into the dark-haired girl, who'd put on a black dress. She said, 'I don't know your name.'

'Rebecca. Rebecca Fenton. Yours?'

'Annushka.'

Together they crept into more bedrooms. The occupiers had either left to see what all the noise was about, or were too engrossed in one another to notice two girls searching the pockets of discarded clothes. Between them they found six more phones. Small, smooth and slippery, it was difficult to hold on to more than two. Annushka peeled the cover from a pillow and they dropped the phones inside.

'I'll check the bathrooms,' Rebecca said. 'Some of them may have left jackets in there.'

The young men's shouts and laughter became a chant as they grabbed the protesting girl's arms and legs and hoisted her, kicking and screaming, above their heads. They'd emerged from the passageway and were progressing along a wide landing that curved above a columned entrance hall. Terrified now, her frantic pleadings mingled with the clamour of male voices echoing around the vast shadowy space.

Alarmed and revolted, but unable to tear her eyes away, Annushka watched from a safe distance. The naked girl was being tossed in the air by a gang of youths made wild and senseless by drink and drugs. Moved by some impulse, Annushka took her own mobile phone from her bag; deft fingers pressed keys, touched icons, then she pointed its tiny eye towards the melee and began to capture the scene.

The jostling became more violent, less controlled; the girl's screams shriller and more terrified. To the sound of cheers and inane laughter, the young men began to throw her higher and higher. She suddenly bounced from their grasp and tumbled, arms and legs flailing, over the balustrade. Hands reached out and snatched at calves and ankles, but she slid free. There was an audible thud when her head hit the chequered marble floor of the hall below. Shocked into silence, the stupefied youths lined up along the marble handrail and peered down at the body.

Annushka pointed her phone towards the sprawling figure of the girl. The head seemed misshapen, flattened, compressed into the shoulders, and blood was oozing over the tiles. Fear aroused in her an instinct to flee. She turned, left the landing and ran back down the passageway, calling Rebecca's name.

The dark-haired girl emerged from a bathroom and dropped two more phones into the pillow case. 'Run,' Annushka insisted. She grabbed the older girl's hand and pulled her along.

'Why?'

'They've thrown Nicole down into the hall. She's got to be dead.'

'Oh my God,' Rebecca moaned, and ran faster.

'Over here.' Annushka steered her through a door and they plunged down winding flights of servants' stairs. 'This leads to the kitchens in the basement. They lock the outer doors and the windows on the ground floor are too high to jump from, but we can climb out of one down there.'

'Aren't there any lights?' Rebecca panted. 'I can't see a thing.'

'Don't know where the switches are, but I know the passage-ways. I used to play hide-and-seek here when I was a child.'

Heels clattering over stone floors, they turned into a short corridor where some light filtered in through a grimy window at the bottom of a glazed brick shaft, then pushed through a door and staggered, panting, into a large and gloomy kitchen.

Annushka crossed over to an old porcelain sink, climbed in and released the catch on the window above it. When she tried to lift the sash it wouldn't move. She glanced around, saw an old iron saucepan, grabbed the handle and swung it at the glass. The crash as it shattered was alarmingly loud, but she continued to wield the pan, breaking away the jagged remnants still lodged in the frame.

'Is that a rug?' Annushka nodded towards a rectangle of dark-ness on the floor beside a big Welsh dresser.

Rebecca lifted a corner and confirmed that it was.

'Bring it here.'

She dragged it across to the sink, Annushka grasped the end and heaved it over the window frame to protect them from splin-ters of glass, then took Rebecca's hand and helped her up. They clambered out of the chilly dampness of the basement kitchen into the fading light and lingering warmth of the summer evening.

A flight of worn stone steps took them up to ground level. Annushka glanced back at Rebecca. 'Have you got a car?'

'Left it at home. Don't like driving when I've been partying, so I asked one of the boys to pick me up in town. Someone called Stoggers – I'm sure that's not his real name. He told me he's the eldest son of the fourth Baron Pelgrove.'

Unimpressed, Annushka said, 'They're all the sons of some-thing or other. We'll take Vincent's. I've got the keys.'

They ran, hand in hand, round to the front of the house where

11

a number of cars were parked, some on weed-invaded gravel, some on a lawn lumpy and coarse for want of care. The facade of the old building towered over them, a dark and brooding silhouette against the evening sky. Not a single gleam of light escaped through the curtained windows; not a sound could be heard. It was as if there had been no revelry, as if a young girl's life hadn't ended, just a few brief moments ago, in the hall behind the impressive entrance doors.

Annushka clicked a key. The lights on a yellow Mini Cooper blinked. She tugged open the driver's door and slid behind the wheel. Rebecca clambered in beside her. Doors slammed, the engine fired, and Annushka crashed her way through the gears as they snarled off down the drive.

'Should we be running away like this?' Rebecca's voice was panicky and scared. 'They'll have to call the police and the police will want to interview everyone who was here.'

Annushka braked hard, sent gravel flying as they spun out on to a narrow country lane. 'The idiots who killed Nicole can talk to the police. And there's coke dust everywhere: on tables, in the bathrooms.' She risked a glance at Rebecca. 'Did you snort any?'

'Just a couple of lines.'

'Well, then, that's another reason to get away. They'll test everyone. If you stay, you'll be charged with possessing. And if they do contact us we can say we got tired of it all and left early and we don't know a thing about Nicole being thrown off the landing. Did anyone see you taking the phones?'

'Don't think so. The one or two that hadn't gone out onto the landing were too stoned or squiffy to remember anything.'

'That's OK then. Charlotte and a girl with blue hair saw me, but I told them I was collecting car keys for a draw.' Annushka braked, negotiated a bend, then changed the subject. 'Did you go to Martha's?'

Rebecca tried to brace herself against the erratic motion of the car. How could Annushka chatter on so calmly about nothing when a girl was lying dead back there?

'Martha's,' Annushka prompted. She stood on the brakes and dragged the car round a sharper bend. 'Did you go to the Martha Hemmingway School for Girls?'

Rebecca let out a breath. 'That's right. And you?'

'I'm still there.'

'Still there?' She gave Annushka a surprised look.

'Going into the sixth form when the autumn term starts.'

'You look much older than that.'

Annushka laughed. 'Everyone thinks so. It can be useful. Who invited you along to the parties?'

'Teddy Farnbeck. We went to Oxford together, met up again at Charlotte's twenty-first, about a month ago.'

'Viscount Farnbeck? He's a bit of a Hooray Henry, don't you think?'

'I think he's rather sweet,' Rebecca retorted sharply.

'They all can be for a while, then they get bored and become rough and you can tell they couldn't care less about you. What did you do after Martha's?'

'Oxford. Took a history degree, then Daddy got me a job as PA to one of the directors of Volmack Financial Services, at their head office in Cheltenham.'

'That where you live?'

'Yes. I used to have a flat there, but last year I had problems and decided to move. Daddy bought me a little house closer to the town centre, in a Regency terrace. It's rather pretty and very convenient. And you?'

'Underhill Grange, in the countryside, east of Gloucester. But I'm away at school during the week and out and about most weekends now Father's away. He's on his honeymoon.' Annushka's voice took on a bitter edge. 'It's his third. He's spirited her away on his yacht. They're cruising in the Aegean.'

'You don't care for your new stepmother?'

'She's a bitch. Even worse than the second. They only want

his money, but he can't see it. And they get younger and younger. This one can't be much older than you. Tatiana Milosovitch, as was. Now she's Tatiana Dvoskin.'

'Your father's Vladimir Dvoskin? CT and T Dvoskin?'

'That's him. Copper, tin and titanium: CT and T. That's the name he trades under in the West.'

'We buy and sell shares in his companies for clients.'

Annushka swung into a bend. A wall loomed in the headlights. She stood on the brakes and heaved at the wheel. Tyres screeched, they mounted the verge then bounced back on the road and swayed on. Her voice unruffled, she asked, 'I presume it was man problems that made you want to leave?'

Rebecca glanced at Annushka. 'Leave?'

'Leave the flat, find another place, move on.'

'You're very perceptive.'

Annushka let out a bitter little laugh. 'My father sent my real mother to the grave, divorced my first stepmother, and now he's got married again. I watch and learn.'

'It became too intense,' Rebecca explained. 'He was possessive, a bit controlling, rather boring. When I told him it was over he was really upset. I'd been giving him hints for weeks but he didn't get the message. I had to be very blunt with him at the end. I was a bit afraid he might become difficult and start pestering me, keep on calling at the flat, so I found somewhere else as quickly as I could.'

'And did he?'

'Did he what?'

'Become difficult?'

'No, thank God. After we'd parted I saw him at our offices once or twice – his firm upgraded the computer system, that's how we met – but when I said hello he just blushed and looked away. He seemed a bit crushed. I suppose he wanted to settle down and I didn't. Anyway, he wasn't husband material. I can't think what Daddy would have made of him.'

They careered around another bend, tyres screeching, road signs flaring in the headlights. 'I really am worried about us running away like this,' Rebecca moaned when she'd got her breath back. 'It could make us look guilty.'

'Guilty of what? *They* threw Nicole down from the landing. Trust me, it's best to clear off. We both left early, remember, and we didn't see a thing.' They crested the brow of a hill, then plunged down into a shallow valley, fences and hedgerows a blur as they flashed past. 'Have you got those mobiles?'

Rebecca lifted the pillowcase from the footwell.

'How many did we find? Count them and make sure they're all switched off or they'll be able to trace them.'

She checked the phones. 'Nine . . . No, ten.'

'You hang on to them. Put them in a biscuit tin and hide them somewhere. And put mine in, too. I videoed them on the landing. It's in my bag.'

'Don't you want to take care of them?' Rebecca, uneasy about keeping the things, groped for Annushka's bag in the gap between the seats.

'The housekeeper and the security men are always nosing around. They'd be sure to find them and start asking questions.'

Rebecca clicked the bag open, found two phones amongst the clutter. 'Which one? The monogrammed white one or the red one?'

'The red. The white one's faulty. Battery always needs recharging.'

Rebecca dropped the red phone in the pillowcase. 'And why put them in a biscuit tin?'

'Grigori told me mobiles had to be put in a tin or wrapped in cooking foil if you wanted to prevent them being traced. Either that or take the batteries out. He said the police and phone companies can sometimes locate them, even when you think they're switched off.'

'Who's Grigori?'

'One of my father's security men. He was trained by the KGB.' Annushka laughed. 'He lusts after me. I torment him, let him catch glimpses of me in my underwear, but he daren't touch me; he'd be dismissed on the spot. He's gone with the party on the yacht. I think he was glad to get away.'

As they climbed out of the valley, the car's headlights probed a tunnel formed by the overhanging branches of trees. 'I'll take you to Cheltenham,' Annushka said. 'If the police come looking for me they'll probably go to Underhill, so I'm going to drive on to our flat in London. Anyway, I don't feel like going to Underhill. The housekeeper's always going on about me being out all the time and threatening to tell Father.' She frowned at Rebecca and made her voice stern. 'Just remember, if the police talk to us, we left early, and we didn't see a thing.'

CHAPTER TWO

SAMANTHA FELT CRISPIN'S FINGERS under her chin, tilting her head. She closed her eyes. Scissors, cool on her brow, began to snip, and wisps of raven-black hair drifted down on to the towel draped around her shoulders.

'You ought to keep out of the sun,' Crispin murmured absently.

She opened her eyes. He was concentrating on the heavy fringe that almost covered her brow, flicking at it with his comb, snipping with his scissors, deftly trimming and shaping. His features were softening, she reflected, becoming less youthful. If anything, it made him even more handsome. She said huskily, 'Natural vitamin D: sunlight's good for you.'

'Take a tablet. The sun will ruin your hair, make it lose its shine, its body. And it ages women. Your skin's too delicate, love. It simply can't stand it.' He frowned down at her while he teased her abundant, not quite shoulder-length hair with his comb. 'You'll do,' he said presently. 'When you comb it, draw the ends inwards and forward a little. It'll keep its shape longer.'

He unwrapped the towel from her shoulders, shook filaments of hair into the bath, then lifted the lever that opened the outlet. 'What was that American woman – Fienburg, Finklestein, or whatever her name is – saying to you when we were leaving the dining room?'

'She said you looked absolutely adorable. She can't take her eyes off you. She's been giving you longing looks ever since we arrived.'

'Poor thing.' He beamed; compliments delighted him. 'Philippe said much the same to me, last night.'

'How's it going?' She watched him wipe the sides of the bath and steer hair clippings towards the outlet.

'It's been pleasant, but it's just a holiday fling, nothing serious. Have you decided?'

'Decided?'

'Which of those two dresses you're going to buy?'

'Can't make my mind up. The skirt on the Vuitton's a bit short and the Moschino's rather severe, but they'd both be OK for the autumn.'

'Your bum and tits really do something for the Moschino. You look sensational in it: sex on legs. You could charge double.'

Samantha laughed. Crispin was convinced she was a high-class whore. She nurtured his illusions.

'And those Escada shoes and bag were made for it,' he chattered on. 'The shade of grey's perfect, and they'd stop it looking quite so plain.' He squeezed out the sponge and stood up. 'Your eyes are the problem, love. Brown or grey aren't difficult, but that green can clash so.'

She studied her reflection in the mirror over the basin. 'It's got to be the Moschino, then.' Crispin was right, as usual. She pursed her lips and began to colour them the same vivid red as her nails. 'I'll collect it this morning. Are you coming?'

'May as well. Philippe's working.' He slid a sleeveless silk dress from a hanger behind the door and passed it to her. Samantha removed her robe, stepped into it and eased the fitted skirt over her hips. A phone began to ring in the bedroom. Crispin picked up the robe and hurried out.

She heard him asking, 'Does she have a name? No. OK, I'll fetch her, just a moment.' His head appeared around the bathroom door. 'It's a woman, for you. Reception are holding the call. She wouldn't give her name.'

Samantha went through, sat on the edge of the ornate ivory and gilt bed and picked up the phone.

'We have a caller for you, madam. She refuses to give her name. May I put her through?'

'Of course.'

The line clicked, then: 'We have met and spoken before. Do you recognize me?'

Samantha had met the woman only a couple of times, but the voice was unmistakable. Clear and commanding, this morning it had a tense, brittle edge to it. She said, 'I know who you are.'

'No need for names, then. I'd like you to come back to England.'

'Now?'

'Now. I want you back as soon as you can get here.'

'My contract ended more than a month ago.'

'You can have another. I need you here.'

'Something's happened?'

'Events are unfolding.'

Samantha closed her eyes. Loretta Fallon contacting her personally: it had to be something catastrophic. She didn't want this right now.

'Your flight's been booked on British Airways: Paris Orly to London Heathrow. Departure's scheduled for twelve noon. When you arrive in London, take a taxi to the Connaught Hotel in Chertsey, it's a couple of miles outside the town, on the Shepperton Road. I'll be waiting for you there, in the cocktail bar. It's the room on your right as you enter the foyer.'

The phone went dead.

Crispin appeared from the bathroom. 'Problems?'

'A friend. She can't keep an appointment with a client. She's asked me to stand in. He's a regular; she doesn't want to let him down.'

'You're going back to England?'

'She's booked me on a twelve o'clock flight. Why don't you stay here? There's no reason why this should spoil things for you.'

'Will you come back?'

'Can't say. I could be gone a few days.' She turned her back to him. 'Come and zip me up.'

He crossed over to the bed, slid the zip up from her waist, then linked the tiny fastening at the back of her neck. 'I may as well say goodbye to Philippe and travel home tomorrow. I don't particularly want to stay on if you're not going to be here, and I ought to get back to the salon.' He glanced at his watch. 'There's not much time. I'll fetch some cases from my room and help you pack. What about all the stuff you've bought?'

'Bring it in the car for me.'

'And the Moschino?'

'Buy the Moschino and the Vuitton, and the bag and shoes. If you see any other shoes and things you think are OK, get them, too. I'll leave you my card.'

'I don't know how I'm going to cram it all in the Ferrari. I'll be ages going through customs. And heaven knows what they're going to make of all the underwear.'

Samantha wandered across a sea of blue and gold carpet, stood by an elegantly curtained window and gazed down the tree-lined boulevard. 'It's been pleasant here, Crispin. Best hotel we've stayed at this year. I think I've enjoyed it more than Venice.'

'You seem a bit down, love.'

She turned and smiled at him. 'Back-to-work blues, that's all. I'm not looking forward to a night and a day, perhaps a few nights and days, of smiling and pretending. I can be myself when I'm with you.'

Lionel Blessed settled himself a little lower, a little more comfortably, into his seat. He was concealed beneath the trees at the back of a tiny car park. His was the only car; the residents of the narrow street had either gone to their places of work or driven away on other business. From here he could study the house where Rebecca lived: bottle-green front door and tall sash window on the ground floor, two smaller windows above. Glass gleamed darkly against cream-painted stucco, and a parapet hid the roof. It was all very Regency, very Cheltenham. He could hear Rebecca saying, 'Such a sweet little house,' in that sexy top-drawer voice of hers. Daddy must have bought it for her, just as he'd bought her the flat and the car. She was letting the flat now. He'd seen it advertised in an estate agent's window. One evening, a few weeks ago, desperate to discover her new address, he'd followed her as she'd driven home from work. This was where she'd led him.

Afraid of the dark things he might uncover, he didn't care to think too deeply about why he was here. His motives, his urges, were too tangled and confused to confront. He came here twice, sometimes three times a week, almost always during the day when the car park was deserted, and spent an hour or so gazing across at the tiny house where Rebecca ate and slept, bathed and dressed. It wasn't rational, he knew that, and he'd always prided himself on being an ordered, rational person: his job demanded it. Quite soon after they'd parted he'd realized it was more than an overwhelming physical attraction he'd felt for her. He'd loved her; he'd loved her very deeply. He still did. She was constantly in his thoughts. In fleeting moments of brutal self-honesty he was forced to admit he was sad, obsessed and unbearably lonely.

The pain and longing wouldn't go away. He seemed to miss her more and more. The six months they'd been together in her flat had been the happiest of his life. Even when she'd stopped being affectionate, when she'd become critical and hard to please, being with her had been preferable to this miserable loneliness. That old proverb, better to have loved and lost than never to have loved at all, was utter nonsense. In his experience it was far better never to have met than have to bear this intolerable pain, this overwhelming feeling of loss. At least he'd been spared the torture of jealousy. She'd not inflicted that on him. On the admittedly few occasions when he'd seen her leave and return home, she'd always been alone, and there didn't appear to be anyone else living here.

They'd met when his firm sent him to Cheltenham to oversee

the upgrading of a computer installation at Volmack's. The offices were luxurious, located in what had once been a Regency mansion close to the town centre. Her manager had had responsibility for the project, and he'd assigned Rebecca to deal with day-to-day problems. Refined, poised, full of public-schoolgirl confidence, she'd bowled him over. And she'd always been so tastefully dressed; dark haired, dark eyed, shapely not skinny, her pale silky skin always so fragrant, and her . . . Lionel swallowed hard, blinked back tears, admonished himself. He was stupid, sitting here, staring at her house, dreaming, remembering, scratching away at the scabs, endlessly reliving the pain. He really must try to get a grip.

She'd asked him to fix her laptop, sort out her internet connection, get her printer working properly. He'd gone round to her flat, she'd given him a meal and he'd offered to do a few jobs for her: fix the sagging doors on the kitchen cupboards, replace light fittings, help her with the redecorating. After a while she'd said it was senseless him travelling to and from Gloucester every day, and he should move in. It was then he'd assumed they were in a serious relationship.

That public-school assertiveness had been very evident in the bedroom. Always the one to take the initiative, she'd been completely uninhibited, shedding her refinement with her clothes. In the end he'd been slow to realize what was happening, that her interest was waning. Her nights out with the girls had become more frequent. When he'd protested, they'd had arguments. When she'd returned, sometimes in the early hours, she'd rejected his advances. And now he couldn't get her, or the things they'd done together, out of his mind. It was like a loop of film, endlessly turning, reviving memories, arousing him, intensifying his sense of loss.

He'd tried to divert himself; to fill his life with other things. He'd moved into a new house, renewed his hi-fi system, changed his car, done some freelance work. And he'd joined an internet group called *Pickcraft*. Its members practised and perfected lock-picking skills. Just as a hobby, of course; their slogan, *Stay Within the Law*, was repeated like a mantra. The craft demanded intense concentration. A mental picture had to be formed of what was happening inside the lock, a delicacy of touch had to be cultivated. It was a distraction that had done more than anything else to soothe and relax him; to prevent him sliding into total despair.

Cylinder locks had been fairly easy to master. After practising for a few nights, he'd become quite adept. He'd bought an expensive set of picks but experience had taught him that two were enough; none at all if you just 'bumped' the lock with a deeply serrated key. No one realized how easy it was to open a cylinder lock. Knowing how, and becoming able to do it with such ease, had given him a great feeling of satisfaction.

Mortise locks were more difficult, but even these soon yielded after the skills had been acquired. Getting hold of locks to practise on had been a problem, but members of the club circulated locks through the post, and they were generous in sharing experience and giving advice. Once you had a selection of picks, it was simply a case of practice, practice and more practice. The lonely evenings had given him plenty of time for that.

An idea had formed in his mind while he'd been honing his skills. Perhaps it had been there from the very beginning, lurking in some dark recess before creeping into his consciousness. He'd begun to contemplate using his newly acquired skills to gain entry to Rebecca's house; explore it, look through the cupboards and drawers, touch her clothes, her underwear, breathe in her fragrance, read her correspondence. He felt that, in some mysterious way, it would enable him to share in her life again, to enjoy, once again, their former intimacy.

The back garden was accessible only from the house; the tiny paved area at the front was enclosed by iron railings and a dense hedge that hid the refuse bin. A couple of weeks ago he'd checked the profile of the key aperture on the cylinder latch, checked the keyway for the mortise lock. There'd be no problems. The locks were conventional. Picking the mortise lock would take no more than thirty seconds; the cylinder lock could be 'bumped'. The street was usually deserted, seldom any pedestrians, just the occasional car going to or coming from a small luxury housing development on adjoining land. And the hedge limited visibility; a person would have to stand in the gateway to see what he was doing at the front door.

But not today. This afternoon he had to commission an installation in Oxford, and once he was inside the house he wanted to linger and savour the experience. No point taking the risk without maximizing the satisfaction.

Rebecca closed and locked the front door, kicked off her shoes and headed down the narrow hallway to the kitchen. She filled the kettle, switched it on, then went up to her bedroom to change. Through the windows she could see the tiny residents' car park where her little white Fiat and Mrs Novak's blue Micra were parked in the shadows beneath the big trees. The terrace was full of single women: working, retired, divorced, widowed. There were no families. The houses were a bit too small for families. In fact, her new home wasn't much bigger than the flat she'd left, but it was more interesting, had more possibilities. She suddenly wondered how Lionel was. Probably still plodding along in his boring old way. He'd have been useful here for all the fixing and decorating, but she couldn't cope with his quiet dullness, his inhibitions, his controlling ways, the jealous anger when she went out on her own and the unpleasantness when she returned. She craved the excitement of new experiences, the freedom to find herself. She shivered. Last night's adventure had been chastening. She didn't want to go through anything like that again.

Rebecca drew the curtains and took off her dress. Her body was still trembling. She'd felt scared and sick all day, unable to concentrate on her work, dreading a call announcing that the police were in reception and they'd like to talk to her. But nothing had happened. No one had tried to contact her. Everything had been normal. Her boss had noticed something was wrong. She'd told him she felt unwell and he'd urged her to take the afternoon off. He was really sweet, very appreciative and considerate, delegated heaps of things to her so her job was never boring. He was retiring at the end of the year. She wasn't looking forward to that. She put her dress on a hanger, pulled on her jeans and a cotton top, then reached under the bed for her comfortable shoes.

The tiredness was really getting to her now. That was probably why she felt so nervy and scared. Annushka had got her home before eleven, but she hadn't fallen asleep until the sky had begun to lighten. She'd just laid in bed, shaking, dreading the knock on the door, dreading the arrival of the police. Ever since she'd been a child she'd been a bit scared of policemen. They were big and faintly menacing, always silent and watchful. Last night her pulse had quickened every time a car had whispered down the street and her ears had strained for the creak of the gate.

She returned to the tiny kitchen, made a mug of tea and a ham sandwich. She'd eaten nothing all day. Hunger could be making her feel nervy and unwell, quite apart from the tiredness. She took them into the sunlit sitting room at the rear of the house, pushed aside swatches of curtain fabric, then sank into the sofa and clicked on the television. Conflict in the Middle East, wranglings in parliament, a scare about processed meat, the flatlining economy; there was nothing on the rolling news programmes about the death of an MP's daughter at Darnel Hall.

Perhaps Annushka had been right; perhaps it had been wise to just drive away from trouble. She slid her mug on to a low table and wandered back to the kitchen for a biscuit. Only three chocolate ones left. She took them all, then re-sealed the plastic bag. The tin box that had held them was down in the cellar, crammed with the mobile phones and hidden under a big stone shelf. It was the first thing she'd done when she'd arrived home last night.

Annushka had seemed so streetwise, so worldly. Perhaps her mother's death, two stepmothers, housekeepers, all of those security men, had matured her, made her older and smarter than her years. Thinking about it, Rebecca wished now that she hadn't let her dump the phones on her. The story about prying housekeepers and nosy security men wasn't all that convincing, but she'd been so assertive. Surely Annushka could have hidden them somewhere? And what were they going to do with them? She reminded herself that one or more could hold images of her doing intimate things with Julian or Timothy, or any one of half a dozen other men if videos had been made at earlier parties. They'd probably been wise to take as many as they could find. The phones were safely hidden. She'd wait a few days, then contact Annushka and discuss what was to be done with them. Perhaps the best thing would be to break them up with a hammer and put the pieces in the refuse bin. Just get rid of the things.

CHAPTER THREE

SAMANTHA STOOD BESIDE THE reception desk in the Connaught Hotel, looking across the foyer into the cocktail bar. Red leather chairs, clustered around low circular tables, formed islands on a carpet of a deeper red. Wood panelling, its varnish darkened by age and tobacco smoke, made the room seem dingy. Loretta Fallon was its only occupant. She was sitting beside a window at the far end, well away from the bar and the entrance, gazing out over sunlit gardens.

Her appearance hadn't changed: iron-grey hair drawn tightly back and tied with a black ribbon, navy-blue suit with a pencil skirt, white silk blouse with a choker collar, black low-heeled shoes. Clothing that was more uniform than fashion statement. Her features, large for a woman, were composed, her posture relaxed. If the Department was in the grip of a crisis, she was betraying no sign of it.

'Can I help you, madam?'

Samantha turned. A tall grey-haired man was smiling at her across the reception desk.

'I'm meeting someone in the cocktail bar. Until we've talked, I don't know whether or not I'll be booking a room. May I leave my cases here for a while?'

'Of course, madam. I'll have them carried into the office.'

She crossed the foyer, passed through the doorway and moved silently over thick carpet towards Loretta. When she was close,

27

she murmured, 'Miss Fallon.'

The woman turned. Cool grey eyes looked up at her and thin lips pulled into a smile. 'Miss Quest.' A long and slender hand gestured towards a chair. 'Thank you for coming.'

'Did I have any alternative?'

'You could have just walked away.'

'Curiosity overcame me.' Samantha sat down and smoothed the skirt of her dress.

'Can I order you some tea? A drink from the bar?'

Samantha shook her head.

Elbows on the arms of her chair, chin resting on linked fingers, Loretta Fallon studied the woman facing her across the table. Marcus Soames was right, she mused. Quite beautiful, but what man would want to wake and find those huge green eyes staring into his? Ice cold and still as death, they seemed to freeze one's mind. Her gaze lowered to slender arms, lightly tanned, the sleeveless dress, perfectly cut and of a pale bluish-grey, the matching bag and shoes. Very elegant. And the gleaming black hair had been exquisitely cut and styled. Perhaps she'd been travelling with the hairdresser, the male model. Loretta sniffed. 'Was your friend Crispin with you when I called?'

'We were holidaying together. I've left him behind. How did you find me?'

'I always know where you are. How did you explain the sudden departure?'

'I told him a friend had asked me to take over an appointment with one of her regulars. He thinks I'm a high-class whore.'

Loretta laughed softly. 'We're all whores, Miss Quest, selling some part of ourselves for food and clothes and shelter. Your hair gave you away. He's shaped and styled it perfectly. And did he choose the dress?'

Samantha nodded.

'Marcus told me he helps you choose your clothes. He has impeccable taste.'

'He has an eye for colour.' Changing the subject, Samantha asked, 'How is Marcus?'

'Fine, as far as I know. He's been taking a few days' leave; spending them with Charlotte and his daughters on the farm. He's driving back to London today.' She straightened herself in the chair. 'We'd better talk about why you're here.'

'I presume it's serious?'

'If it's not handled deftly, it could assume catastrophic proportions.' Loretta drew a breath, then began. 'I was called to number ten in the early hours of this morning and taken into the Cabinet Room. The Prime Minister, the Home Secretary, the Foreign Secretary and the Metropolitan Police Commissioner were there. I could feel the tension the moment I stepped through the door.

'It seems the night before there'd been a party at a place called Darnel Hall, a run-down old house owned by Earl Farnbeck. It was a gathering of the offspring of the elite: cabinet ministers' sons, a couple of viscounts, possibly a more elevated member of the aristocracy. They couldn't, or wouldn't, give me a list of the people who'd been at the party, but I gathered that the young men had all attended a very exclusive public school called Conningbeck, and the young women had been educated at the Martha Hemmingway School for Girls.' She saw the shadow of a smile touch Samantha's lips. 'You know it?'

Samantha nodded. 'School motto is *Educate, Enlighten, Empower.* I've had dealings with one of its former pupils.'

Loretta hurried on. 'During the course of the evening a girl died – the PM kept referring to it as a tragic accident – and one of the young men, Viscount Barksdale, contacted his father. His father conferred with Earl Farnbeck, and they passed the problem up the line. An hour later, Buckingham Palace had dispatched one of the Queen's Lord Lieutenants, Major Sir Kelvin Makewood, to the hall. I wasn't told what transpired while he was there, but by the time he'd left, Sir Nigel Dillon, the Police Commissioner, had visited the scene with one of his senior officers, the dead girl had been taken away in an ambulance and Alfred Mortmane had been lined up to do an early-morning post-mortem. The partygoers all insisted they hadn't seen her fall from the landing, but they did say she enjoyed sliding down the marble handrail of the stairs. They could only think she'd lost her balance and tumbled down into the entrance hall.'

'There was a forensic investigation?'

Loretta shook her head, 'There was no forensics team. Sir Nigel and the plain clothes officer went unsupported. I've got someone in the Met. He's trying to find out what he can, but as yet there's no incident report in their system and no gossip about it amongst the force. Mortmane released his report on the autopsy about 9 a.m. It confirmed that death had resulted from a fall from a considerable height, with the impact to the crown of the victim's head. He also recorded extensive bruising to the limbs and torso of a kind caused by rough handling, and an unusually large quantity of semen in the vaginal canal. He suggested this was consistent with the deceased having had sexual intercourse with several men shortly before her death. He was told to edit the report by removing all reference to the bruising and the semen.'

Samantha raised an eyebrow.

'Presumably they thought bruising wasn't consistent with an accidental death. The girl was the daughter of Lucas Manning, an MP considered to be a rising star in the party; no doubt they wanted to spare him and the party the embarrassment of the comment about semen.'

'The politicians told you all this?'

'They told me as little as they could. After I left the meeting I gave instructions for all communications between the parties to be monitored, round the clock. Mortmane faxed his handwritten report on the autopsy through to number ten, the PM phoned him back within minutes, then faxed him a copy of the report with the offending statements redacted. He took pains to make clear to the pathologist what he was expected to write. We intercepted and printed out the exchanges.'

'And Mortmane went along with all this?'

'Protested vehemently when the PM phoned him. When he was reminded he'd been pencilled on to next year's Honours list, a knighthood, he decided to go along with it.'

'Have the girl's parents been told?'

'Dillon gave them the news, told them the girl's features had been badly distorted by the fall, said she'd been identified by friends and by documents in her handbag, and they need only view the body if they wished.'

'And how have they reacted?'

'We've heard nothing so far. Lucas Manning has his political career to consider and, quite apart from that, the family might not want to kick up a fuss and have the media nosing around.'

Samantha smiled. 'It seems the establishment's closed ranks and stitched things up very neatly. Why involve you?'

'There's a little more. Vincent Fairchild, the Foreign Secretary's son, was given a grilling by his parents when he arrived home. He'd had to beg a lift because someone had taken his car. When his father asked him why he didn't phone so he could be collected, he said his phone had been taken, and that most, if not all, of the young men at the party had lost their phones, too. He was with a girl called Annushka Dvoskin. Apparently when she learned that boys had been taking intimate photographs and videos of couples, she snatched his phone and car keys and ran out of the room. He presumed she'd gone through other rooms, grabbing what phones she could, then driven off in his car.

'His mother contacted Dillon at the Met, told him the girl who'd taken her son's car had also taken phones that held embarrassing images. By that time the police had picked her up on the M25 and were going to charge her with taking the car without consent and driving without a licence. The girl told the police she knew nothing about phones, said hers wasn't working because the batteries needed charging, then became truculent and defiant.

When they checked her phone it was completely dead. They found nothing in the car and returned it to the Fairchilds within the hour. They were instructed to take the girl to a secure children's unit just outside Gloucester, not to charge her, and not keep any record of the incident.'

'This Annushka Dvoskin,' Samantha murmured, 'does she have any connection with the Russian oligarch, Vladimir Dvoskin?'

'His only child.' Loretta reached down beside her chair, lifted an attaché case onto her knees and clicked it open. She leafed through a folder, plucked out a glossy ten-by-eight photograph and passed it across the table.'

Samantha studied it. 'Very pretty: she's going to be a beautiful woman.'

Loretta retrieved the image. 'I understand she has her father's temperament: Slavonic grit and determination combined with a boldness that verges on arrogance. People who've met her say she's smart and extremely precocious, the product of a difficult child-hood. Her mother and father were forever raging at one another and she was cared for by a succession of nannies and minders. The atmosphere in the home was so poisonous, the child so wild and rebellious, none of them stayed long. When the mother died the father settled her in England and sent her to boarding school.'

'Has her father been informed? Incarcerating a wealthy Russian's daughter without legal process could prove embarrassing.'

'I made that point. He's honeymooning on his yacht, a vessel of considerable size, with his third wife. They're cruising – Black Sea, Mediterranean, Aegean – and not easy to contact. His daughter was heading for their London flat when the police picked her up. The family home's near Gloucester, a place called Underhill Grange; there's a housekeeper and security men in residence. They told the police they'd no means of contacting Vladimir; I gather they were less than helpful. The police have been instructed to say the girl was agitated and difficult, her parents were absent, so they put her in a secure children's unit fairly near to her home for her own safety. We've started intercepting all communications to and from the yacht. They're heavily encrypted, but we're working on it.'

Samantha gazed across the table at Loretta. The sound of adult laughter and children's voices drifted in from the foyer. Lift doors opened then rumbled shut and the place fell silent again. She said, 'I'm still not clear about your involvement in all this?'

'They've instructed me to recover the mobile phones – we should be able to identify at least some of the people at the party from the list of numbers they gave me – and they want me to arrange the discreet questioning of the girl, the transcript of the conversation to be for the PM's eyes only.'

'Why not leave it with the Metropolitan Police?'

'If they involve Sir Nigel Dillon he may feel he has to let the law take its course. They think a more covert investigation's appropriate, otherwise they could lose control of the situation.'

Samantha frowned. 'It's delicate, but there's been worse. And they've covered it up rather well. I'm surprised they're quite so concerned.'

'There are two possible reasons. One involves a member of the Cabinet, the other's conjecture on my part.' Loretta slid two more photographs from the folder and passed them over the table.

'Well, well.' Samantha's eyebrows rose when she glanced at the first image. Annushka's pert little posterior was perched on the pedestal of a statue, the hem of her skimpy pleated skirt drawn up to her hips, her long legs wrapped around Alexander Fairchild's waist. White linen shorts around his ankles, underpants around his knees, he was holding her tightly, his handsome head thrown back, his eyes closed, his lips parted. She turned the photograph so Loretta could see it. 'Where was this taken?'

'Tennis party at some big country house. The statue of Apollo is at the centre of a maze. One of the officers in the security team was ours. He followed them and took the photograph.'

Samantha studied the second image. Annushka Dvoskin was straddling Alexander Fairchild who was sprawled across a rumpled bed. They were both naked. The photograph was less clear, a little grainy, but the identity of the parties was unmistakable. 'And how did you get this one?'

'They're in a flat, Fairchild's pied-à-terre in Mayfair. Tripod mounted camera with a telephoto lens located in a hotel room on the opposite side of the street. We put him under surveillance when we discovered he was interested in his son's girlfriend. Foreign Secretary having an affair with the underage daughter of a Russian oligarch; it could pose quite a security risk.'

'She's below the age of consent?'

'She was when these photographs were taken. She's sixteen now.'

'And very well developed for her age,' Samantha murmured. 'You said there could be two reasons for their excessive concern. What's the other one?'

'I think they might be trying to hide something bigger. Why did the palace send one of the Queen's more formidable Lord Lieutenants to Darnel Hall? Would they be so concerned about a couple of viscounts the public have never heard of, or was there someone more important at this party? And the account of events doesn't ring true. I had the researchers locate a photograph of the hallway and stairs at Darnel Hall. They found one in Blackwell's *Historic Houses of the Home Counties*. The stairs aren't steep, they sweep down very gently, and the marble handrail's almost a foot wide. It would be difficult to fall off.'

'Drink, drugs?' Samantha suggested. 'Perhaps she was hardly able to stand.'

'Then she wouldn't have been able to hitch her bottom on to the handrail; the balustrade's quite high. And how did she get all the bruising?'

A motor mower appeared between shrubs at the far end of the garden and began to drone towards the hotel. Loretta went on, 'Something serious happened at Darnel Hall last night, and the sons and daughters of the great and the good are mired in it. Just how great and how exalted, we don't know. This girl, this Russian oligarch's daughter, may have seen something that frightened her, that made her run away. And there could be incriminating videos and images on the phones she took. She could be in considerable danger.'

'You think they might do a Diana?'

Loretta gave Samantha a knowing look. 'Someday I'll let you look through the Diana files. If you remember, the Queen was reported to have said at the time that dark powers, of which she had no knowledge, were at work. I think she's very astute; far more aware of things than one might imagine.'

'Dark powers?'

'Perhaps she had in mind a group of zealous royalists, men obsessed with preserving the institution of monarchy. The establishment were very concerned about Diana's behaviour; her stepmother was scathing about it. Would they have wanted the mother of the heir to the throne, a woman who should have become queen, to marry one of the commoners she was involved with; marry him and bear him children?'

'The House of Windsor's weathered worse storms.'

'But none involving the mother of a future king. And the winds are colder now, Miss Quest, and blowing harder. Australia's voted to become a republic. Next year Canada holds a referendum; other Commonwealth countries are thinking along the same lines. Right now any scandal involving a member of the Royal Family would be particularly unwelcome.'

The noise of the mower grew louder. It reached the path that ran beneath the window, then turned and headed back down the strip of lawn. When the sound had faded, Samantha asked, 'What is it that you want me to do?'

'Get the girl out of the secure unit, hide her and keep her safe while you uncover the truth and retrieve the mobile phones.'

'She'll think I'm crazy. She won't want to be hidden. The only offence she's committed is driving without a licence. And surely your people can trace the mobile phones.'

'They're trying, but the devices don't respond to signals. Either the batteries have been removed, or the phones have been disabled in some way. And you'll just have to impress on the girl how much danger she's in.'

'She might not be in any danger. Why not do as they ask?'

'That's precisely it, Miss Quest. I'm afraid of what they might ask me to do.' They gazed at one another across the low table. Presently, Loretta said, 'I have a duty to maintain the security of the state and safeguard its institutions. I don't see that as being consistent with having a young girl murdered to protect the reputations of the great and the good.'

'You think it could come to that?'

'We won't know until you've questioned her and recovered the phones.'

'Are you going to keep Marcus Soames informed? He is your number two; he's the person who normally briefs me.'

'He might already know. If he does, it would tell me that you and I are very much on our own with this.'

Samantha gave her a questioning look.

'Marcus Soames and the Queen's Lord Lieutenant, Sir Kelvin Makewood, both served in the Guards and the Household Cavalry. They share a passionate loyalty to the monarch. They also attend the same London club as Sir Nigel Dillon, the Commissioner at the Met. The three of them may also have other affiliations in common with Earls Barksdale and Farnbeck, the Prime Minister and the Foreign Secretary.'

'Affiliations?'

'Masonic affiliations.'

'I take it you intend to keep my part in this secret?'

'I do, but I'll have to involve Marcus, or questions might be asked.'

'Is the girl to be removed from the secure unit in the Department's name?'

Loretta shook her head. 'I want it to appear as if she's been sprung from the place by parties unknown. When I return to London, I intend to instruct Marcus to arrange for someone to visit the unit and interrogate the girl. By that time I expect you to have removed her.'

'They'll have been told to increase security. It might be difficult to get inside. Am I allowed to show the Serious Crime Unit card?'

'Find some other way. I want them to be in no doubt that she's been snatched and neither the police nor the Department had anything to do with it. It's a privately run place so it's not likely that they'll deploy many staff through the night, probably no more than a man and a woman – it's a place where they keep boys and girls.' She clicked the attaché case shut and slid it across the table. 'Take this. There are two mobile phones inside, one for your major use – it's registered to an address in Poland in a Polish name – and one that's encrypted so you can maintain contact with me. Keys to a farmhouse in Wales, a flat in London and a house in the north, close to the Scottish border. And there's a collection of banking cards.'

'I don't have a car.'

'Take the one I drove down in. It's new; signed into the pool last week. There are three different sets of clip-on plates in the boot; alternative licence discs in the compartment under the dash.' She laid the keys on the briefcase. 'It's decent: black Mercedes coupé, six litre. I'll hire a taxi for the ride back to London.'

'And I don't have a gun with me.' Samantha caught Loretta's uneasy look. 'I'll need one. I may have to intimidate people. I may have to protect myself and the girl.'

'We're not dealing with terrorists or the criminal classes. I expect you to exercise restraint.'

'Restraint or no restraint, I'll need an intimidator, a persuader.'

Loretta smiled, despite herself. 'There's a 9mm Heckler and Koch semi-automatic in the case with two boxes of shells. New issue, unregistered, can't be traced.'

'You understand that if the girl comes under my protection, I'll protect her and go on protecting her no matter what that involves, no matter where it leads,' Samantha warned.

'I'd expect no less.'

'Even though I may be confronted by crazy monarchists, the Metropolitan Police, agents assigned by Marcus?'

'Do what has to be done, but always exercise restraint, and remember, you're on your own. You're not employed by the Department and we've never met.'

'My contract's been extended on the same rates?'

'There is no contract, no record of your involvement. When the issues have been resolved, you'll be paid in cash, by me, twice your usual rate.'

'And if they're not resolved?'

'One way or another, they have to be. I think the stolen mobile phones are going to provide the answer. The girl must be kept safe and protected until they're recovered and we've seen what they contain.'

Tatiana rose from the lounger, gathered her flimsy cotton robe around her and crossed over to the rail that enclosed the upper deck. The sun was sparkling on a choppy sea and she found the scintillating brightness painfully dazzling. Half closing her eyes, she studied some dark shapes on the horizon. Too big for ships, she decided; probably islands.

The gleaming mahogany deck was warm under her feet. Through it she could feel the faint vibration of the engines, hear a deep rumbling whispering up from the bowels of the ship. On her second day aboard, the chief engineer, proud of his gleaming pipes and dials, had taken her on a tour of the engine room. The size and power of the great machines that propelled Vladimir's yacht had frightened her. Vladimir frightened her a little, too, but the crew, from the captain down to the cabin staff, were deferential. They were in no doubt that she was the new Mrs Dvoskin. Wary of Vladimir, they kept their eyes discreetly averted from her, but sometimes, when she caught them unawares, she saw their lingering glances.

There was a cooling breeze up here. It was parting her robe, exposing her legs and thighs, the blue satin pants of her skimpy bathing suit. She turned and looked back at Vladimir, reclining under the awning. He was reading through the narrow strips of yellow paper that held the decoded transcripts of messages transmitted to the ship. In the morning it was always papers, papers, papers. At noon they would have a lunch of many delicacies, prepared by an Italian chef and served by two Malaysian waiters, their black trousers neatly pressed, their Mao-collared jackets freshly laundered, their hands covered by white cotton gloves. After the meal, Vladimir would take her by the hand and lead her to their suite of rooms. His appetites were voracious. His paunchy body might be succumbing to middle age, his sandy hair receding, but he had the energy and vigour, the insatiable sexual urges, of a teenage boy. Such a pity he was so low on tenderness, that he was so lacking in sensitivity. The concept of romantic love was as incomprehensible to him as the movement of the stars.

He was frowning in a worried way at one of the slips of yellow paper. Deciding to distract him, she untied the ribbon securing her robe, allowed it to fall open, then struck a pose; leaning back with her elbows on the rail, her body curving towards him, her breasts, of which she was justly proud, barely concealed. 'You seem concerned, Vladimir. Is it something serious?'

When he glanced up, his frown dissolved in a smile. His gaze lingered for a moment on her breasts, then slowly descended to her hips and thighs. 'It's troubling, no more than that. A message from the housekeeper at Underhill Grange – that's a house in England – we'll be going there after the honeymoon. Annushka's been in trouble with the police: taking a car without the owner's consent, driving without a licence. They've put her in what they call a secure children's unit. I can't decide what to do.'

'Why not tell one of your London lawyers to deal with it, then forget about it.'

'I could, but I'm inclined to do nothing; let the police keep her until we get back, then look into it. She needs teaching a lesson. I told her to behave while we were away. I give the child everything she asks for, yet she's always so petulant and ungrateful.'

'I don't think she likes me,' Tatiana observed.

Vladimir sighed. 'That makes two of us. She hates me.'

'You're her father. How can she hate you?'

'She was very close to her mother, and her mother and I lived like cat and dog. Annushka thinks I treated her badly.'

'And did you?'

'I behaved abominably. I'm not proud of it. After Annushka was born, we no longer had a marriage. The birth was difficult, Ekaterina was traumatized, we no longer slept together, I strayed and she became insanely jealous. And she was too clever for her own good; a smart-mouthed harridan who was forever riling me. Annushka takes after her.'

Tatiana pouted and softened her voice. 'Do I rile you, Vladimir?'

'You enchant me.'

She let out a surprised little laugh. This was the closest they'd ever come to a flirtatious exchange. 'But do I ever irritate you?'

'You calm me, you make me feel at peace with the world.'

Deciding to quit whilst she was ahead, she turned and pointed towards the smudges on the horizon. 'What are they?'

'The Cyclades; tiny islands. You're seeing some of the outer ones: Milos, Sifnos, Serifos, Kythnos. We're sailing north, heading for Piraeus, the port of Athens. In a few hours we'll dock there. Tonight we'll go and see the Acropolis by moonlight.'

'There might not be a moon.'

'The moon will shine for you.'

Flirting a moment ago, and now he was saying the sweetest things to her. Whatever next? 'And tomorrow we can go shopping?'

He laughed gently. Women were perceptive and smart, yet they could be so childlike. 'Tomorrow we will go shopping.'

'And I must visit a hairdresser.' She ran her hand into blonde curls, brushing them away from her face. 'My hair's in such a mess.'

'There was never a woman who needed a hairdresser less, but I'll have one brought to the ship when we dock.' He stuffed the yellow slips into a folder, then rose from the lounger and reached for her hand. 'Lunch,' he said. 'Let's go down and see what the chef has prepared for us.'

'Will you let me steer the ship?'

He roared with laughter. 'It would be wrecked. We would all drown.' Still laughing, he slid a huge and hairy hand beneath her robe and caressed her buttocks. 'You can go up on the bridge when she's being brought into harbour. That's the closest you're going to get to steering the ship.'

'Have you decided?'

'Of course I've decided. That's my last word. You are not steering—'

'I mean about Annushka.'

'Oh, her . . . I think I'll leave her where she is. When we arrive in England, you can take charge of Underhill Grange while I deal with the problem. She'll have been to court by then, maybe fined and put on probation. The humiliation will be good for her. She's arrogant, just like her mother, and too clever by half. She needs to be humbled.'

They abandoned the heat and brightness of the upper deck for the air-conditioned coolness of the ship. Still holding her hand, Vladimir led her down a stairway to the dining room in their suite on the deck below. She was quite looking forward to their lunch: the meals relieved the boredom of endless sunlight, of a world bound by the confines of the ship, of their uneventful journeying through calm seas. The certain prospect of what would come after the meal did not excite her at all. Why were rich and powerful men invariably middle-aged and unattractive; their conversation, limited to money and business, so dull and boring? Why were all the handsome and sensitive young men poor and at the beck and call of the rich? Her father had told her not to make trouble; to submit willingly to her husband and be a good wife. He'd promised that her release would not be long in coming, but she must be patient. Questions might be asked if it came too soon.

CHAPTER FOUR

Having declined Loretta Fallon's invitation to have a meal with her, Samantha took the car and headed west along the M4. She broke her journey at Reading, bought a blonde wig and a mesh wig cap, a cheap blouse and skirt, a pair of flat shoes and a summer raincoat, then had an early and indifferent dinner in a hotel before disappearing into the powder room and locking herself in a cubicle. Once inside, she removed her dress and put on the blouse and skirt. Concealing and flattening her hair beneath the flimsy gauze cap and adjusting the wig proved difficult with only a tiny handbag mirror to guide her. Eventually she ran a comb through the synthetic curls. The effect was untamed and rather tawdry, but quite convincing.

After folding her dress and sliding it into the bag that had held the blouse and skirt, she drew on the raincoat, stepped into the shoes and emerged from the cubicle. A stranger gazed back at her from the long mirror ranged above the hand basins. She took her comb, tidied wayward curls, then slid on a pair of steel-framed sunglasses she'd bought in a chain store. Small, round and blue-tinted, the lenses were just big enough to hide her eyes; unusual enough to draw attention from the rest of her face. The blonde hair and rather strange glasses would be the only things people remembered if they were asked to describe her.

The powder-room door swung open and a pair of girls clattered in and approached the mirror. Engrossed in conversation and their reflections, they didn't spare Samantha a glance. She gathered up her bags, headed down a carpeted corridor, across the rather grand foyer and emerged into the now quiet city street. The hot brightness of the afternoon had faded; the evening light was softer and more diffused, the air cooler, as she walked to the car.

Eating the meal, changing her clothes and fixing the wig had taken more than an hour. It was almost seven when she turned on to the motorway and resumed her journey; a little after eight when she neared Gloucester. This was a strange and messy business that Loretta Fallon had embroiled her in. It required some thought. Getting the girl out of the secure unit shouldn't be too difficult; persuading her to stay with her and keeping her safe once she'd been released were different matters.

Sleepy eyes half open, her mind still wandering the shadowland between dreaming and waking, Annushka Dvoskin gazed across the pillow. She felt bewildered. This wasn't her grandmother's dacha. She wasn't sitting in the red rocking chair, holding the skein of wool between parted hands while Babushka wound it into a ball. Where was she? Reality crashed over her like an icy wave: she was still in the miserable hole they called Sternwood. She swung long and slender legs down from the bed and groped for a shoe. Armed with it, she rose, avoided fragments of broken crockery as she squished through meat and potatoes and overcooked cabbage, and began to hammer on the door with the heel.

'I am Annushka Dvoskin!' She punctuated every word with a blow that reverberated down the corridor. 'I am the daughter of Vladimir Dvoskin, one of the most powerful men in the whole of Russia. I have done nothing wrong. You must charge me or release me.' Her voice, young and refined, faded in a fit of coughing. She was becoming hoarse. She'd been banging and shouting for most of the day. Gripped by a sudden frenzy, she began to flay the door and her words poured out on a rising torrent of anger: 'I am Annushka Dvoskin! Daughter of Vladimir Dvoskin. Charge me or release me. Charge me or release me. If you do not release me, you had better be very afraid.'

Samantha was driving through suburbs made only a little less drab by the fading sunlight. The car Loretta had given her was silent and powerful, its thick carpets and leather interior luxurious. She was heading towards the Sternwood Secure Children's Unit. Located well away from Gloucester's more affluent areas, it was in a part of the town where the main through road linked long terraces of grimy red-brick houses. Some of the dwellings had been cleared to make way for huge windowless metal sheds, ringed by barbed-wire-topped fencing. Old railway bridges spanned the road, advertisement hoardings hid lorry parks, tiny shops afforded their owners a meagre livelihood.

She turned left at a filling station, drove past a small public library with boarded-up windows, a mother and baby clinic, a newsagents, an off licence, then slowed as she approached the unit. Built of biscuit-coloured bricks, it was set behind a tarmac fore-court. The gates were open and pegged back; the entrance door was flanked by narrow windows through which visitors could be viewed before it was opened. Cameras, mounted on the walls, covered the forecourt and the entrance. Two wings projected at the rear: probably bedrooms, arranged above communal dining and recreation rooms and a kitchen. Windows were small, square and barred behind the glass. High steel fencing enclosed a rear yard that extended across a derelict area to the blind wall of an abandoned warehouse.

After sweeping over a bridge that spanned a canal, she turned into the parking area of an all-night supermarket, then locked the car doors and lifted the attaché case on to her lap. She studied the few documents and photographs in the slender file, then slid the gun from a pocket in the lid. New and unused, its unsullied blackness had an oily gleam. She ejected the magazine, took shells from a box, pressed nine, one by one, into the clip, then slammed it back into the butt with the flat of her hand. When she screwed the silencer on to the muzzle, the weapon became unbalanced: unbalanced but very intimidating. Using a nail file, she poked a hole in the pocket of her raincoat and slid the long barrel into the lining; she found its cold hardness against her thigh reassuring.

Samantha checked the dashboard clock: it was almost nine. She'd wait another two hours. By that time the inmates should have been dispatched to their rooms and, as Loretta had said, being privately run, there'd probably be no more than two wardens on the night shift, a man and a woman, to cope with the teenage boys and girls. She slid the attaché case beneath the seat, settled herself into soft grey leather, and waited.

When she eventually stirred, the car park was deserted save for a few late-night shoppers, its darkness relieved by illuminated trolley bays, the light spilling from the entrance, the blood-red sign blazing like a beacon above it. Samantha stepped out of the car and began the short walk to the secure unit.

As she crossed the canal bridge she opened her raincoat, unbuttoned her blouse, eased straps over her shoulders and drew down the zip of her skirt. When she reached the iron railings that fronted the secure unit, she began to run. Holding her skirt up with one hand, waving frantically with the other, she turned through the gates and began to scream, 'Help me! Help me! I've been attacked!' She pounded on the door with her fists, then saw a bell push and pressed it long and hard. Still screaming, 'Help me, help me!', she stepped in front of one of the narrow windows and hammered on wired glass. She peered inside. A stocky bald-headed man had rounded a reception desk and was coming towards the door. He stared at her through the narrow window, took in the tousled blonde hair and tiny tinted glasses, then his gaze dropped to her open blouse and lingered on her breasts. The tip of a pink tongue appeared, circled fleshy lips, made them glisten. He looked up into her face.

'There's a man!' Samantha screamed, gesturing towards the

gate. 'He grabbed me and tried to drag me under the bridge. He's following me. Don't let him find me.' She pounded on the glass. 'Let me in! Please let me in! I want to call the police.'

He snatched another glance at her breasts, then disappeared from view. A key turned in a lock, bolts slid, the door swung open. As she crossed the threshold she drew the gun from her raincoat pocket and levelled it at him. Grey shirt transformed into a uniform by epaulettes, grey flannel trousers neatly pressed, the plastic identity tag clipped to his shirt pocket told her he was called James Harvey.

'Peep show's over, James.' She tugged up the zip of her skirt and buttoned her blouse. 'Don't be a hero. They don't pay you enough to be a hero. Hold out your hands.'

He did as she asked, his eyes wide with shock, his fleshy mouth hanging open.

'Where are the other staff?' She flicked a handcuff over one wrist, clicked it shut, then captured the other.

'Other staff?' His eyes were darting nervously between the gun and her face.

'The people you work with. It's a mixed sex unit. Surely there's a woman on duty?'

He ran his tongue around his lips again and swallowed hard. 'I'm here on my own. Janet's gone home because her kid's ill. I told her to slip away after we'd cleared the recreation room, come back before the morning shift starts.'

'You're not telling me porkies, are you, James? If you start telling me porkies, I'll get very annoyed.'

'It's the truth. I'm the only member of staff here.'

'What's in there?' Samantha nodded towards an open door behind the reception desk.

'It's the office. Just a few filing cabinets, a photocopier, stuff like that.'

She reached for the two-way radio clipped to his belt, tugged it free, dropped it on the floor then crushed it under her heel.

'Where are the video recorders?'

'Video recorders?'

'The machines that record the images on the security cameras.' She brushed a fall of blonde hair from her face. 'You've got the entrance and the grounds covered. There must be cameras in the corridors and communal rooms.'

'In the office, in a cupboard above the filing cabinets.'

Samantha gestured with the gun, then followed him into the tiny room behind the reception desk. He raised his hands, swung the cupboard doors open and exposed a pair of video recorders.

'Eject the disks.'

He pressed buttons. Trays glided out of the machines.

'Take them off the slides, put them on this cabinet and stand back.'

He turned and scowled at her. 'It's difficult with my hands—'

'Do it.'

James reached up, restrained hands fumbling, and somehow managed to remove the disks and drop them on the filing cabinet. He stepped clear.

She pocketed the disks, then inclined her head towards the door. When they emerged from the office she saw the monitor screens, mounted on the reception desk, each one split to display four views. The forecourt and yards, the corridors and communal rooms, were all deserted.

'There's no money, nothing of value,' the man bleated. 'You're wasting your time. There's not even—'

'Annushka Dvoskin. I want the Russian girl. Take me to her.'

He stared at her for a moment, a sudden understanding glimmering behind the fear in his eyes, then turned, led her across the entrance hall and down a corridor. He paused by a heavy door, punched a code into a pad, bolts clicked and he shouldered it open.

'Don't let it close.' Samantha unhooked a fire extinguisher from the wall and used it to wedge the door open. They walked on. Glazed partitions gave her a view of a long room equipped with snooker tables, a pinball machine, a large television; then the man led her up a flight of terrazzo-covered stairs.

'She's up here?'

He glanced back. 'Can't you hear her?'

When they pushed through a pair of unlocked fire doors the sound of screaming and banging was suddenly very loud. Speaking in Russian, Samantha called out, 'Annushka, Annushka Dvoskin, I have come to take you from this place.'

The banging and shouting stopped. 'My father has sent you?'

'People concerned for your safety have sent me.'

Cream painted walls gleamed in the hard fluorescent light as they progressed down the corridor, their footsteps deadened now by some coarse grey carpet. On one side, windows overlooked a courtyard. On the other, six blue doors were spaced evenly along its length.

'How do the others cope with the noise?'

'We were lucky. Only three girls were on the wing when she was brought in. The police moved them out the same night. She's been up here on her own.' He stopped outside the last door, tried to tug a bunch of keys from his trouser pocket, but his restrained hands couldn't grab the chain that attached them to his belt.

Samantha pressed the gun into his back, tugged the keys free and separated them from the chain. She held them up. 'Which one?'

'The brass key, the long one.'

She slid it into the lock and called out, 'Speak only in Russian, Annushka,' as she opened the door.

Blonde hair tousled, her short black skirt crumpled, the girl was sitting on the edge of an untidy bed, wiping her feet with a towel.

'Are you ready to go?'

'When I've cleaned this mess from my foot.'

Samantha gave her a questioning look.

'I threw my dinner tray at the wall and everything spilled over the floor. I trod in it.' Her long legs were bare, her skirt hitched high enough to expose her knickers. James the jailer was standing just inside the room, his bright nervous eyes taking in the scene. Annushka rose, slid her feet into her shoes, then tugged down the hem of her crimson sweater. When she stepped out into the corridor and saw the gun, she froze. 'Hey, what's going on here?' Scowling at Samantha, she demanded, 'Who are you?'

'I've been sent to take you out of this place. While you're in here you could be in danger.'

'Maybe I'll be in more danger if I come with you.'

A smart girl, Samantha reflected, with plenty of attitude. She was beginning to feel edgy. The longer they lingered here the more likely it was they'd be challenged, but taking the girl by force would make it impossible to form a relationship and she might never uncover the truth of events at Darnel Hall. Making her voice urgent, she said, 'I've travelled a long way and taken risks getting inside this place. If you're coming, come. If you want to stay, get back in the room and I'll lock you in. But just ask yourself, why are you being held without charge, without documents? No one knows you're here; they can do what they want with you.'

'*They*? Who are *they*? I have no enemies; I have many friends.'

'People you've endangered, powerful people who won't tolerate their comfortable lives being threatened. You should believe me when I say I've been sent to take you from this place and protect you.'

Annushka thought of the dead girl and the video she'd made of her being tossed from the landing, remembered the stolen mobile phones. Maybe she should go along with this.

'Are you coming or staying?' the husky voice demanded.

She shrugged. 'OK, I'll come. Anything's better than this miserable hole.'

The bald-headed man had been watching them, his expression bemused, his gaze shifting from one to the other as they conversed in a language he didn't understand.

Samantha turned to him. 'Move over to the bed.'

He shuffled through the remains of Annushka's meal. 'Surely you're not going to lock me in?'

'Take a nap. They'll let you out in the morning.'

'There could be alarm calls. Some of the kids are coming off drugs, some of them are self-harmers.'

She swung the door shut and locked it. Seconds later he was banging on it and yelling, 'You can't do this! Let me out, you must let me out!' When they reached the double doors they heard him calling, 'I need the toilet! I need it bad. How do I clean up if my hands are tied? At least unfasten my—'

They clattered down the stairs, headed along the half-glazed corridor and passed through the door Samantha had propped open with the fire extinguisher. As they crossed the reception area, Annushka said, 'My bag. They took my bag and my watch.'

'What does this bag look like?'

'Red leather, fairly large, with a gold catch shaped like a G. It's a Gucci bag. And the watch is a gold Rolex with diamonds on the dial. They made me leave them on the desk.'

The reception desk was no more than a counter where a security man could sit and view the monitor screens. Behind it cables dropped to a trunking in the floor and a single shelf carried forms for recording admissions and departures; accidents and misdemeanours.

They stepped into the office and began to pull open metal drawers. Most of them held slender files on the young people incarcerated in the place. There was no file for Annushka Dvoskin in the drawer reserved for current inmates. Large manila envelopes, each one bearing a name and lumpy with small items, filled three drawers. There was no envelope for Annushka. Samantha slid open the bottom drawer, saw a red bag nestling beside a stack of Bibles and a couple of copies of the Koran. She handed it to Annushka, who clicked it open and began to check the contents.

She flicked through a tiny diary that had cards and folds of paper sandwiched between the pages, then opened a red leather purse. 'Money's all here, and the banking cards,' she muttered, then rummaged amongst the clutter at the bottom of her handbag and lifted out a watch by its strap. 'And my Rolex.' She shook the contents of the bag while she peered inside. 'My mobile phone's there, too. At least they're honest. In Russia the cash, the watch and the phone would probably have gone.'

'Switch the phone off,' Samantha insisted. 'Switch it off now.'

'It is off. It's completely dead. The battery goes flat after two or three hours. I'd have got it fixed if I hadn't been locked up in this place.'

Samantha held out a gloved hand. 'May I see it?'

Annushka took the phone out of the bag and passed it over. Samantha examined it. Tiny diamonds studded the back of its pearly cover and formed an intertwined AD. She pressed the on button. The screen remained dark: no icons, no low-battery warning. 'Whatever you do, don't charge it. If you activate the thing, we can be located.' She handed it back then took Annushka's arm and led her out of the office, tossing James Harvey's keys on the reception desk as they passed it on their way to the entrance door.

'Where are we going?'

'To a flat in London.'

'We could go to my father's flat.'

'The police will have it under surveillance. It's the last place you should go.' They walked out into the coolness of the night, crossed the forecourt and headed down the dimly lit road.

Annushka gave Samantha a searching look before asking, 'Who are you?'

'We'll talk when we're in the car.'

'I'm starving. I was too angry to eat the food they brought me.'

'There's a Kentucky Fried Chicken place on the road out of Gloucester. How about a takeaway?'

'Perfect,' Annushka sighed. 'Absolutely perfect.'

Tatiana Dvoskin looked around the crowded restaurant, searching for the sign of the skirted woman. Eventually she saw it, at the rear of the room, half hidden behind an ornamental screen. She gathered up her bag and smiled across the table at her husband. 'I have to go to the powder room.'

He nodded. 'Grigori will accompany you to the door.'

'Must he? I find it so embarrassing.'

'I have to protect you. If something happened to you, your father would never forgive me.'

She patted her elaborately coiffured blonde curls; the Greek hairdresser's efforts had pleased her. 'So, you protect me only because you do not wish to anger my father?'

He smiled indulgently. 'There are other reasons.'

She gave him a coquettish look.

'Because you enchant me,' he added.

'Is that all?'

Questions, questions; just a simple statement and she had to pick away at it like this. He laughed softly. 'Isn't that enough?' Then, lowering his voice until it could scarcely be heard above the conversations going on around them, he whispered, 'Because I love you.'

The smile froze on her face. This was the last thing she'd expected Vladimir to say. She felt an unwanted rush of tenderness towards him. Such great wealth, so much power, yet deep down he seemed to have a need to give and receive affection that was almost childlike. Keeping her voice teasing, she asked, 'And will you still love me when I'm old and wrinkled?'

'I shall be dead long before you are old and wrinkled.' He caught the eye of the security guard called Grigori. The man immediately stopped eating and leaned across the gap between the tables. 'Mrs Dvoskin wishes to powder her nose.'

Grigori wiped his mouth on his napkin, tossed it down, then rose to his feet and drew Tatiana's chair back from the table. He followed at a respectful distance as she trotted down the room.

Vladimir relaxed back in his chair. He felt content. Tatiana had fulfilled all his hopes. And she did enchant him; they were not merely kind words, spoken to please her. She was attractive, very attractive, but not what one would call beautiful. Ekaterina, Annushka's mother, had been beautiful, and look at the terrible life she'd given him. Beautiful, smart-mouthed, mean and frigid: that just about summed up Ekaterina. He sighed. Annushka was beautiful and smart-mouthed, like her mother, but he suspected she was far from frigid and by no means chaste.

Perspiring in the humid warmth, he closed his eyes, lulled by the murmur of voices all around him. Yes, he reflected, Tatiana most certainly did captivate him. Such a splendid body: long-limbed, warm, voluptuous and fragrant; incredibly arousing when naked, so enticingly elegant when clothed.

He stifled a yawn. He'd had enough of wandering along crowded streets. Impatient now to be back on board his ship, he was looking forward to relaxing in its air-conditioned coolness, taking a shower, lying beside Tatiana in their vast bed with its silk sheets. He summoned a waiter over and asked for the bill, then turned to the guard called Boleslav. 'When I've paid, we're leaving. Phone the drivers, tell them we're going to stroll down through the Plaka; tell them to bring the cars to Hadrian's Arch.'

The man rose, steered his massive bulk between crowded tables and stepped out, through open doors, on to the pavement. Vladimir watched him key numbers into a mobile phone, press it to his ear, then study the night-time crowd drifting along the street they called Kydathineon while he muttered into it.

Vladimir settled the bill, adding only a meagre tip. Tatiana appeared and headed towards him, the full and finely pleated skirt of her white dress swirling, the gaze of the ever-vigilant Grigori sweeping the room as he followed her.

When they'd all assembled in the street, Vladimir reached for Tatiana's hand and linked her arm in his. Moments later, as they were making their way out of the crowded labyrinth of shops and bazaars called the Plaka, he glanced at her and asked, 'Did you like it?'

'Like it?'

He gestured towards the rocky mound rising above the rooftops. 'The Parthenon, up there, on the Acropolis. The moon came out for you, just as I promised.'

'It was OK.'

'Only OK?'

Tatiana shrugged. 'It's a floodlit ruin on a hill. What more do you want me to say?'

Vladimir's laughter was affectionate, not mocking. He whispered in her ear, 'Beautiful women do not have to think of smart things to say. OK is fine.' He squeezed her hand.

His compliments, his charming words, were unsettling her. They were unwelcome. The last thing she wanted was to find herself feeling sympathy or affection for this man. Half teasing, half serious, she said, 'You promised you would take me shopping tomorrow and let me buy lots of things.'

Women! She'd journeyed to the cradle of civilization and all she could think about was shopping. He patted her arm. 'Tomorrow you shall go to the Kolonaki, all the exclusive shops are there, and you must buy whatever you want. And we'll dine at Milton's. I think you'll like that. It's modern and international and very stylish.'

Tatiana glanced over her shoulder, caught the guard, Grigori, staring at her hips and thighs. She sensed a growing boldness in him. He made her uneasy, even a little afraid. He gave her a respectful nod, then directed his gaze over the crowd. Grigori and Yegar were walking behind them, and there were two guards in front and one on either side, keeping the crowd at bay, always alert and watchful, ready to protect them from harm. Wherever they went they were always surrounded by these huge and powerful men; men who could absorb terrible beatings and still kill with a blow. What woman would want to spend her honeymoon under the constant gaze of these great brutes? It was torment enough spending it with a man she felt no affection for, a man she had little in common with, apart from language and a background of ruthlessly acquired wealth. Who better than her to understand Vladimir's fears; the fears of a man who must have made many enemies in his struggle to become obscenely rich?

They were emerging from the Plaka now, strolling along a broad pavement beside a road where the traffic was heavy and fast moving. She could see Hadrian's Arch up ahead and, just beyond it, the Temple of Zeus. She thought them even worse ruins than the Parthenon, up there, above the city. Why, she wondered, did people flock from all over the world to stare at rows of flaky old columns, the decaying remnants of buildings that no longer had roofs or walls?

Two black limousines swept past, indicators flashing, and drew up beside the kerb, a dozen yards ahead.

Vladimir muttered, 'Thank God. My feet ache like toothache,' then quickened his pace, limping ahead of the guards, craving the comfort of a seat in the air-conditioned car.

'No, Mr Dvoskin, no!' the guard called Boleslav roared.

Tatiana felt an arm encircling her waist, tugging her from her husband's grasp, holding her back. She suddenly found herself face down on the pavement, covered by the huge and hard body of a guard. Cheek pressing against cool stone, she peered out from beneath a massive shoulder, but could see only running legs and scrambling feet.

A voice shouted, 'These are not our cars, Mr Dvoskin! These are not—'

A door swung open, a gun barked, a pair of legs buckled, then her husband dropped into her field of view. Tatiana screamed, tried to struggle free, tried to rise and go to him.

Grigori growled in her ear, 'Don't move. There's nothing you can do.' Then his entire weight bore down on her, imprisoning her, squeezing the breath from her lungs. His arms encircled her face, his huge hands covered her head. She could see nothing now, but she could hear feet scuffling, the sound of someone being dragged along the pavement, frenzied shouts, more gunshots. Then car doors slammed, engines roared, tyres screamed on tarmac.

The crushing weight lifted from her. Tatiana felt a hand beneath her arm, helping her to her feet. She teetered along the pavement on her high heels, then dropped to her knees beside the bodies of two men. Her husband was lying on his back, mouth hanging open, eyes half closed. The guard called Boleslav was sprawling, face down, on top of him, his body perfectly still. Hysteria gripped her. She began to whimper her husband's name, 'Vladimir, Vladimir,' began to pat his cheek in a futile attempt to rouse him. Grigori crouched down beside her, laid his fingers on Vladimir's throat for a moment, then gently drew them down the lifeless face and closed his master's eyes.

'Your husband is dead, Mrs Dvoskin.' He whispered the words in her ear. 'There is nothing you can do.' He reached out and laid his hand on the neck of the guard, feeling for a pulse. 'And so is Boleslav.' He helped her to her feet, retrieved her bag and handed it to her.

Two black limousines, the cars Boleslav had phoned for, drew up beside the kerb. Vladimir's enemies, listening and waiting, must have intercepted his call and rushed there in their own cars. Four of the guards encircled the bodies, standing with their backs to them, looking out over the gathering crowd. Grigori keyed numbers into his phone, then muttered, 'Send police, an ambulance. There's been a shooting, beside Hadrian's Arch. Two men are dead.'

Overcome by shock and fear, tears streaming down her face, Tatiana began to shake uncontrollably. There were flashes from amongst the crowd; opportunists were using cameras and mobile phones to record the scene. A hand touched her arm. As if from a great distance, she heard Grigori say, 'Could you get into the car,

Mrs Dvoskin. We must take you back to the ship.'

'My husband. I ought to stay with him, go with him when they take him away.'

'Stanislav, Yegar and Dimitri will remain here and deal with the authorities. Vasila and I will take you back to the *Empress*. You will be safe there.'

'The police will want to talk to me.'

'Then they must visit the ship.' She felt his hand grip her arm and draw her towards the car. 'Come, I have to take you to a place of safety. It's not easy to protect you here. God knows who is in these crowds.'

Vasila opened the rear door of one of the limousines. She lowered her head, climbed inside and moved over to the far seat. Grigori settled himself beside her, Vasila sat next to the driver, doors slammed and they sped off, merging with the flow of traffic, heading for Piraeus.

Samantha tossed the blonde wig on to the bed and peeled off the gauze cap. When she shook out her hair the relief was immense. She could hear Annushka singing a popular song in the shower across the landing. She was probably enjoying a fleeting moment of happiness at her escape from the secure unit. The girl's smart but rather inane chatter, her irrepressible I-know-everything attitude, were becoming tiresome.

The so-called safe house was a tiny mews flat in Chelsea. Its one external door opened on a narrow flight of stairs that led up to some modest accommodation above what had once been a coach house and was now the garage: just a kitchen, tiny sitting room, bedroom with twin beds, a cramped bathroom. She'd already checked the bedroom door. It had a lock and the key was in it. When they'd settled down for the night, she'd lock them in and remove the key.

Annushka's red bag was lying on her pillow. Samantha opened it, found the brown leather diary and leafed through its tiny pages.

Here and there Annushka had scribbled times and near illegible notes and initials, but it would require much more than a quick glance to make any sense, discover patterns, in the entries. The monogrammed white mobile phone was half hidden beneath a card of contraceptive pills. Once again, nothing happened when she switched it on: no icons, no low-battery symbol. Its batteries were completely exhausted. A careful search didn't reveal a charger, it couldn't be used to make a call, so she dropped it back, picked out a purse and clicked it open: half a dozen banking cards, about £200 in notes, a bunch of keys and some small coins were making its red leather bulge.

There was a faint bleeping. Samantha lifted her attaché case on to the bed, raised the lid and snatched up the encrypted phone.

A cold and commanding voice demanded, 'Where are you?'

'In London.'

'In the flat?'

'Yes.'

'And your friend is with you?'

'Yes.'

'Things went smoothly?'

'Yes.'

'And no one was harmed?

'No.'

'Good. I have some news for you; for your friend, really. Her father is dead. Murdered, in Athens, about a couple of hours ago: a drive-past shooting. No doubt the media will be reporting it in the morning. Have you learned anything?'

'Not yet.'

'Keep me informed.' There was a click and the faint hissing of the encryption faded. Samantha switched off the phone, dropped it back in the case, then took the gun from the pocket in the lid and slid it under the pillow of the bed nearest the door.

CHAPTER FIVE

ANNUSHKA KEPT STEALING GLANCES at Samantha across the two-seater breakfast table while she ate her kippers and toast. The table was hinged to the wall between the refrigerator and the door. When raised and in use it took up much of the free space in the tiny kitchen. She sipped her coffee, then said, 'You look quite different without the wig and tiny spectacles.'

Samantha smiled.

Annushka buttered another slice of toast. 'Where did you find the kippers?'

'In the freezer. It's small but well stocked.'

'Reminds me of Martha's.'

'Martha's?'

'Martha Hemmingway School for Girls. I go there. They serve kippers for breakfast on Fridays.'

'Do you like it?'

'The breakfast or Martha's?' Annushka picked up her knife and fork; she ate and drank with enthusiasm. Her blue eyes were clear and bright, her long blonde hair was uncombed, her pert and pointed breasts were thrusting at the wool of her red jumper.

'Martha's.'

'It's OK.' She bit into the toast and forked up some more of the kipper. 'Sending me there was one of Father's better ideas. The teachers know their subjects, they're patient and there's plenty of them; one to one if you're finding something difficult. Discipline's sensible, food's not too bad, we each have our own room, the girls are pleasant, and there's a swimming pool and good sports facilities.' She reached for another slice of toast. 'Most of us share the same problem.'

Samantha raised an eyebrow.

'Dumped there by divorced parents rich enough to afford the fees.' Annushka frowned. 'I've forgotten your name. I'm sorry . . .'

'I didn't tell you my name.'

'May I ask what it is?'

Samantha smiled. 'It's best you don't know.'

'I've got to call you something.'

'Then call me Georgie.'

'Short for Georgina?'

Samantha nodded.

'Are you a very heavy smoker?'

'I don't smoke. I never have. Why?'

'Your voice, it's so husky and whispery: a heavy smoker's voice.' Annushka laughed. 'But it's jolly sexy; I should think it very useful if you're trying to seduce someone.'

'Not so good if you want to be assertive, but I've learned to live with it.'

Annushka bit into her toast and chewed while she stared across the table at Samantha. 'And your hair's fabulous,' she went on. 'You look heaps younger. The blonde wig made you look a bit like Gerda Lundgren, our games mistress. She's Swedish; plays for the other side.' Annushka picked up her cup. 'Are you into men, or do you play for the other side?'

Samantha smiled. 'I'm a widow.'

'A widow!' Annushka gulped at her coffee. 'You're rather young to be a widow.'

'I'd been married only six months when my husband died. A sniper's bullet. He was a doctor, attending a patient on the Gaza Strip. We lived in Jerusalem.'

'You're a Jew, then?'

'My husband and my father were Jewish. I'm not.'

Annushka was eyeing her steadily over her cup.

'My mother was Irish,' Samantha explained. 'Catholic, very devout. I was baptized by the Bishop of Dublin, confirmed by the Patriarch of Jerusalem, educated by nuns.'

Annushka nodded. 'My grandmother's religious. Russian Orthodox. She has a little dacha outside Moscow. You can't see the walls for icons. When she lights candles, the gold and silver gleam. I like to go there. My father, my mother, me: all godless. We are Lenin's children.'

'Your father seems to have forsaken Lenin and pursued wealth.'

Annushka's expression soured. 'Men like my father are ruthless and greedy. They become rich by using their cunning to exploit the knowledge and skills of others. And there were many desperate people for my father to trick and exploit when the Soviet Union fell.'

'In the West we call them entrepreneurs.'

'I've done economics. I know how capitalism defines such men. I still think that cunning people who plot and scheme, who use the labour and talents of others to make money, are parasites.' She frowned at Samantha for a long moment, then asked, 'Can you tell what I'm thinking?'

Samantha laughed. 'Of course not.'

'It's your eyes: they're such a vivid green, so calm and still. They scare me a little.'

'Are you always so open and direct?'

Annushka shrugged. 'It's just the way I am. I suppose we're all a bit like that at Martha's. We say what we think, and if we want to know something we just ask.' She rattled her cup down on its saucer. 'Thanks for the breakfast.'

'You're welcome. I think it's the first time I've cooked since my husband died. If you can call boiling kippers in a bag cooking.'

'I'm honoured. Don't you do domestic stuff?'

'I don't cook, I don't clean, I don't do washing and ironing.

I mostly dine out and I have a friend who attends to household matters.'

'She lives with you, this friend?'

'It's a he, not a she, and no, he doesn't live with me.'

'Cool.' Annushka seemed to approve.

'There's something I have to tell you,' Samantha said. 'I've been wondering how to say it while you've been having breakfast, but there's no easy way, so I'm just going to come out with it.'

Annushka shrugged, as if urging her to go ahead.

'I'm sorry to have to tell you that your father died last night.'

'My father's dead? How? Where?'

'A drive-by shooting, in Athens.'

The girl closed her eyes and her body became very still. After a moment her mouth and chin began to tremble. Samantha reached over the table and laid her hand on hers. Annushka snatched her hands away and pressed them into her lap. Her head drooped. She was weeping.

'I'm so sorry,' Samantha whispered.

Annushka nodded, sniffed loudly, then looked up. 'His new wife, Tatiana, was she . . .'

'The only information I have is that your father was killed. I think I'd have been told if your stepmother had been harmed. It should be on the news channels by now. Do you want to switch on the television?'

She shook her head. 'How do you know this?'

'The people who engaged me to protect you keep me informed.'

'What people? And why do I need protecting? I keep on asking, but you tell me nothing.' Tears were trickling down Annushka's cheeks. Her face was white with shock, but already her mouth had stopped trembling and that brash assertiveness was creeping back into her voice. Loretta Fallon had been well briefed. The girl had inherited her father's toughness.

'I told you when I took you out of the secure unit,' Samantha reminded her. 'You need protecting because you've become a threat to the comfortable lives of rich and powerful men.'

'Me, a threat? I'm not a threat to anyone. My father was a threat to many people, but not me. Who have I harmed?'

Opening with something she was certain of, Samantha said, 'You've been having an affair with Alexander Fairchild, your boyfriend's father.'

Annushka was taken aback. She drew a breath, then demanded, 'So what? And Vincent Fairchild isn't my boyfriend. He's one of several boys I know. He's not what you'd call a *boyfriend*. And how do *you* know I'm involved with Alexander?'

Samantha ignored her question. 'We're splitting hairs. The bottom line is, you've been having sex with his father, a government minister, the Foreign Secretary no less, on a fairly regular basis.'

'Has Alexander been talking about me?'

'The last thing he'd do is talk about having sex with his son's underage girlfriend.'

Annushka seemed mollified. She stared at Samantha for a moment, then asked, 'Has his wife found out?'

'Not as far as I know.'

'Then so what? I don't see what harm's been done.'

'He's the Foreign Secretary. He's been conducting an amorous liaison with an underage Russian girl.'

Annushka's expression was still uncomprehending.

Samantha went on. 'It's a security risk: indiscreet talk, the possibility of blackmail.'

'That's stupid.' Annushka's tone was scathing. 'We never did any serious talking, it was just flirty, intimate stuff. He said nice things to me and I teased him a little, but that's about all. We just made love. We never did anything else together, never had a meal, except when we were at a wedding or a party, and then he was always with his wife, so that doesn't count. Does he know other people know?'

'He may have been informed and warned. If he has, he'll be

very concerned about the possibility of exposure and what it would do to him.'

'Alexander would know I'd never do anything to harm him.'

'He might not be so sure. He could be very worried. If the affair became known, he'd lose everything.'

'He should have thought about that before he kissed me and put his hand on my leg. And I still don't see how all this is a threat to me.'

'He might not be prepared to take the risk. The government might not be prepared to face the fallout from a scandal. Remember, you were picked up by the police, but they didn't charge you. No documents, no paperwork, no records. They locked you away in the secure children's home until they could decide what to do with you. They even removed the other girls from the wing. You were there on your own. You were probably in considerable danger.'

'That's why you came and got me out?'

Samantha nodded.

'Who sent you?'

'You don't need to know that.'

Collecting her thoughts, recovering her composure, Annushka said, 'There have been scandals before. Loads of them. A politician has an extra-marital fling. So what? In Italy, France, no one cares. I don't think anyone here really cares anymore.'

The girl was stubborn and not easily scared, Samantha reflected. She'd have to try harder. Pretty sure that lies had been told about the death at Darnel Hall, deciding to confront her with it, she said, 'There's something even more damaging, isn't there, Annushka?'

'I can't think what you mean.'

'The party you went to a couple of nights ago, at Darnel Hall. You witnessed a girl falling to her death; stole mobile phones that held unsavoury images. Perhaps one of them holds a record of the girl's death.'

Annushka stared back at her, her face bleak, her pretty mouth pressed into a hard line. 'Who says so?'

'People who were there say so.' There was fear in the girl's eyes now. Her composure was slipping. Sensing she'd touched on the truth, Samantha went on, 'The sons of senior politicians were at the party, and a couple of viscounts. Who else was there? Was a duke or a prince enjoying himself? A princess, perhaps?'

'I don't know what you mean.'

'You know very well what I mean. Was a prominent member of the Royal Family letting his or her hair down?'

'They're just people to me. I don't bother about titles, or who they are, or what they are. I go for a good time. We have a meal, sometimes one of the boys runs a disco, we dance, we pair off. It's all very discreet, very select. The girls go to, or went to, Martha's. Most of the boys go to, or went to, Conningbeck.'

'There's drink and drugs?'

'I don't drink and I don't do drugs.'

'But some of the others do?'

'There's wine and beer with the meal. A lot of weed's smoked, some snort a few lines of coke, others take pills.'

'And things got a bit wild. They started fooling around. They were so doped up and stupid they threw the girl off the landing and you videoed it?'

Annushka glared at her. 'This is why you came for me, why you got me out of the Sternwood place: you want the phone with the video.'

'If I had the video I could make you safe.'

'And if I had this video, which I don't, how would giving it to you make me safe?'

'You'd no longer have it, so you'd be less of a threat. And if that weren't enough, the contents could be put in the public domain and the damage would have been done. There'd no longer be any point in them silencing you.'

They gazed at one another across the remains of the meal. The refrigerator clicked and began to hum, the faint sound almost hidden beneath the rumbling-roar of a jet plane crossing the sky above the city. Annushka's expression was inscrutable, her face pale and tear-streaked. Presently she said, 'I don't want to talk about this anymore. There's too much to think about. My father's dead and my stupid stepmother might try to interfere with me.' Her body suddenly tensed. Something had occurred to her. 'I must go to the flat. I must go there now.'

'The flat?'

'The family flat. It's close, in Belgravia. I could walk there.'

'It's too dangerous,' Samantha protested. 'They'll be watching the place round the clock.'

'I must empty the safe, take papers and my mother's jewellery. And I need clothes.'

'It's out of the question. I can't risk you being arrested again.'

Annushka's tone became determined. 'Get me in there and safely away, and I'll tell you where you can find the mobile phone with the video.'

Tatiana Dvoskin was sitting in Vladimir's high-backed swivel chair, her trembling legs hidden behind his massive desk. This was the first time she'd lingered in the cabin he'd used as an office. Awnings projected above the long viewing windows; books lined the wall behind the desk. Purchased by the metre, they were intended only for decoration – Vladimir had never read a book in his life. The awnings, the old leather bindings, the dark wood that lined the walls, muted the bright Mediterranean light, made it the calming, peaceful place where Vladimir used to come to think and make decisions, the place where he'd contemplated the vastness of his business empire, the enormity of his wealth.

She'd slept badly. She was still in a state of shock. Only a few days ago her father had said she must wait a while before he ordered her husband's death. On reflection, she'd needed that time to learn how Vladimir dealt with things, observe the way he controlled the entourage who travelled with them and attended to their needs. They had all feared and respected him. Now she was in control, would they fear and respect her? She would have to begin as she meant to go on. She would have to hide her fear and assert her authority, to speak and act appropriately, to distance herself from this retinue of people. She was going to be very alone.

The Dior suit she was wearing was the only item of black clothing she'd brought with her on the cruise. Its tailored jacket had narrow lapels and tight sleeves, the fitted skirt was calf length. It was smart yet austere, appropriate for a bereavement. She'd pinned up her hair, clipped black pearls to her ears, shadowed her eyes but left off the lipstick, concealed her spectacular cleavage beneath a black silk blouse.

Andrei Potamin, the captain of the *Ocean Empress*, had already been to see her. Braided cap tucked under his arm, he'd stood stiffly in front of the desk while he'd offered his condolences and the condolences of the crew. They were all anxious to serve her; he awaited her instructions. At the request of the police, he'd extended their stay in the harbour by another ten days. The Russian ensign was being flown at half mast. If there was any way in which he could assist her, she had only to ask.

He had been followed by Vladimir's secretary, a young Englishman by the name of Cecil Trope. Educated, cultured, something of a linguist, he spoke fluent Russian, German and French and had a smattering of Greek and Italian. Tatiana suspected repressed homosexuality. Wasn't that sort of thing prevalent amongst the English? His devotion, his attentiveness to Vladimir had been excessive. She'd sensed his coolness towards her; a coolness she'd interpreted as sexual indifference, possibly even jealousy. His sorrow at his master's death was evident. Brown eyes wet with tears, small pointed chin trembling, he'd offered his condolences, expressed an earnest wish to continue to serve her, assured her of his dedication. She reminded herself that he was clever, that he had a knowledge of Vladimir's business dealings and how his empire was run. He could be very useful to her. No doubt he'd be able to put aside his aversion to her sex; Vladimir had paid him well and good jobs were hard to find.

He'd brought with him that morning's yellow slips, the transcripts of messages sent to the ship. She'd asked him if there were any he couldn't deal with, any that required her decision. He'd said only one, and passed her a message from the housekeeper at Underhill Grange. Apparently her stepdaughter, Annushka, had disappeared from the secure unit. She hadn't returned home and the police were searching for her. The school had written, complaining of her absence and expressing concern. Tatiana instructed him to send an encrypted reply, advising the housekeeper of Vladimir's death and informing her that she would arrange for a search to be made for the girl. Before dismissing him, she'd asked him to send in Grigori, the head of security. She was waiting for him now.

She had a desperate need to talk to her father, but she daren't use her mobile phone or the systems on the ship. She wanted his advice and guidance, and she wanted him to explain why he'd changed his mind and acted so quickly, without giving her any warning. All those months ago, when he'd urged her to be pleasant and welcoming to Vladimir, to consider him as a possible husband, he'd promised her she wouldn't have to endure the marriage for long. As he'd said, marriage is the perfect way to resolve enmities and consolidate the wealth of families. Vladimir had been the cause of much trouble for him – many of his activities had been financially damaging. When she'd protested about marrying him, her father had pointed out that it would make her a wealthy woman in her own right. And he'd reminded her she was no longer a young girl; that at thirty-two she ought to be married. As her father had predicted, Vladimir had insisted on a pre-nuptial agreement; to protect his daughter, he'd said, and to provide for his mother. Through the long and wakeful hours of the night, she'd read and re-read the document, begun to realize that if she acted swiftly and decisively she could inherit all of Vladimir's wealth. Annushka's disappearance was auspicious. She had to seize the opportunity it presented.

There was a gentle tapping, she called, 'Enter,' the door opened and Grigori advanced across the green and gold carpet towards her, his grey hair close cropped, his broad face impassive. Dark suited, his massive shoulders and huge body blocked her view of the harbour. Tatiana nodded towards a chair. He lowered himself into it and folded his hands in his lap.

She cleared her throat. 'I want to thank you for protecting me last night. You probably saved my life.'

'It was my duty. Whilst I am in your employ I will do whatever is necessary to protect you from danger.'

She remembered his legs imprisoning hers, his arms enclosing her head, the crushing weight of him, and felt a rush of heat to her cheeks. His narrow, pale-blue eyes were fixed on hers. His thin-lipped mouth was grim.

'I'm sorry about Mr Dvoskin. I feel that we failed him, but he would not allow us to carry guns, and he moved out of the cordon and walked on ahead.'

'He was tired,' Tatiana murmured. 'Tired of walking. He wanted to relax in the car.'

'Boleslav pulled him back, tried to step in front of him, but . . .'

'Boleslav died for my husband,' she said softly. 'That's one of the things I wish to talk to you about. Did he have a wife?'

'He had a wife, but they were divorced.'

'Did he have any children?'

'One, a boy. When the child was four he discovered he wasn't the father, hence the divorce. It was acrimonious. He was very bitter.'

'Parents?'

'He never spoke of parents, but he did have a relationship with a woman in Odessa. She had a child from a previous marriage. He used to support them.'

'Can we find her?'

'I'll look through the things in his cabin, check his wallet and the clothes he was wearing when the police release them later today. He carried a photograph of the woman and the little girl. We should be able to trace her.'

'Talk to me again when you have an address and telephone number. I want to speak to her personally and make some financial arrangement. Presumably Boleslav would have wished that?'

'He would have been grateful to you. And he would have admired you for it, as we all will.' They gazed at one another across the gleaming top of the desk. Presently the silence was broken by the deep bellow of a siren, a chorus of shrieking gulls; a ship was leaving the harbour. When the sound had faded, he said, 'You mentioned other matters, ma'am?'

She nodded. 'I think you know that my stepdaughter is in some trouble with the British police. Vladimir was worried, but he felt it best to wait a while before becoming involved. The housekeeper at Underhill Grange, I gather she assumes some responsibility for the girl when Vladimir is away, has sent another message. It seems Annushka has absconded from the place where she was being kept, but she hasn't returned to her home and her headmistress has written to say she's still absent from school.' Tatiana realized she was toying with Vladimir's big black fountain pen. She laid it on the blotter, then linked her fingers to keep them still. 'I've had a message sent to the housekeeper, telling her I'm going to organize a search for the girl.' She paused, uncertain how to put into words the thing that she wanted him to do.

Grigori was eyeing her expectantly, his bushy eyebrows raised. When she didn't speak, he asked, 'You wish me to arrange a search?'

'More than that.' She cleared her throat. 'Vladimir once told me that, from time to time, you undertook special tasks for him?'

He nodded.

'Would you be prepared to do things of that kind for me?'

'I would be pleased to serve you in any way that I can.' He gave her a quick respectful smile. 'Of course, Mr Dvoskin always recognized the special nature of the tasks. He was invariably generous.'

'As I would be.' She leaned forward and lowered her voice. 'I want her found before the British police find her, and I want her killed. An accident of some kind. It is most important that the authorities recover and identify her body.'

Grigori's face remained impassive. He was having some difficulty concealing his surprise at the request, but it didn't displease him. Annushka was smart-mouthed, arrogant, precocious. Since she was little more than a child she'd mocked and tormented him, forever flaunting herself, humiliating him, pretending to offer what he dare not take.

'Does that give you any problems?' Tatiana asked.

'None that I can think of.'

She continued to gaze at him across the desk. It was uncluttered: just the blotter, Vladimir's pen and two telephones, one red and one black. 'When could you travel to England?'

'The police want to go over my statement with me today. After that I should be free to leave. But I have concerns about your security.'

'You think I am in danger?'

'You will always be in danger. Boleslav is dead, I am to travel to England, that will leave Stanislav, Yegar, Dimitri and Vasila. They will have to be vigilant, and you must avoid risk. When you are in public places, the four of them must surround you at all times. And you should put one of them in charge whilst I'm away so their work can be coordinated.'

'Who do you suggest?'

'Vasila is the most capable, the most experienced, and he is respected by the others.'

'He would be loyal?'

'He would die for you; they would all die for you.'

'Our conversation,' Tatiana said, 'it stays with us, it is our secret.'

'Of course. For both our sakes.'

'Thank you, Grigori, that is all. Send the other guards to me. I must thank them, tell them that you are to go to England, and put Vasila in charge.'

He nodded, rose, and headed for the door. When he reached it, she called after him. 'There must be a body, Grigori. There must be clear and tangible proof that the girl is dead.'

CHAPTER SIX

L IONEL BLESSED STOOD AT the kerbside, waiting for a break in the flow of traffic. Dark hair neatly barbered, the open collar of his blue shirt turned down over the neck of his grey sweater, black trousers, black trainers: he was smart, but comfortable. His lock-picking equipment was in an old canvas shopping bag along with a packed lunch and a flask of coffee. If he was able to get inside the house he intended to linger for a while.

The traffic along London Road was still heavy: mothers returning from the school run, workers driving into and out of Cheltenham. From where he was standing he could look across the main road into Orchard Street. It was deserted. He was tingling with excitement and his pulse was quickening, but his hands were steady, there was no shaking. That was important if he was to maintain a delicacy of touch, a sensitivity in his fingertips, when he exercised his much-practised skills.

Traffic lights further down the road halted the flow of traffic. He crossed over, entered the narrow street and glanced into the residents' car park. Only one car: a blue Nissan Micra. There was no sign of Rebecca's tiny white Fiat. He heard the sound of an engine behind him, turned and saw a grey van approaching. It slowed as it passed him, then stopped. The cab window lowered and a head craned out. 'I'm lookin' for Parkside Close, mate. Know where it is?'

Lionel felt a twinge of alarm. He hadn't wanted to be seen, let alone stared at and spoken to. 'Don't you mean Parkside Villas?'

The man studied a delivery docket. 'Yeah, that's it, Parkside Villas.'

Lionel pointed towards a gap in the row of terrace houses. 'Through there; that's Parkside Villas.'

'Thanks, mate.' The van pulled away and disappeared through the opening.

Lionel walked on for another twenty yards, then paused and looked across at Rebecca's house. Through the gateway he could see her green front door and part of the big sash window beside it; a gleaming rectangle of darkness, it was reflecting the refuse bin and the tall privet hedge that enclosed the small paved area in front of the house. He glanced up. The curtains were still drawn across the bedroom windows. That was nothing to worry about, she often left them that way.

He crossed the street, pushed through the groaning iron gate and gently closed it behind him. Concealed by the hedge now, he crouched down beside the door and swung a new-looking escutcheon aside. Bright metal gleamed at him when he peered into the keyhole; the lock had recently been changed. Something decent would have been fitted, probably a curtain-lever job. He straightened up and stood there for a moment, listening. The only sounds he could hear were the rumble and swish of traffic moving along the main road fifty yards away. As a precaution, he pressed the bell push, heard a faint ringing from within the house, then realized he'd be unbelievably embarrassed if Rebecca appeared. She didn't.

No use dithering. If he was going to do it, he'd better get on with it. He groped in the shopping bag, pulled out the wallet of tools and selected the two-piece pick that would open the mortise lock. He inserted the spindle into the keyhole, turned it until a narrow groove was uppermost, then slid the slender steel pick along the groove and into the lock. He closed his eyes. It was all down to delicacy of feel and touch now. He began to probe the mechanism. One by one, he located and lifted the levers, all the time adjusting the torque on the grooved spindle to prevent the raised levers dropping back. It was a delicate business: if he applied too much pressure the mechanism would become impossible to pick, too little and the levers would fall and he'd have to start all over again. There was a faint click as the fifth lever lifted. The lock no longer resisted. When he withdrew the pick and turned the grooved spindle, the bolt slid out of its keep.

Just the cylinder lock now. He'd already decided to 'bump' it. He replaced the pick in the wallet and took out an evenly serrated key. His earlier inspection had been fruitful: he'd correctly matched the profile and it slid into the lock. Things were going well. Gripping the key between finger and thumb, he eased it a little way out of the lock, applied a gentle turning force, then began to tap it rapidly with a hard rubber block, vibrating it in and out of the cylinder, bouncing the pins up to the shear-line. The key suddenly turned. When he reached down and pressed the handle, the door opened.

He snatched up the tool wallet and shopping bag, stepped inside, then closed the door and leaned against it. His legs were shaking. This was illegal entry. If he'd been discovered, he'd have lost everything. He'd never have got a decent job again. But he hadn't been seen, he hadn't been challenged. Getting inside had taken little more than thirty seconds. No one had passed along the street. The tall hedge had hidden him from watchers in the adjoining houses. He could relax now; enjoy the experience, explore the rooms, look through Rebecca's things and, in a secret and mysterious way, become one with her again. He breathed in the lingering aromas of cooked food, fresh paint, the mustiness of the old house.

The narrow hallway extended down the side of the stairs and ended in a door, half glazed with rippled glass that was sparkling with sunlight flooding the room beyond. The stairs ascended to the shadowy darkness of an upper landing. He left his trainers on the door mat, gathered up his shopping bag and went through the half-glazed door. The sunlit kitchen was small but tastefully fitted out: gleaming black floor, white cupboards, grey granite work tops. He crossed over to a window above the sink and looked down a back garden enclosed by high brick walls. The grass was long, flower beds were overgrown with weeds, ivy climbing over the end wall needed trimming. He could have helped her so much; just a few evenings and weekends and he'd have put things in order.

Leaving his bag on the drainer, he wandered out of the kitchen and into a small sitting room at the rear of the house. He recognized the cream and gold striped sofa and chairs that crowded the tiny room. Swatches of curtain fabric, wallpaper samples, paint colour cards, were scattered over a coffee table; decorating magazines were piled up beside the sofa. The television set was on the window side of the fireplace and books were stacked on sagging shelves that crossed a recess on the other side. There were so many things that needed fixing here. If only she'd . . .

Lionel swallowed hard, wandered back down the passageway and peered into the room at the front. A dining table and chairs had been pushed against the far wall. Rolled-up rugs, packing cases, boxes, suitcases, covered what was left of the floor. He ascended the stairs, ignored the half-open bathroom door at the end of the landing and entered a small rear bedroom. Curtains, blankets and winter coats were piled on an unmade single bed. Cardboard boxes were stacked on and beside a chest of drawers.

Heart pounding, legs trembling, he pushed open the door to the larger bedroom at the front. White curtains, drawn across the windows, gave the light a misty, spectral quality. He stepped inside, closed the door, then stood there, wriggling his toes in the deep pile of an ivory-coloured carpet while he glanced around the room. Rebecca seemed very near to him now. This was her private place: the room where she dressed and undressed, the room where she slept.

She was still using the big double bed with the white satin headboard, still using the big pillows with the frilly edges, the white Laura Ashley duvet that matched the curtains. The counter-pane was neatly folded back, the sheet and duvet tossed aside, the pillows on her side of the bed rumpled. Moving closer, he gazed for a while at the faint depression in the mattress that had been made by her body. He took a deep breath and let it out in a sigh. He could smell her perfume, her cosmetics, her warm silky skin; her fragrance permeated everything.

On a sudden impulse, he lay down on the bed in the very place where she had laid, settled his head on the pillow where her head had rested, and was reminded of the aroma of her shampoo, clean and faintly astringent. Presently, the feeling of unutterable loss that had dogged him for weeks began to fade, erased by the over-powering sense of her nearness. Intensely aroused now, his body seemed to burn and his breathing became rapid and shallow. He closed his eyes and kept perfectly still until the intensity of feeling passed. He was sad, he was lonely but he had to get over her. He wanted to so desperately, but no matter how hard he tried, he couldn't. She was the first thing he thought of when he woke; the memory of her was the last thing on his mind when he drifted off to sleep.

She was living here alone. The thought comforted him. She hadn't left him for someone else; she'd spared him the unbearable agony of sexual jealousy. Feeling a sudden unease, he rose from the bed and crossed over to the wardrobe. It was crammed with her clothes, most of which he recognized. He stared down at the shoes beneath the rack of garments, searched the floor beneath the bed. There were no men's things. He sighed out his relief.

The dressing table was crowded with creams and cosmetics, tiny ornaments, a leather jewellery case. He pulled open the shallow central drawer and gazed down at her collection of knickers; silk of many hues, lace-trimmed, embroidered, beribboned, all neatly folded. A white pair, satin, unadorned by lace, larger than the rest, caught his eye. He gently eased them from beneath the others and unfolded them on top of the dressing table. He remembered her wearing them. The others hardly covered her pubic hair, but these rose up to her waist, clinging to her buttocks and the gentle swell of her stomach in a most provocative way. His fingers stroked the silk, then trailed down and lingered on the gusset.

A feeling of revulsion swept over him. He snatched his hand away. He was sick, he was pervy. Endless nights of loneliness and longing had reduced him to this. He folded the knickers, attempted to replace them between the smaller, frillier items. Then, surrendering to impulse, snatched them back, stuffed them in his pocket and closed the drawer. She wouldn't miss one pair amongst so many.

Consumed by shame at what he'd done, he left the bedroom and went into the bathroom at the top of the stairs. Pink tiles covered the walls; a pink bath, basin and WC took up most of the pink-carpeted floor. There was no shower. Rebecca wouldn't like this. It wouldn't be long before she had it all replaced. The intense gaze of a face staring at him out of the mirrored doors of a wall cabinet startled him: the brow was damp with perspiration, the stubble-darkened cheeks flushed, the fleshy lips parted and glistening. Not liking what he saw, overwhelmed by self-loathing, he turned and thudded down the stairs, heading for the kitchen.

He leaned against the drainer and looked out over the garden while he ate corned beef sandwiches and drank coffee, all the time trying to compose himself, trying to rationalize why he was here. After the meal he felt calmer, less tense and nervy. He checked his watch: it was a little after twelve. He'd been in the house for almost two hours. Time to leave before his luck ran out. He put his lunch box and flask in the bag, swept crumbs from the drainer with the palm of his hand, and left the kitchen. When he reached the front door he remembered there was a grate over a light well in the paved area: the house had cellars. After going to all the risk and trouble of getting in, he may as well take a look. He turned and retraced his steps down the hall.

A door had been formed in the panelling beneath the rake of

the stairs. Lionel pushed it open, felt for a switch and clicked it on. An unshaded bulb illuminated whitewashed walls and stone steps that descended to a brick-paved floor. He trotted down, hunching his shoulders beneath low ceilings, breathing in cool musty air. A grimy window let some light into the cellar at the front, where dusty Kilner jars, an old mincing machine and discarded crockery filled shelves that crossed the far wall; probably things abandoned by previous owners. Gas and electricity meters and some ancient fuse boxes were mounted beside the window that looked into the light well. The house needed rewiring. If they'd still been together he could have done it for her and saved her a packet.

He turned down the side of the cellar steps and peered into a small chamber at the back. Bridged by a heavy stone slab, it had once been used for keeping perishable food cool. As he turned to leave, a glint of red and gold caught his eye. He crouched down and peered beneath the slab. A biscuit tin had been placed on an upturned bucket. He lifted it out, removed the lid, folded back some white linen and exposed a number of mobile phones. Like the tin, they were clean and new-looking. Everything else was covered in a fine grey dust, so they hadn't been down here long. Rebecca must have put them here. What on earth was she doing with a collection of mobile phones? Intrigued now, he rose to his feet and carried them into the light at the foot of the steps.

He picked out a phone, keyed it on, and was surprised when icons appeared on the screen. Even more curious now, he touched the 'photo' icon then scrolled through images too tiny to yield any detail. He saw one that carried a video symbol, touched it, and was rewarded by a picture of two girls sitting in a pool of light, one with blue hair, the other a blonde wearing black satin underwear. He touched the start symbol. The women began to kiss and caress one another, their movements slow and languid, their fingers gliding down cheeks to linger on breasts before descending to thighs. They turned to face the camera; they must have realized they were being watched. Amused rather than annoyed, they laughed, made vulgar gestures, and refined female voices mouthing expletives whispered out of the phone.

There was a blur of movement and the scene shifted to a sofa in a dimly lit room. Despite the poor light, the moving image of the embracing couple was startlingly clear. Both were naked and both were young. The girl was laughing helplessly; the boy's face was brick-red and beaded with perspiration. Either they didn't know, or didn't care, that they were being watched.

Lucky beggar, Lionel thought: the girl was blonde, small breasted, slender and pretty. He'd encountered this sort of thing whilst he'd been at university – parties where there was plenty to drink and a few of the girls, a world away from home and family, felt free to cast aside their inhibitions. But unspoken rules had always been observed; anyone caught taking photos or making videos would have been given short shrift.

Another blur of movement, then the camera steadied on a door. It opened slowly to reveal a couple on a mattress covered by a sheet. The observer crept closer. A dark-haired, pale-skinned girl was lying beneath a tall muscular youth. Oblivious to everything except themselves, his big hands were busy, his buttocks were heaving.

The girl raised her knees, began to caress the youth's back and run her fingers into his hair. His efforts became more vigorous, the girl more responsive. She turned her head and her face came into view. Eyes half closed, lips curved in an abandoned grimace, it was Rebecca!

Lionel stared down at the screen. The image was vividly clear. There could be no doubt about it. Her face, what he could see of her body – her plump thighs, her shapely legs – were things he remembered all too well. The girl on the mattress really was Rebecca. Sickened, he switched off the phone. The shock was making him dizzy. A maelstrom of emotions – dismay, disenchantment, a jealous rage – was seething up inside him. He'd adored her, he'd been deeply in love with her, and now the feeling of betrayal was utterly overwhelming. Tears stung behind his eyes, then, in a sudden moment of lucidity, he reminded himself that she'd dumped him. She'd told him to go. As far as she was concerned, it was all over. He had no claim on her. She was free to do as she pleased.

He dropped the mobile back in the tin, folded the cloth over it and replaced the lid. He ought never to have entered her home: it was a bad thing to have done. Intending to put the tin back in its hiding place, he made for the tiny chamber, then paused. He'd take the phones, all of them, search them, discover what she'd been up to. There had to be some reason why she'd collected them and hidden them down here. They weren't likely to be something she'd look for every day, and if she did discover they'd been taken, so what?

Scales were falling from his eyes. He realized now that the expensive clothes, the posh voice, the perfect manners, had hidden a wantonness. Hadn't she always been the one to take the initiative in their lovemaking; who'd been so uninhibited in the bedroom? A smarter, a more experienced man, would have read the signs and not been taken in. She'd probably been deceiving him whilst they were together: all that talk about nights out with the girls and her colleagues from the office. He recalled how pleasant and accommodating she'd been when he began to help her, how she'd cooled when the jobs had been done, how arrogant and nasty she'd been when she'd finally told him to go. He'd been in relationships before. The initial ardour always faded, but he and Rebecca had remained friendly and companionable. When she'd finally spelled it out to him, when she'd demanded that he clear out of the flat, he'd been stunned; almost as stunned as he was now.

The chilly cellar had made his bladder ache. He climbed back to the hallway, put the box in his shopping bag, then dashed up the stairs and stepped into the bathroom. Desperate, he lifted the toilet seat, relieved himself, then pressed the flush. While he was checking the rim of the pan for splashes he remembered he had her knickers in his pocket. What on earth had possessed him? He felt only revulsion now, at himself for having taken them and for the things themselves. After he'd lowered the toilet seat, he dropped them in a wicker linen basket behind the door and descended to the hall.

Seconds later he was standing in the fresh air, using the two-piece pick to secure the lock. That done, he passed through the groaning iron gate and strode off down Orchard Street. The sky had clouded over and rain was beginning to fall. He quickened his pace, heading for the car he'd parked some distance away.

Sir Nigel settled his apron over his lap, placed his huge white-gloved hands on his knees and allowed his gaze to wander around the room. Softly lit by wall lights, furnished with leather chairs arranged around low tables on a russet-brown carpet, it was a comfortable place where the brothers could assemble before, and relax convivially after, their meetings in the lodge on the floor above. In an alcove, glasses sparkled and the brass and mahogany of a well-stocked bar gleamed. Its shutters were down. When the meeting was over, stewards would raise them and do their best to cope with the crush.

The dark-suited members were gathering. Most were attired in the garb of the Master Mason: aprons edged with a band of blue silk and decorated with rosettes and tassels. A few, holders of the Royal Arch degree, wore aprons embroidered with the Triple Tau – three linked Ts within a triangle – on the lowered bib.

He felt secure and relaxed here, amongst brothers who would never speak ill of him; at least, not to the profane, to cowans, to uninitiated men ignorant of the mysteries of the craft. And they would do him no harm; indeed, they would most generously assist him should he be in any kind of need.

The Queen's Lord Lieutenant was late. Sir Nigel wanted to have a quick word with him before the meeting began so he could leave immediately it was over. Evelyn was becoming very edgy about his never being at home. His police work she accepted; the lodge meetings she was less inclined to tolerate. Indeed, she viewed his Freemasonry with a contempt that sometimes spilled over into anger. He caught sight of Sir Kelvin, waved to catch his attention, then watched him make his way between the groups of chattering men towards him.

Sir Kelvin Makewood lowered his stocky frame into the adjoining chair and leaned towards him. 'You wanted a word?'

'Just to bring you up to date. The girl's been taken by force from the secure unit. Happened last night. A woman tricked the warden to gain entry, then pulled a gun and handcuffed him. When she had the girl, she locked him in the girl's room.'

'This woman, is she known to you?'

Sir Nigel shook his head. 'Warden gave the investigating officer a description: blonde, about five-five, husky voice, wore tinted glasses with tiny round lenses. He said the glasses were like the things John Lennon used to wear in the sixties.'

'John Lennon?'

'Musician, the Beatles, the famous pop group.'

Sir Kelvin sniffed. 'Anything else?'

'Handcuffs she used to secure his wrists were Polish, and she conversed with the girl in Russian, so the warden had no idea what they were saying to one another. You know the girl's father's been killed?'

'Read about it in *The Times* this morning.'

'He owned the factory that makes the cuffs, a place in eastern Poland: exports body restraints and riot control gear, mostly to former Soviet Bloc countries.'

A frown shadowed Sir Kelvin's florid features. 'Could the father have arranged it?'

'It's possible. Warden at the secure unit said the girl went willingly with the woman; there was no coercion. There's usually a female officer on duty as well as the man, but she'd had to dash home because her child was ill. He wasn't found until seven the next morning, so the blonde woman and the girl had plenty of time to get away. They could be anywhere now.'

'It's all rather worrying,' Sir Kelvin muttered. 'Things seem to be sliding out of our control.'

'It's a mixed blessing.'

'Don't follow you, old man.'

'If the girl's disappeared, the situation could be easier to deal with.'

'You mean . . .'

Sir Nigel gave the Lord Lieutenant a grim smile. 'We'll just have to make sure she's not found.'

'Dear God, I didn't think it could come to that.'

Nigel leaned forward and laid his hand on Kelvin's arm. 'Don't worry, whatever happens, we won't be tainted. PM's passed it on to the Security Services; he wanted a covert investigation by people less restrained by the law. Marcus Soames, Fallon's number two, is dealing with it. He was making arrangements for someone to go and question the girl when the message came through that she'd been taken from the children's unit.'

'Could the girl's escape and the father's death be linked?' Kelvin said thoughtfully.

'Possibly, but why rescue the girl and then kill her father? And the woman who did the job was almost certainly a Russian. It's more than likely the father arranged it before he was killed.'

'There's something strange about it,' Kelvin muttered. 'Why would the father feel he had to resort to those measures? Surely he could have sent in a lawyer? Holding her for her own safety was little more than a pretence; you'd have had to let her go.'

'He's prodigiously wealthy, Kelvin. Few men could become so rich, so quickly, without straying outside the law. He might not react to situations in the way that you or I would.'

'I take it the security people are searching for the woman and the girl?'

'Diligently. I spoke to Marcus before I left Scotland Yard.

Ports and airports are being watched; a flat the family owns in London, their house in Gloucester, the girl's school, are all under surveillance.'

'What about the mobile phones?'

'They're still putting out trace signals, but there's not been a cheep from the things so far.' Sir Nigel frowned down at his apron, then added, 'We must retrieve those phones. If the press or some anti-establishment lefties get hold of the things and publish the images all hell will break loose. And there could be more than images of copulating couples.'

'You're talking about the death?'

Sir Nigel nodded. 'That tale about the girl losing her balance when she was sliding down the handrail on the stairs is utter nonsense. The body was lying in the centre of the hallway; she must have gone over the balustrade on the landing. And Mortmane's autopsy didn't reveal any trace of drugs or alcohol; she had her faculties, so she wouldn't have been inclined to do anything senseless. And there were bruises all over her body.'

They sat in thoughtful silence for a moment, then Sir Kelvin asked, 'How did her father take it when you gave him the news?'

'Badly. The mother was absolutely devastated.'

'Did they view the body?'

'The father did. Mortuary attendant was told to keep the torso covered, just expose the face, so he couldn't see the bruising. Face is a ghastly mess: the skull was crushed by the fall and the features are badly distorted. He phoned me afterwards, said he was going to demand a full investigation. I managed to calm him down – he's one of us, attends a lodge in north London. When I told him about the semen and how the PM had leaned on Mortmane to keep the sordid details out of the autopsy report, he saw sense. What man wants his daughter's dirty linen washing in public? And he's got his political career to consider. He's not going to make waves.'

'Where would we be without the brotherhood?' Sir Kelvin muttered. They sat in silence for a moment, listening to the low murmur of male voices all around them. Presently Nigel Dillon asked, 'Do you think we should question the people who were at the party again? We've lost the girl. Without her it's going to be virtually impossible to find the phones. Surely there's someone who was at Darnel Hall that night who could give us a lead?'

'Waste of time, old boy. I gave them a good talking to, a good grilling, before you arrived on the scene. They were either dopey with cannabis or coming down after taking cocaine. Most of them were too stupid to think, too stupid to even speak coherently. They only knew the names of their immediate friends. They'd no clear idea who was at the party or who they'd had sex with. Some of them weren't sure where they were. If we talk to them again we could alarm them, make them start blabbing about it. I impressed on them that they had to keep mum; that if any of this got out we'd no longer be able to help.' Anger suddenly exploded in his voice. 'It's an absolute bloody disgrace, Nigel! They've had every advantage, every opportunity, and if we can't contain the situation they'll have brought shame on themselves, their families and the entire establishment. They'd been having an orgy, dammit; a bloody orgy!' His complexion had deepened from pink to puce.

Sir Nigel decided to let it go. This was one of those times when being Commissioner of the Metropolitan Police gave him no satisfaction. He noticed groups of dark-suited men drifting towards the foyer where the stairs swept up to the lodge. 'We'd better go,' he said. 'They're moving off. Meeting starts in a few minutes.'

They rose, joined the crush in the foyer and began to climb the stairs. When they neared the top, Sir Kelvin asked, 'What's on the agenda?'

'Chap being raised to Master Mason. One of my men, actually. Vernon Greenwood, a Detective Chief Inspector. You've met him. He was the officer who came with me to Darnel Hall. He's very sound, understands the big issues; knows when to tread softly, when it's wise to look the other way.'

They passed through heavy doors, into the lodge with its

sky-blue vaulted ceiling, oak-panelled walls, black and white cheq-uered marble floor. The Inner Guard was already seated beside the entrance. In a few minutes the chamber would be secured and then the Tyler, the Outer Guard, would take up his station beyond the doors.

Sir Nigel breathed a sigh of contentment. He liked this ancient lodge. The impressive furnishings and decorations inspired a feeling of awe, even reverence. Long, leather-upholstered benches were arranged on either side of the ceremonial floor. The lodge tracing boards, visual and allegorical instructions on the three degrees of Masonry, stunningly executed by John Harris two centuries earlier, were displayed behind the junior warden's table. Everywhere, on the blue vault of the ceiling, the panelled walls, the high back of the Worshipful Master's chair, were the signs and symbols – level, square, compass, column, orb and sunburst – that spoke to the initiated of the mysteries of the craft.

He and Sir Kelvin took seats at the eastern end of the room, close to the dais and the lodge banner. Soon the Worshipful Master and the Grand Officers would take their places, the chap-lain would say the opening prayers and the proceedings would begin. There would be an exchange of knocks on the door, from without and within, then the blindfolded initiate would be led in by his left arm, a rope around his waist, naked save for a pair of white linen briefs. The ritual of initiation into the Third Degree would then be enacted on the chequered floor.

He settled himself in his seat, straightened his apron, adjusted his gloves. He felt at ease here, amongst this gathering of honest and respectable men, where fellowship and loyalty were assured. He and Sir Kelvin had to do their best to assist brothers Barksdale, Farnbeck and Fairchild. Why should the children of these distin-guished men have their lives ruined by a youthful indiscretion; why should important and high-ranking families, special people, be shamed and brought low? This Russian girl and her liberator had to be found; the incriminating phones had to be recovered.

Tomorrow he'd talk to Marcus Soames, discuss the possibility of some liaison between the Met and the Security Services. Of course, any help he gave would have to be covert – he was reluctant to become involved in actions that might be beyond the law – but he knew he could trust Marcus. The man was devoted to the monarchy, to the concept of aristocracy; passionate about protecting the Queen and her family. But then, he'd expect no less from a man who'd been a Major in the Household Cavalry.

Until this dreadful business had been resolved there would be no security, no peace of mind, for Earls Barksdale and Farnbeck, Foreign Secretary Fairchild, and all the other men of worth whose children had attended that party at Darnel Hall.

CHAPTER SEVEN

Annushka Dvoskin opened her eyes. The bed nearest the door was empty and she could hear water cascading in the tiny bathroom across the landing. The woman who'd said her name was Georgina was taking a shower.

She yawned and stretched. Being shut up in this pokey little place was beginning to drive her crazy. It was three days since the woman had promised to go with her to the flat. Every time she asked her when it would be, she'd smile and say, 'We'd better wait another day, until the watchers become bored and less attentive.'

Georgina did a lot of watching herself: at the window of the tiny sitting room, at the kitchen window that overlooked back yards. And she was endlessly flicking the television to the security cameras so she could check the entrance to the mews. The intense, icily calm gaze of those green eyes scared her a little. The woman was like a tigress stalking her prey: always alert, vigilant, ready to pounce. And she had the knack of encouraging confidences, saying little herself, just deftly steering the conversation by asking the occasional question. Several times she'd had to stop herself saying too much. When she did that the woman smiled, the green eyes blinked slowly and held her in a knowing stare.

Going to Belgravia, getting inside the flat, was becoming really urgent. She had to remove things from the safe and find fresh clothes to wear. She couldn't wait any longer. Her bitch of a stepmother could be plotting and scheming. She needed to see her father's will and study the pre-nuptial agreement. Had he bothered to remember her? She couldn't say she'd been a loving or even a dutiful daughter. Yet, despite her rudeness, her cutting remarks, her failure to show him any love or affection, he'd gone on being kind to her, and loving too, after his fashion. Now he was dead she could no longer make amends: she couldn't even say she was sorry. Cold fingers began to crawl up her spine. She shivered. She'd lost his protection. When she was threatened or in trouble she could no longer scream my father is Vladimir Dvoskin, one of the most powerful men in the whole of Russia. She was motherless, too. She had no one; no one except Babushka, and she was too old and frail to help her. Tears began to trickle down her cheeks and she could feel her chin trembling. She threw back the duvet, swung her legs from the bed and padded out on to the tiny landing, just as Samantha was emerging from the bathroom.

'Can we go to the flat?' Annushka demanded tearfully. Blonde hair tousled, dressed in pyjamas, she looked less like a woman and more like the child she still was. 'You promised we'd go to the flat, but it's—'

'What's the matter?'

'Nothing's the matter. I just want to go to the flat.' The girl's eyes were bright, her chin was quivering.

Samantha put her arms around her and drew her close; felt the feverish warmth of her body. 'Is it your father?' she asked softly.

Annushka sniffed back tears. 'And my mother. I feel so alone. I have no one.'

'And you're frightened?'

'A little . . . More than a little, a lot.' Her voice wavered. 'I'm in so much trouble, I'm so alone and there's no one I can turn to.'

'I understand,' Samantha murmured. 'My mother died when I was eight, my father when I was twelve. But life goes on, and I'm protecting you, and I'll get you out of the mess you're in if you'll co-operate.'

'I want to go to the flat. I have to find a copy of Father's will.

There could be problems.'

Samantha released her. 'Perhaps we've waited long enough. We'll go today.' She felt uneasy at the prospect, but this wretched business was dragging on and it was time she moved things forward.

'We can go this morning?'

'Not this morning. We need clothes and transport.'

'We have clothes and transport. And Belgravia's less than a mile away from Chelsea; we could walk.'

'It wouldn't be safe to walk to a place that's being watched. They could snatch us in the street, and I don't want the car to be seen near the flat. How is the building arranged? How do you get inside?'

'A lot of steps up to the front door, a big entrance hall, then up a flight of stairs. The building's been converted into two flats. One takes up the semi-basement and ground floor, ours is on the first and second floors. The flats are spacious and quite grand.'

'Is there a caretaker?'

Annushka shook her head.

'Who does the cleaning?'

'Two women, from a cleaning firm. They come most days when the flat's occupied; about once a month when it's not. The people who manage the park in the square attend to the entrance hall and the rear yard.'

'You can get into this rear yard?'

'You enter through security gates set inside a recess in a high brick wall. They open with a remote control. There are parking spaces round the back, and an enclosure for refuse bins.'

'You have this remote control?'

'It's on my keyring. It's quite small.'

'So,' Samantha mused, 'the front of the house overlooks a private park; I take it there are more big houses around this park?'

Annushka nodded.

'And at the back of the house?'

'Just the narrow access road, then more high walls and gates to the rear yards of the houses that face the other way.'

'We'll go as cleaners,' Samantha decided. 'We'll pin your hair up, I'll leave off the wig, and we'll both wear headscarves. When we've had breakfast we'll drive over the river and cruise past used car lots until we see one that sells second-hand vans. Then we'll park the car somewhere, buy a van, a hoover and buckets and things.'

'Seems a lot of bother just to get into the flat.'

'Trust me, they'll have it under surveillance, round the clock. They know what you look like. They know a blonde woman got you out of the children's unit. Going as cleaners in a van is the best I can think of. We can buy suitable clothes from a charity shop.'

'Clothes from a charity shop?'

'The sort of clothes elderly women who clean flats would wear.'

'The cleaners sent by the firm aren't elderly and they wear matching overalls.'

'What about the cleaners who do the shared entrance hall?'

Annushka shrugged. 'I've only seen them once or twice, but I suppose they did look a bit old and they didn't wear uniforms.'

'We'll find some clothes in a charity shop. We need to look nondescript.'

Annushka grimaced. 'I don't care to wear some other woman's cast-off clothes.'

'You're wearing my pyjamas.'

'I don't mind your Clements Ribeiro silk pyjamas.'

Her Majesty the Queen frowned into her Tupperware boxes. There were hardly any apricots and only one fig. They should have been replenished. The household staff were slipping. And it wasn't just her dried fruits; the bowls of nuts and Bombay mix left out for her around the palace were emptying much too quickly again. She must remember to ask Sir Lawrence to send out another warning to the protection officers, telling them to keep their sticky fingers to themselves. It wasn't just the theft of one's nibbles, there was also the question of the men's personal hygiene. Heaven knows where they put their fingers before they dipped them into her little treats.

Her Majesty spooned the two remaining apricots and some prunes on to her cornflakes, then glanced up. Her expression brightened. 'This is pleasant, Philip, breakfasting together. You've usually eaten by now.'

'Felt a bit off-colour. Thought I'd have a lie-in.'

Jason, the under butler, laid a warm plate in front of His Highness and Henry, the butler, served him scrambled eggs from a silver dish. Jason supplied a rack of toast, Henry poured coffee into the Duke's cup and Jason placed a jug of warm milk beside the sugar bowl. Both butlers faded away.

The Queen touched the corners of her mouth with her napkin. 'Sir Lawrence mentioned something rather troubling to me yesterday, when we were going through the diary. I forgot to tell you.'

'Jolly good scrambled eggs.' The Duke hadn't heard her. He chewed and swallowed. 'That new chef was a find.'

'He's from the Cameroons.'

'He makes macaroons?'

The Queen raised her voice. 'He's from the *Cameroons*. Lattimer engaged him.'

'Cameroons, macaroons; he knows how to scramble eggs.'

'The eggs are organic, dear. It makes a difference.'

'Charles and his chickens, I suppose.'

'Charles is having all of our eggs and dairy produce delivered from the Duchy Estates, and most of the meat and poultry.'

'Do we have to have so much of this organic nonsense? It's ages since I tasted a decent sausage. That butcher in Cheapside knew how to make a sausage. Your father gave him a Royal Warrant.'

'That was more than seventy years ago, dear,' the Queen said patiently. 'As far as I'm aware, the firm no longer exists.'

They ate in companionable silence for a while, then the Queen touched the corners of her mouth with her napkin again and repeated, a little louder this time, 'Sir Lawrence mentioned a rather worrying incident when we were going through the diary yesterday.'

'Sir Lawrence?' The Duke forked up the last of the perfectly scrambled eggs.

'Sir Lawrence Jenkins is my new private secretary. Bainbridge retired last month.'

'Worrying incident, old girl?' He poured milk into his coffee.

'Yes, dear. He said Earl Farnbeck had telephoned him a few evenings ago. It seems there'd been a party at a place called Darnel Hall, attended by his son and Earl Barksdale's boy, together with a few of their friends. I'm sure you remember them: Teddy Farnbeck and Julian Barksdale. They joined us at Sandringham last year. Julian's a friend of Harry's, he's a first-class polo player, and Teddy's awfully good at tennis.'

Her husband rattled his cup down on its saucer. He'd finished his eggs and drunk his coffee. He could be more attentive now.

The Queen went on, 'There was an accident. A girl was larking about, sliding down the handrail on the stairs. She fell off, hit her head on the floor and died.'

'Good God, how awful. Do we know the girl?'

'I think not. Daughter of a minor politician; not a person one would know. Earl Farnbeck was concerned about the media getting hold of it. There were a couple of viscounts there, the Foreign Secretary's son, the granddaughter of one of my ladies-in-waiting.'

'Was Harry there?'

'I think Sir Lawrence feared he might be, but he was on his way to New Zealand. Security Services had rescheduled his flight. Sir Lawrence spent some time on the telephone the next day, making sure no other members of the family were there.'

'Then I can't understand what Farnbeck was fussing about.'

'I suppose he was just being cautious; that dreadful referendum in Australia, the people voting for a republic, Canada moving in the same direction. One's realm is diminishing by the day.'

'Ungrateful beggars,' the Duke muttered. 'Whatever happened to loyalty and respect? What's become of tradition?'

The Queen sighed. 'Quite so, dear, but at the moment anything that presents us in a bad light is a cause for concern. Sir Lawrence contacted one of my Lord Lieutenants, Major Makewood, asked him to go over to the hall and do what he could to deal with the situation.'

'Sensible move. Makewood's a shrewd old devil. What happened?'

'Sir Lawrence couldn't say. He received no further calls, so he presumed Makewood had dealt with it.' The Queen folded her napkin, placed it on the table and rose to her feet.

'What's in the diary?'

'Charles and Camilla are opening a waste-sorting and recycling plant near Rotherham. The largest in Europe, apparently.'

The Duke's shoulders heaved with a wheezy laugh. 'They couldn't have put it in a better place.'

'I'm going to walk the corgis around the gardens. What about you, dear?'

'I think I'll just potter.'

They crossed the river on Vauxhall Bridge and entered Belgravia via Grosvenor Place. The battered Mercedes van reeked of tar and cigarette smoke, but its high cab imparted a feeling of supremacy in the heavy traffic. Samantha had told the young and enthusiastic Cockney salesman they were Polish women, sisters; she was leaving her husband and they were returning to Poland. 'Would it get them and their possessions to Poland?'

'Poland? No problem, darling.' He'd patted the bonnet. 'Take you round the world, this little beauty. Heavy chassis, strengthened floor, German know-how. And it's taxed until the end of the month. I'm giving it away.'

They'd had no problems with it so far, and no difficulty finding nondescript clothing in a charity shop: wrap-around aprons, two summer dresses, one green and flower-patterned, one blue and plain; headscarves, a pair of low-heeled shoes and an arm-covering cardigan for Annushka. Despite the warmth of the day, Samantha was wearing the raincoat she'd purchased before releasing Annushka from the children's unit; her gun was nestling in the pocket, its silencer projecting through the tear into the lining.

'Turn right here, then sharp left,' Annushka directed. They were rumbling past terraces of tall, elegant houses. Decorated with columns and pilasters, pediments and cornices, their stuccoed walls were blindingly white in the strong sunlight. Annushka was guiding her to the flat, making sure they avoided the square at the front and approached down the narrow access road at the rear. 'Slow down now,' she warned, then pointed, 'That's it, that's the opening. Turn through there.'

Samantha braked, swung the battered white van through the gap, then drove more slowly between high brick walls, pierced at intervals by steel security gates.

'The one that's coming up now, with the brass number plate,' Annushka directed. When the bonnet of the van was inside the recessed opening, she keyed the remote control and the heavy gates swung slowly open. They advanced into the rear yard, then climbed out and made a show of unloading their buckets, mops and box of cleaning things, their upright vacuum cleaner.

'This dress smells,' Annushka muttered, as she unlocked the rear door of the house.

'It's only camphor. Whoever had it must have put mothballs in the wardrobe.' Samantha, clutching the box filled with bottles and cloths, was glancing around. Despite the high enclosing walls, the top-storey windows of houses beyond the access road were visible. Someone could be watching.

'Don't know why she bothered.' The rear door opened and they stepped inside.

'Bothered?'

'With the mothballs. The dress wasn't worth it.'

Struggling with the vacuum cleaner, brushes and buckets, they headed down a tiled corridor, across an impressive entrance hall, then up a curving flight of stairs. The landing at the top had been decorated to reflect the importance of the Dvoskin household. A strip of deep-blue carpet, laid on white and gold tiles, marked the approach, and tall oriental vases stood, like sentinels, on either side of panelled doors in the pedimented entrance. Bit ostentatious, Samantha reflected, as Annushka unlocked the doors and disabled the alarm.

Abandoning the pretence, they dropped their cleaning things in the inner hallway and Annushka began to climb a second, somewhat less impressive, flight of stairs.

'Don't use suitcases,' Samantha called after her. 'Put the things you want to take in these sacks.' She tossed her a roll of black plastic bin-liners. 'I'll join you in a few minutes. I want to look out over the square at the front and the yard at the back, check for signs of our having been followed.' When the girl had disappeared around the top of the stairs, Samantha returned to the entrance doors, opened one, then crept to the edge of the landing and peered down into the shared hallway. It was deserted.

Back in the flat, she wandered into a large sunlit room that extended across the front of the house. Boldly patterned yellow wallpaper decorated the walls, and an oatmeal-coloured carpet covered the floor. Three floor-to-ceiling windows were framed by yellow and gold curtains and tasselled pelmets. Samantha crossed over to the nearest window and concealed herself behind roped-back folds of damask. She peered out. Most of the houses around the square appeared to be embassies now, but a few remained as the homes of the wealthy. Trees, one large, three small, cast dark shadows across the grass in the private park that filled the square. Everything seemed to be sleeping in the heat. There were no cars, no pedestrians, no signs of life.

She returned her attention to the room. A Tompion clock on the high mantelpiece of a white marble fireplace was big, black, ugly and priceless. Tick silent, its hands rested at five past four. A large oil painting of a futuristic-looking white ship surging through blue seas was hanging above it: no doubt a picture of Vladimir's yacht. Ornaments and lamps with large and tasselled yellow shades were arranged on low tables scattered around the room. Suspended from the high and ornate ceiling were two huge chandeliers, their lustres sparkling with tiny beams of reflected sunlight.

Samantha checked a smaller, cosier sitting room at the back, where a television had been installed beside a rather plain fireplace. The pale-blue sofa and armchairs, the darker blue flower-patterned carpet, made it a more feminine room. When she looked through the window she could see the van in the yard, but high walls prevented her seeing anything of the access road and restricted her view of the yards and gardens of the houses beyond.

The kitchen was large and lavishly appointed; the dining room comparatively small. A tiny office off the hall was furnished with no more than a desk, a chair, a copying and printing machine. She returned to the sitting room at the front and positioned herself behind the curtains. She'd watch the square for signs of activity, give Annushka a little time and privacy to find the things she needed before joining her and helping her down with the bags. The sooner they were away from this place the better.

Annushka crossed the landing at the top of the stairs, pushed through a door at the end of a passageway and entered a small room crammed with discarded things: a chest of drawers, suit-cases, a dolls' house, a bookcase filled with children's books, tennis rackets, a hockey stick. She stepped over a box filled with dolls and lifted the lid of a battered plywood desk. Old mobile phones and chargers lay amongst pencils and crayons, hair slides and dog-eared exercise books. She selected a charger with a connector that looked right for her phone, untangled it from the rest and dropped it in the pocket of her apron.

Having found the thing she wanted, Annushka returned to the landing and entered the master bedroom. It hadn't been used since her father and her first stepmother had become estranged. As far as she was aware, Tatiana had never even seen it. The white four-poster bed was unmade, its mattress protected from dust by a single sheet. Tall gilt lamps still stood on the bedside cabinets, but the top of the dressing table had been cleared. She shivered. The silence of the place, the desolation of the unmade bed, were chilling reminders of her father's death.

A large electric fire, cast in bronze, decorated in the Art Deco style, was mounted in the opening of a delicate marble fireplace. She padded over pale-blue carpet, knelt down, pressed a concealed catch and swung it aside to expose the door to the safe.

Thoughts of her father were filling her mind as she leafed through her tiny diary, searching for the page where she'd written the combination. On the eve of his wedding he'd come to her room in their Moscow flat and done his best to give her a fatherly talk about behaving well while he was away on honeymoon. He hadn't admonished her for refusing to be a bridesmaid; he hadn't criticized her coolness, her rudeness, towards Tatiana. She realized now that he'd been showing his concern for her. It was during this conversation that he'd told her about the contents of the safe and given her the combination. Perhaps he'd had a premonition.

She found the page where she'd scribbled the seven numbers, set the dial on the safe door to zero, lifted the brass lever, then entered the sequence. When she pressed the lever down and pulled, the heavy door swung open. She peered inside the tiny space, saw ribbon-tied documents, a small black velvet bag, a slender black imitation leather case, and money, in new bills – pounds, dollars, Euros – all in neat, paper-banded bundles. Georgina had told her to be quick. She tore a sack from the roll, scooped the entire contents of the safe into it, then closed the heavy door and swung the electric fire back in place.

Her heart lurched. He must have been as silent as a cat. He was standing very close, his massive bulk towering over her. She opened her mouth, but before she could gasp his name, he'd covered it with one huge hand and encircled her throat with the other.

'I've been waiting for you,' he said softly. 'I was sure you'd come here. You are alone?'

She stared up at him, blue eyes wide with terror.

Grigori squeezed her throat. 'You are alone?'

She managed to nod.

'You're lying. I heard voices, women's voices.'

'It was the woman who lives in the ground-floor flat. She was saying hello, saying it was a while since she'd seen me.' She mumbled the words into his hand.

He gazed down at her for a dozen heartbeats, his flat Slavonic features expressionless. Then, narrow eyes glittering, thin lips hardly moving, he whispered, 'You're mine now, Annushka. Mine to do with as I wish. What a provocative little tease you've been. Did you enjoy taunting and arousing me? Did you enjoy humiliating me with your smart little mouth?' His hand still clamped over her face, he dragged her out on to the landing and into the bedroom that was hers.

The bed had been slept in. Cups and plates, an overflowing ashtray, littered her dressing table. A leather travelling bag, unzipped and disgorging socks and underwear, lay beside the bed. He reached into a side pocket, took out a syringe, then tumbled her down on the crumpled sheets and knelt astride her. 'You have no need to be afraid, Annushka. I'm not going to take what you've endlessly flaunted, I'm not going to hurt you.' He put the syringe to his mouth, gripped the red plastic sheath covering the needle between his teeth and drew it off. He spat it out, then laid the hypodermic by the pillow.

When he pulled up her dress, anger and outrage overrode her fear. She tried to sink her teeth into his hand, but his flesh was leathery and unyielding, soured by sweat and nicotine. She began to flail his chest with her fists, but the futility of it dismayed her: it was like hitting a brick wall.

Fearful of marking her, Grigori was restraining her gently. Her body must bear no signs of trauma, no marks of an assault. And the injection had to be made at the top of her inner thigh, hidden amongst her pubic hair, where the prick of the needle wouldn't be noticed. He eased a massive knee between her legs, forced them apart, then grabbed the waistbands of her tights and knickers and dragged them down her thighs. He reached for the syringe. It had slid into a fold in the sheet. She was writhing violently now, still aiming pathetic blows at his face and chest. His groping fingers touched the syringe, he smiled down at her and whispered, 'This won't hurt, Annushka. You won't feel a thing.'

'Enjoying yourself?'

He jerked round, saw a black-haired woman standing in the doorway, saw a quick stab of flame. He didn't hear the dull thud of the silenced gun. Before the sound could reach him the bullet had destroyed his right eye and ripped through his brain. The floor shook when his vast bulk crashed down from the bed.

A dazed Annushka slowly sat up; Grigori's blood and brains were splattered over her face and hair, the pillows, the bed's carved headboard.

'Did you know him?' Samantha asked.

'He was one of the security guards who was travelling with Father and my stepmother on the yacht. He was called Grigori.'

Samantha glanced around the room, at the cups and plates, the full ashtray, the unmade bed. 'He's been keeping watch, looking out over the park while he waited for you.' She slid the gun inside the pocket of her raincoat and helped Annushka to her feet. 'Let's clean you up, then we'll get away. Did he hurt you?'

'He seemed to be trying not to.' Annushka drew her hand across her cheek and grimaced with disgust when she saw it was covered in blood. Legs shaking, she rose from the bed, lifted her skirt and pulled the waistband of her tights over her hips.

Samantha picked up the syringe and read the small print etched into the glass. '*KCl 100m,*' she muttered; then, glancing at Annushka, said, 'Potassium chloride, it's absorbed into body tissues after death. Unless the pathologist's very vigilant it's seldom traced, and this dose would have caused heart failure: Grigori was trying to kill you. Where's the bathroom?'

Annushka gestured across the landing. As Samantha led her through the door, she whimpered, 'Why would he want to kill me? He's known me since I was a child. He was Father's head of security.'

Samantha sat her on the rim of the bath. 'He was probably sent to kill you.' She wet a towel and began to clean the blood from the girl's face and hair.

'Sent to kill me?'

'We'll talk about it later.' Samantha dried her face. 'That'll have to do for now. You can take a shower when we get back to the flat. Did you get what you wanted?'

'I emptied the safe. I was about to look for clothes when he grabbed me.'

'We've been here too long,' Samantha muttered anxiously. 'Go and get what you want while I search through the man's pockets and bags, then we'll be off.'

'I can't.'

'Can't?'

'Not with Grigori in there.'

'He's dead, he can't harm you.'

Annushka gave her a terrified look.

'OK, just stand outside the bedroom door and tell me what you want. Where are the plastic sacks?'

'In the master bedroom.' Annushka lunged forward, gripped the edges of the basin, and vomited.

Samantha drew the girl's hair back from her face. When the retching had subsided, she handed her a clean towel. 'Wait here. I'll collect some things for you and search Grigori, then we must go.'

The flat had been made secure and Annushka's belongings placed in the van. Samantha slid the loading door shut, climbed into the cab beside her and backed out on to the rear access road. Up ahead, a black car was reversing across the exit. She glanced in the rear-view mirrors. Behind them, another car was slowly advancing along the narrow roadway, blocking their escape.

'Fasten your seatbelt and brace yourself.'

Trembling hands fumbled helplessly with the metal tag. Samantha reached over, secured it, then released the clutch and pressed the accelerator to the floor. The van surged forward. Annushka began to scream, the sound rising in pitch, louder and louder above the roar of the engine, until they hurtled into the side of the black car and heaved it across the tarmac. The sound of the crash was deafening; seatbelts cut into their shoulders, airbags exploded into the cab in a cloud of chalk dust, then began to deflate.

Samantha crumpled hers into her lap, then slid the gears into reverse. They lurched back. Walls and gates became a blur. In the mirrors she could see a horrified male face behind the wheel of the car looming up behind them; see his passenger making a frantic attempt to open a door. The van lurched and shuddered, and the crash of crumpling metal and breaking glass reverberated around the backs of the houses.

She pumped the clutch and pushed the gear stick over. Tyres screeched and Annushka screamed as they hurtled back towards the mouth of the access road. This time the impact pushed the obstructing car clear, the van scraped past and they bounced out into the street, exhaust pipe trailing along the tarmac. The unsilenced engine emitted a throaty roar as they sped through the quiet residential area, heading west towards Knightsbridge. When they neared the main road, Samantha parked the van down the side of a terrace and unclipped Annushka's seatbelt. 'Out,' she demanded, 'quick as you can,' then dropped down from the cab, slid open the cargo door and pulled out the sacks. She handed one to the girl. 'Sloane Street: it's just beyond the next terrace. Run.'

'What about the van?' Legs shaking, Annushka trotted off, clutching the bulging sack to her chest.

'It's wrecked and it's making a terrible racket. If we try to drive it through London we'll be stopped by the police.'

'The Knightsbridge tube station's quite close,' Annushka panted. 'They'd never find us down there.'

'The underground's full of surveillance cameras. We'll take a taxi.'

Traffic noise grew louder as they ran past the end of the last row of houses, rounded a small park and merged with the shoppers on Sloane Street. The bright afternoon sun, the sweltering heat, the traffic fumes, made their cheap shoes and second-hand clothes feel even more uncomfortable and out of place. Annushka had lost her headscarf; her young face was deathly pale, her eyes were haunted. The silencer on the gun in Samantha's raincoat pocket was chafing against her thigh.

This was the street of a thousand fashion houses. They'd already struggled past Chanel, Emilio Pucci, Yves Saint Laurent and Valentino. Up ahead lay others of equal fame. All had minimalist window displays, some of which involved mirrors. Samantha glanced at their reflections: two bedraggled women carrying plastic sacks and looking like a couple of fleeing shoplifters. She began to fear the taxi drivers might not stop when they beckoned.

A black cab veered out of the traffic and pulled up fifty yards ahead. The passenger, a tall elegantly dressed woman carrying a tiny dog, climbed out. 'Run,' Samantha urged. Annushka rallied, and they began to dash along the crowded pavement. Under the surprised gaze of the woman with the dog, they clambered into the back, heaved the bags in beside them and slammed the door.

'Where to, ladies?'

'Lewisham.'

'Where to in Lewisham?'

Samantha tried to clear her mind of the events of the afternoon, recall the location of the place where they'd left the car. Suddenly it came to her. 'Sydenham Road,' she said. 'The junction with Gurton Road.'

'I know it. It's near Crystal Palace.' Brightening at the prospect of a decent fare, he swung out into the traffic, then kept glancing at them in the rear-view mirror, intrigued by their unkempt appearance, their plastic sacks. 'It looks as if you've had a busy afternoon, ladies.'

The twilight had deepened into a sultry darkness; lightning flickered and thunder rumbled as rain fell steadily over the city. Annushka, clad in green silk pyjamas, was curled up on the tiny sofa, head and shoulders in a circle of light cast by a table lamp. She was studying the documents she'd taken from the safe.

Samantha abandoned her vigil by the window, let the curtains fall back and settled in an armchair. 'Mind if I switch the television to the security cameras?'

'Go ahead. I wasn't watching anything.'

Samantha keyed the remote control. Black and white images appeared: the opening on to the road, the cobbled mews, the tiny enclosed yard behind the flat. They were all deserted. It would seem that no one had followed them. There'd been no mention in news broadcasts of a disturbance in Belgravia, no talk of a dead body. It must have been found. The Met, the Counter Terrorism Unit, the Security Services: one or other of them had seen them arrive at the house and tried to prevent them leaving. The flat would have been searched after they'd escaped.

'You never stop watching,' Annushka murmured.

'Our lives could depend on it.'

The girl laid the papers on her lap, gazed across at Samantha and said softly, 'I'm sorry.' She sounded contrite and somewhat forlorn. The bravado, the youthful arrogance, seemed to be deserting her.

'Sorry? Why are you sorry?'

'For refusing to tell you where the phones are, for not believing you when you said they'd be watching the flat. And I still can't think why Grigori tried to kill me. I teased and tormented him, badmouthed him sometimes, but you don't kill someone for that.'

'You tormented him?'

'Let him see me in my underwear or draped in a bath towel. Sometimes I'd let the towel slip.' She laughed. 'He really lusted after me.'

'Didn't your mother tell you that wasn't the way to behave? That it wasn't fair to Grigori?'

'Wasn't fair? I was doing him a favour; he liked to look. And I didn't have a mother because she was dead, and by that time my stupid first stepmother was too busy complaining to me about my father to pay any attention to what I was doing.'

'You deliberately aroused the man. It was like waving a piece of meat in front of a chained dog, raising appetites he couldn't satisfy.' Samantha glanced back at the images on the television screen. A man and a woman had emerged from a house further along the mews. She watched the man unfurl a large black umbrella and draw the woman beneath it. For an instant they disappeared from the screen as they moved past, then flicked back into view when another camera picked them up. The man's hand moved slowly down the woman's back and caressed her thigh through tight blue jeans. The woman snuggled closer, then they turned out of the mews and faded into the rain and the night.

Samantha glanced at Annushka. 'Have you learned anything from the papers you took from the safe?'

'Things in the pre-nuptial agreement seem to be duplicated in the will, and they're both dated a month before the marriage. In the event of my father's death, Tatiana gets the flat in Moscow, a house in Switzerland and three million US dollars a year, index linked. If she remarries, the payments stop. I inherit everything else, held in trust until I'm twenty-one. Four trustees are listed: an accountant and a lawyer, they're both British with offices in London, and two senior members of the board of CT and T, they're based in Moscow. If I die before attaining the age of twenty-one, everything goes to Tatiana. There's stuff about a pension for Babushka, what would happen if I die without issue, whatever that means, and if they'd divorced. I'm pretty sure I've got it right, but I wouldn't mind if you'd read it through.'

'Now you know why Grigori tried to kill you: Tatiana sent him.'

'But he'd known me since I was a child. He'd have refused to harm me.'

'And since you were little more than a child, you tormented him and verbally abused him. Your father's dead, Tatiana was his new employer; presumably she treated him with some respect. He would have wanted to ingratiate himself with her, do her bidding, stay on the payroll.'

'And the men watching the flat, what did they want?'

'You, so they could question you, find out how much you know about the murder at Darnel Hall and the mobile phones that went missing. And I think it's time you told me where the phones are.'

'When you have the phones you might abandon me. You might even kill me, like you killed Grigori.'

Samantha sighed, summoned her last reserves of patience, made her voice gentle, as she said softly, 'We've talked about this before, Annushka. I've been sent to protect you because two things have put you in danger. First, you witnessed and videoed the sons of powerful men murder a girl. You also stole phones that hold images they wouldn't want exposing to public gaze. Secondly, you've had sexual encounters, some when you were below the age of consent, with Britain's Foreign Secretary. That, by itself, might not have put you in danger, but it does increase the pressures on them to deal with you. You've become a thorn in the establishment's side. When I've recovered the mobile phones, I can make you safe.'

'How do I know *you're* not in the employ of these people? Grigori was supposed to protect me, but he tried to kill me. And when you killed him, you didn't seem to give a damn about it.' She snapped her fingers. 'It was just like that. Maybe you wouldn't have a second thought about killing me.' She fixed Samantha in a baleful stare. 'Have you killed many people?'

'A number of men. I've never killed a woman.'

'Five, six?'

'More than a hundred.'

Annushka's face paled; her voice dropped to a whisper. 'More than a hundred?'

'Probably many more. I no longer bother to count.'

'It doesn't seem to affect you.'

'It affects me deeply. Often, when I'm drifting off to sleep, I see their faces, like the flickering images cast by an old black and white film: fair skinned, dark skinned, old, young, bearded, clean shaven. See the light fading from their eyes as death claims their bodies.'

'That's awesome,' Annushka whispered, in a shocked little voice.

'You must get it into you head that I've been sent to protect you.'

'Who sent you? Was it my father?'

'It was someone who believes in the universal rule of law; someone who's not prepared to allow you to be silenced by powerful men so they can go on enjoying lives of privilege and influence.'

Annushka frowned thoughtfully for a moment, then shrugged and said, 'Why should I put up with this? I have money, I have my passport. I could fly to Athens, board the *Ocean Empress*, and just sail away.'

'And confront the woman who's tried to have you killed?'

'OK, so I'll take a flight to Moscow and stay with Babushka for a while.'

'You'd be arrested at the airport. They wouldn't let you out of the country. And if you managed to get to Moscow, how would a little old lady protect you from your stepmother, Tatania, and the killers she controls?'

The girl's shoulders sagged. Bottom lip trembling, eyes suddenly bright with unshed tears, she lowered her gaze and began to toy with the hem of her pyjama jacket. Presently, a tremulous little voice asked, 'And will you abandon me when you have the phones?'

'I've been sent to protect you. I won't leave you until you're safe. Getting my hands on the phones is part of making you safe, nothing more, and I think you'd better stop shilly-shallying around and tell me where you've hidden the things.'

Annushka sniffed. Blue eyes swept up and held Samantha's gaze for a moment, then she said, 'A girl called Rebecca has them.'

'Rebecca who? What's her surname?'

'I can't remember her second name. I probably never knew it. The girls don't bother with surnames. The boys do. They all address one another by their surnames. It's a silly public-school affectation.'

'And where is this Rebecca?'

'She lives and works in Cheltenham. When Vincent told me some of the boys had been taking pictures of people having sex I—'

'Vincent? Presumably that was Vincent Fairchild, the son of the man you're having an affair with?'

'That's right. Anyway, when he told me, I ran out into the corridor, saw Rebecca and told her. We went into bedrooms, gathering up mobile phones. We had to put them in a pillowcase because we'd collected quite a few. While Rebecca went off to search the bathrooms, I went out on the landing where all the commotion was.'

'Commotion?'

'One of the boys had pictures on his mobile of a girl having sex with him. She was begging him to give it to her. He was holding it above her head and she kept trying to jump up and grab it. She was frantic. The other boys were jostling around them, laughing and jeering. Nicole was very upset.'

'Nicole?'

'The girl who was trying to get the phone; the girl who died.'

'I take it they were all in a state of undress?'

'Nicole wasn't wearing any clothes, nor were most of the boys. They'd all left bedrooms and come out on the landing to join in the fun. In the end, the boys grabbed her, hoisted her up and started throwing her in the air and catching her. She was absolutely terrified – they were completely out of control. I don't really know why I did it, but I got my own phone out and videoed what was happening, right up to her going over the balustrade and falling down into the hall. I was really scared then, so I ran back down the passageway and found Rebecca. They lock all the doors before the party starts, so we got out through a kitchen window and drove away in Vincent's car. I took her to Cheltenham and left her at her front door.'

'She kept the phones?'

'I persuaded her to. She lives alone, in her own home, so there's no one snooping around. If I'd taken them to Underhill, the housekeeper or one of the security guards might have found them. And I couldn't have hidden them at the flat. The housekeeper drives up once a month with one of the security men. He makes sure the place is OK, and she checks on the cleaners. She's always looking through my things. I think Father told her to spy on me because he thought I might be doing drugs.'

'This Rebecca; you have her address?'

'No, but I could take you to the house. And she told me she works for Volmack Financial Services, at their head office in Cheltenham.'

'We'll go tomorrow, arrive early, before she leaves for work.'

'Will we come back here?'

'I don't think so. When you're being hunted it's wise to keep moving.'

Samantha watched the deserted scenes from the security cameras for a while, then joined Annushka in the bedroom. She was in bed, asleep, oblivious to the flicker of lightning beyond the curtains, the thunder rolling over the city, the rain pelting down on the slates above their heads. The slender leather case and velvet bag she'd been holding had slid from her grasp. Samantha picked up the bag and shook the contents into her hand: a wedding ring, an engagement ring, a diamond brooch and matching earrings, a string of pearls. She slid them back and tugged a cord to close the bag. The case opened to reveal a photograph of a man and woman on their wedding day. The man was youthful, stockily built, not much taller than his bride. He stood very erect, his large masculine features confident and self-assured. The woman was beautiful, exceptionally so, but her eyes were apprehensive, her body stiff and tense. Annushka's mother hadn't radiated any happiness on her wedding day.

CHAPTER EIGHT

WITH EVERY SHRILL RING, Tatiana Dvoskin's irritation mounted. Who could be calling at this hour, and why didn't Vladimir answer the phone? It was on his side of the bed; the calls were always for him. She turned, reached out to shake his shoulder, but felt nothing. Her eyes fluttered open. She was alone. Sleep had erased the memory of her husband's death. His body, lifeless and cold, was lying in a mortuary in the basement of the Alexander Hospital. He would never lie beside her again. She slid into the coolness on what had been his side of the bed, and groped for the phone.

'Maxim here, Mrs Dvoskin. I'm sorry to—'

'Maxim?'

'Maxim Gaidar, your radio operator, your communications officer.'

'Maxim . . . Maxim,' Tatiana mumbled, struggling to clear her mind.

'Maxim Gaidar, ma'am. I'm sorry to disturb you at this hour but I have messages I think you would consider urgent.'

'Messages?'

'Messages, ma'am.'

'Go ahead.'

Gaidar's voice lowered. 'I think it would be best if I gave them to you on the red phone.'

'The red phone?'

'On the desk in your study. It's connected directly to the bridge and my radio room. It's not linked to the ship's telephone system. Shall I wait five minutes, then call you on the red phone?'

'Please.'

Tatiana crawled from the bed, drew on her robe, then yawned her way to the study at the far end of the suite of rooms. She lowered herself into Vladimir's chair then gazed through the observation windows while she waited. Dawn was breaking over Piraeus. The first rays of watery sunlight were gleaming on the white walls of the hotels and flats and offices that crowded the harbour; infusing some colour into the drab greyness of the sur-rounding hills. Frightened and lonely, she found herself missing Vladimir. The coarseness, the insensitivity of his lovemaking had repelled her, but he'd been a strong protector, someone who'd made decisions, relieved her of all the nagging worries. And he'd been incredibly sweet to her that last day they'd spent together. Perhaps he'd sensed that something bad—

The red phone began to bleep. Tatiana swung round to face the desk and picked it up.

'Mrs Dvoskin?'

'I'm here.'

'I've had a message from the housekeeper at Underhill Grange. The police called, late yesterday evening, showed her photographs of a dead man and asked if she could identify him. It was Grigori. They told her his body had been discovered in your Belgravia flat following an incident at the rear of the premises involving two women. They asked her if she could throw any light on the matter. She said the only women who would have been at the flat were women sent by the cleaning company, usually in pairs. Other than that, she knew nothing. They asked her if your stepdaughter had returned home. She told them she hadn't. They said they were investigating the death, and they'd probably want to talk to her again.'

Tatiana slumped back in the chair. Wide awake now, she was

struggling to grasp the implications of what she'd been told.

A deferential, almost timid voice interrupted the silence. 'Ma'am? Are you still there, ma'am?'

'I'm here, Maxim. Please go on.'

'I presumed you would wish me to report the communication directly to you rather than enter it on a yellow slip for your secretary to deliver.'

'You presumed correctly. Thank you, Maxim. I think you said there was another message . . .'

'Your father wishes to speak with you. Would you like me to make the connection now?'

'Would it be secure?'

'Completely. I'll activate the encryption.'

'Surely that would make it unintelligible to my father.'

'He has the encryption algorithms. He is able to decode our communications. Shall I make the connection?'

'Please. How long will it take you?'

'Just a few moments. I will try to be quick.'

The line went dead. Tatiana replaced the handset and sat back, pondering on the duplicity of men. Who had killed Grigori, and who had given her father the means to decode Vladimir's communications? Was there anyone she could trust? The phone began to bleep. She snatched it up.

'Tatiana?'

'Daddy.'

'How is my beautiful daughter?'

'Frightened. Vladimir's death was a great shock. You said it would be a while before you ordered the killing, but you acted so quickly.'

'A window of opportunity arose, as they say. When I learned that his only child is missing and in trouble with the police, I decided to bring the takeover forward. The girl is the only remaining obstacle to our taking control of Vladimir's enterprises; so, first the father, and now the daughter. She's staying away from home, she doesn't attend her school – fewer suspicions are raised, fewer questions are asked, when a missing person has an accidental death. And with her father dead, there's no one to express concern, no one to make demands on the authorities.'

'You've arranged for her to be killed?'

'Men boarded flights to England within an hour of Vladimir's death. Don't concern yourself. It has to be done.'

Tatiana stroked her forehead. So much was happening so quickly. What should she tell her father? Some things might be best not mentioned. Perhaps there was nothing he didn't already know. She said, 'The girl could be difficult to find.'

'We located her yesterday. There's a flat in London, in a part of the city called Belgravia. I had two men watching it from a nearby house; two others cruising the neighbouring streets in a car. They heard a crash, drove towards the noise, saw two women in a white van ramming a car, trying to escape from an alleyway. The women smashed their way out and drove off. My men followed, saw them abandon the van, run towards the main road and hail a taxi. They followed the taxi to a car park outside the city where the women recovered their car, then followed them to a flat in a district known as Chelsea. The place is being watched. At the first opportunity, the girl, and her companion if needs be, will be killed.'

'And there will be a body? There must be a body.'

'Of course there will be a body.' Leonid Molosovitch struggled to keep the irritation out of his voice. Did his daughter think he was stupid?

'The car they rammed – it was a police car?'

'She's in trouble with the authorities, so presumably it was.' His tone became brisker. 'How are you coping with the captain and the crew and the people on the ship?'

'Very well, so far. They've all assured me of their loyalty and their wish to serve me. They're all respectful; at least, they are to my face.'

'Good. Immediately the police say the *Empress* can leave port, I want you to instruct the captain to sail for Odessa. When you dock there I'll join you, arrange the appointment of a new captain and crew, and begin the takeover of all Vladimir's enterprises.'

Take everything over? Surely it was hers? It was all hers. Her father had promised her the marriage would make her one of the wealthiest women in the world; now he was proposing to take her inheritance from her. She'd been used, used by her father to entice a business rival; used like a whore by a husband of only thirty days. Suddenly close to tears, she blurted out, 'Vladimir treated me badly, Daddy. He would never leave me alone. He did dirty things to me. He wanted me to do dirty—'

'Enough! These are not matters a daughter should speak of with her father. All marriages have secrets. If you must talk about these things, discuss them with your mother when you return home.'

Tatiana sniffed back tears. 'I understand Maxim Gaidar is your man.'

'He's been in my employ for three years. He can be trusted. If you need to contact me, he can arrange it; any hour of the day or night.' Leonid sighed and affection replaced the anger in his voice. 'It will be good to have you home again, Tatiana. Your mother and I have missed you.'

'And I you,' she murmured dutifully. 'Thank you, Daddy.'

She put down the phone, suddenly feeling even more vulnerable, even more isolated and alone. She had to protect herself, to hold on to what was rightfully hers. She'd bathe and dress, then summon the captain and instruct him to arrange for their stay in Piraeus to be prolonged, to make it appear that this was at the behest of the police and port authorities. Then she'd speak to Vasila, her new head of security, tell him that Maxim Gaidar must not return from his next trip ashore. That would hold the situation, give her time to decide how best to safeguard her interests. And she'd tell Vasila she wanted the guards to accompany her to Athens, to the place called Kolonaki where the fashion houses had their boutiques, and the shops sold the most expensive and luxurious things. She needed new clothes, clothes that were smart and fashionable, yet restrained; the sort of things a newly bereaved and wealthy young widow would be expected to wear.

Loretta Fallon followed the attendant down the strip of red carpet that crossed the entrance hall to Number 10. They passed through half-glazed doors with delicate fanlights, then headed down a wide corridor lit by windows that looked over an inner courtyard. It led them to an antechamber to the Cabinet Room. Loretta glanced through an open doorway, into an office on her left. A white-haired woman wearing a black dress with a white collar and cuffs was sitting behind a desk, frowning down at papers through heavy horn-rimmed spectacles. When she looked up she smiled, left her desk and joined them.

'I'm so sorry, Miss Fallon, the Prime Minister's decided to hold the meeting in the study rather than the Cabinet Room.' The woman turned to the attendant. 'Could you escort Miss Fallon to the study, James?'

'Of course.'

'So sorry, Miss Fallon,' the woman gushed. She removed her spectacles and smiled again.

'The study's over the entrance hall, ma'am, so we could go back the way we've come and use the front stairs, or we could slip through the door over there and take the grand staircase. Which would you prefer?'

'Grand staircase is fine.'

He led her through the doorway and they began to ascend some dog-legged stairs. Not very grand, Loretta mused: the scroll work on the balustrades was very ordinary, the lamps on tall black and gilt poles somewhat grotesque. It was utterly outclassed by the sweeping staircase at Darnel Hall where Nicole Manning had fallen to her death. Black and white photographs, set in white mounts and thin black frames, lined the ascent. Carefully posed, artfully lit, the photographers had done their best to make their subjects, all Prime Ministers, appear wise and statesmanlike. As they neared the top of the stairs they encountered the only image of a woman. Tight lipped, blonde haired, her cold myopic stare challenged them as they passed.

'You're taking me on the grand tour,' Loretta said, making conversation.

The man turned and smiled. 'Are you very well acquainted with the premises, ma'am?' He led her around the landing and through an opening at the top of a short flight of stairs that descended to yet another passageway.

'Not really. I've visited a few times, that's all.' She was dissembling. She'd memorized the plans of the place, attics to basements, arranged for it to be swept for surveillance devices and had devices installed. It was a warren of rooms and stairways and passages; a security nightmare.

'The room they call the study used to be called the library, but that was before my time. Prime Ministers Wilson, Heath and Thatcher liked to work in it.'

'Is that so?' The staff seemed to enjoy trotting out these trifling titbits of information about their former masters.

After more twisting and turning, they emerged in a wider passageway. The attendant knocked gently on a door and swung it open. 'Miss Fallon, Prime Minister.'

Loretta swept past him, into a large sunlit room where tall windows looked out on Downing Street. White-painted bookcases lined three walls; a black and white marble fireplace dominated the fourth. The Prime Minister was sitting at a round table with Sir Nigel Dillon, the Metropolitan Police Commissioner, Alexander Fairchild, the Foreign Secretary, and Bernard Markham, the Home Secretary. She heard the door close behind her as she strode towards them.

'Thank you for joining us, Miss Fallon. Sorry about the early start.' The Prime Minister's countenance was grim and unsmiling.

And it was Miss Fallon today. When she'd been summoned to the dawn meeting it had been Loretta.

She drew out one of the chairs. Upholstered in some nondescript blue material, its seat had sagged badly. Perhaps its springs and webbing had surrendered under the onslaught of Harold and Edward's portly posteriors. She thought it surprising that Margaret hadn't insisted the chairs be reupholstered, the rather ordinary table replaced with something grander, the tired-looking Persian carpet renewed. Loretta settled herself into the depression and placed her briefcase beside her feet.

The four men were eyeing her warily. She gazed back at them, her grey eyes calm and untroubled. Sir Nigel Dillon was tall, broad and powerfully built, his massive head crowned by a mane of greying hair, his black and beribboned uniform immaculate. A swagger stick, ebony with silver tips, together with a silver-braided cap, lay beside him on the table, a pair of black leather gloves nestling inside it like a couple of dead bats. Loretta found his sheer physical presence brutish and rather overwhelming.

Alexander Fairchild met Loretta's cool gaze with apprehensive eyes. Wearing a blue pinstripe suit, he was leaning back in his chair, a blue silk handkerchief bursting out of his top pocket, his arms folded across his chest. Without a doubt he was extremely handsome in that mature and urbane kind of way many women find attractive. Bernard Markham, the Home Secretary, a smallish man with thinning hair, a long face and nervous eyes, stared at her for a moment, then glanced down and began to shuffle through his papers.

The Prime Minister cleared his throat. 'The Dvoskin business, Miss Fallon.' His voice had a reedy, nasal quality. 'Did your people discover anything when they questioned the girl? Are you any nearer to recovering the mobile phones?' Small and deep-set eyes searched her face.

Devious bastard, Loretta mused. Dillon would have briefed him about the girl's escape from the secure unit and the debacle in

Belgravia. She rested her elbows on the arms of her chair, linked her fingers and smiled. 'I thought you would have heard, Prime Minister; the girl was freed from the secure unit within hours of your placing the matter with me. Since then I've had the family home, her boarding school, and a house in Belgravia where the Dvoskins have a flat, kept under surveillance. Yesterday, two women in a white van entered the Belgravia premises via the rear yard and carried cleaning paraphernalia inside. Operatives were instructed to move in and prevent their escape from the rear access road. After about thirty minutes the women left, carrying plastic sacks, and used the van to batter their way past the obstructing cars. They abandoned the van in a side road close to Sloane Street.'

The Prime Minister sniffed. 'Your people allowed them to escape?'

'The cars were a write-off, incapable of being driven. One of the agents had concussion, another a broken wrist, and they all suffered severe bruising.' Loretta studied each of the men in turn. Dillon's lips were arranged in a smile that verged on a sneer, Alexander Fairchild's expression was inscrutable, the Home Secretary's right eye had begun to twitch, the Prime Minister looked peevish.

'Agents entered the flat after the incident,' Loretta went on.

'You had a warrant?' the Home Secretary interrupted.

Loretta's smile widened. 'Covertly.'

He gave her an exasperated look.

'They found the body of a man in one of the bedrooms. All means of easy identification had been removed. The body was still warm. Death had probably occurred at the time of the women's visit to the premises.'

'They killed him?' the Prime Minister demanded.

'It would seem so. The Serious Crime Unit at the Met were notified. Presumably they carried out the usual scene-of-crime investigation and removed the body.' She glanced at Dillon.

He drew breath, then said, 'We found some evidence that he'd been using the bedroom to watch the approach to the front of the building; cups and plates on the dressing table, a full ashtray on the window sill. And we found the plastic cover of a syringe needle in the bed, but no syringe. The housekeeper at the family home in Gloucester identified the body from photographs as that of Grigori Malkin, one of Vladimir Dvoskin's security men.'

'And Vladimir Dvoskin was murdered in Athens a few days ago,' the Prime Minister muttered. 'How did the girl escape from the secure unit?'

'She was freed from the place by a woman who tricked her way inside,' Dillon explained.

'Tricked her way in?'

'She made herself look dishevelled, exposed her breasts and hammered on the door, screaming she'd been raped by a man who was still chasing her. When the warden on duty let her in, she threatened him with a gun, handcuffed him and made him take her to the girl. The girl went with her willingly, there was no duress, and the warden was imprisoned in the girl's room. The girl and the woman conversed in Russian; the handcuffs were manufactured by a Polish firm owned by Dvoskin.'

'The girl's rescuer was Russian?'

'It would seem so. Probably a professional employed by the girl's father.'

The Prime Minister returned his gaze to Loretta. 'And how is the search for the stolen mobile phones going?'

'We've abandoned the electronic search; there was absolutely no response to signals. Either the batteries have been removed or the phones have been disabled in some other way; they may have been destroyed.'

He gave Loretta his displeased look. 'We must recover those phones, Miss Fallon. God knows what's recorded on the things. I can't contemplate the consequences of them falling into unsympathetic hands. The women who arrived in the van; did your men get a good look at them?'

'One wore a dress and overall; the other a raincoat and dark glasses. Both were wearing headscarves. The cab of the van was high, it was driven at speed towards the cars; it wasn't possible for the agents to note more than that.'

The Prime Minister gave Dillon a smug little smile. 'Why would Dvoskin hire someone to kill his own security man?'

Dillon shrugged. 'Everything's conjecture, Prime Minister. We can't be sure the woman was in his employ. Then again, he may have wanted the man killed. Who knows?'

'Aren't we playing a little fast and loose with the law here?' the Home Secretary demanded.

'Can't think what you mean, Bernard?'

'Confining the girl in a secure unit. She wasn't formally charged with anything, she wasn't arrested, nothing untoward was found in the car she was driving, there's no paperwork, no records.'

'We've been over this, Bernard,' the Prime Minister snapped tetchily. 'Her parents couldn't be reached so she was put in a secure unit near her home for her own safety.'

'Well, I'm unhappy about it. Don't forget, she's the daughter of an extremely wealthy Russian. We might be faced with a legal challenge.'

'The Met will face any legal challenge. Nigel will take it in his stride. And her father's dead, dammit. I'm sure his widow's got more to think about than a wayward stepdaughter.'

'Very well then,' the Home Secretary ploughed on, 'forget the way the girl was treated. What about the undocumented and unprocedural response to the events at Darnel Hall?'

The Prime Minister's expression darkened and irritation sounded in his voice. 'That's a completely separate issue we can discuss later, if you wish. But just remember, you attended that early-morning meeting. You went along with what was decided. You can't walk away from this now.' He stiffened his shoulders and glared at the faces around the table. 'And perhaps we should all remind ourselves of what we thought was at stake that night, and the oath we took when we assumed office. We were trying to safeguard our most precious institution; we were protecting the monarchy at what seems to be a particularly sensitive and difficult time.'

'And we've since learned there were no high-profile members of the Royal Family at Darnel Hall.'

'Since learned, Bernard. We didn't know it at the time. The Queen's private secretary was being cautious when he asked Makewood to go there and contain the situation. And it's not just members of the Royal Family we have to consider. What about Manning's daughter, the girl who died? He's one of our rising stars. Would you want information like that revealing to the public? And Barksdale and Farnbeck's boys were there, and Alexander's son, not to mention the granddaughter of one the Queen's ladies-in-waiting. It had to be contained, Bernard, not just to protect the monarchy, but in the interests of stable government.'

The Home Secretary met the Prime Minister's gaze for a long moment, then said softy, 'And perhaps we should remind ourselves that we've just emerged from an expenses scandal, and that several members of parliament are currently embroiled in a paedophile investigation. Are we going to be confronted with yet another unspeakable mess in a few years' time?'

'I'm sure our predecessors always endeavoured to act in the best interests of parliament and the nation, Bernard.' The Prime Minister's tone had become patronizing. 'Democratic institutions have to be safeguarded, public confidence maintained. There will always be things that are best concealed.'

'The rule of law – shouldn't that be upheld?' the Home Secretary demanded.

The Prime Minister leaned towards him. 'For the last time, Bernard, you attended that early-morning meeting, you went along with what was decided. We're not going to change course now.' He took a breath, paused to calm himself, then, one by one, glared into the faces around the table, trying to assert his authority.

The Home Secretary looked down at his papers, subdued but unconvinced.

'We have to do something for the girl's sake,' Alexander Fairchild said softly. They were the first words he'd spoken. 'We've no idea what her relationship with this woman is. Her father's dead, presumably she'll inherit; it could be coercive. It would have been better if she'd not been stopped by the police, if she'd just driven home to the flat.'

'I believe it was you who informed the police she'd stolen your son's car,' Dillon muttered.

'His mother contacted the police. He was in a state of some distress when he arrived home. A girl had died at the party, Makewood had scared the living daylights out of them, his car had been taken, he'd had difficulty finding transport. I told him we'd recover his wretched car, that if the girl had taken it, it was probably just a simple misunderstanding.' Alexander Fairchild shrugged. 'Anyway, it's happened now. But we ought to find the girl, for her own safety.'

'And to discover what she's done with the mobile phones,' the Prime Minister added. 'But you're right, Alex.' He turned towards Loretta. She raised an eyebrow and gave him an encouraging smile. 'The rather low-key response you've taken to the situation hasn't produced a successful outcome, Miss Fallon. All we have are injured operatives, wrecked cars, and questions being asked about a disturbance in Belgravia. The girl's become involved with a woman who seems to be on the rampage: threatening officials with guns, killing foreign nationals, ramming cars to escape arrest. One could reasonably say these are acts of terrorism. One could—'

'Criminal acts, Prime Minister, not terrorism,' the Home Secretary interrupted. His right eye was twitching noticeably now. He'd become quite agitated.

'As I was saying,' the Prime Minister went on, 'these could be taken to be acts of terrorism, and I'm handing responsibility for the problem to Sir Nigel to be dealt with by his Counter Terrorism Unit.'

'One could hardly describe that as a measured response,' Markham protested.

'The terrorism legislation will free Sir Nigel to act in a more robust way.'

'She's a young girl, Edward.' Alexander Fairchild's tone was pleading, almost fearful. 'She's probably innocent of any wrong-doing. She was just caught up in events, like the other young people at the party. They may have been behaving rather stupidly, but that's in the nature of the young.'

'And I'll say it again,' the Home Secretary insisted, 'using counter terrorism legislation can't be regarded as a measured response; it's going to make us even more vulnerable to legal challenge.'

'I heard you the first time,' the Prime Minister snapped. 'And I'm sure Nigel's taken Alexander's comments about the girl on board. But just remember this: if anyone knows the whereabouts of those wretched mobile phones, she does.' Turning towards Dillon, he snapped, 'Deal with it, Nigel. Deal with it robustly and deal with it quickly.' He rose to his feet. 'That's it, everyone. Thank you for attending. Now, if you'll forgive me, I've another meeting I'm already late for.' He pushed back his chair.

'Prime Minister . . .' Loretta called him back. 'I have informa-tion I must give you. Now. For your eyes only.'

'Surely it's not that urgent?'

'I think you'll agree that it is.'

'A risk to national security?'

'And to the government.'

He turned to his Home Secretary. 'Would you stop by Cynthia's office before you leave, Bernard. Ask her to give my apologies to James Walton, tell him I've been unavoidably delayed and arrange another meeting.'

Loretta waited while the room cleared and the door closed. She was in a dilemma. What she was about to do would put Quest and the girl in even greater peril. She clicked open her briefcase, drew out a glossy ten-by-eight, and slid it across the table to the Prime Minister.

When he glanced down at it his face registered surprise, then became grave. When he finally looked up, the flesh around his mouth was white. 'Where was this taken?'

'At some big country house. A tennis party.' She slid a second photograph over the table.

He snatched it up. 'And this?'

'They're in the bedroom of his Mayfair flat.'

'Does anyone else know about this?'

'Not as far as I'm aware. They've been very discreet.'

'How long have you known?'

'Almost a year. When the first photographs were taken, she was below the age of consent.'

'You've waited some time to tell me.'

'These things often burn themselves out and they're forgotten.'

'Then why tell me now?'

'I understand there's to be a meeting of European Foreign Ministers in Moscow next week. Would it be appropriate for a man who's been having an affair with the underage daughter of a recently murdered Russian oligarch, a girl who's being hunted by the police, to attend?'

'Of course it wouldn't be appropriate.' He studied the first photograph again. 'The fool,' he muttered. 'The bloody fool.' He glanced up. 'But she is very lovely, Miss Fallon. If it was on offer, any man would find it difficult to refuse. I'm loath to stand in judgment.'

'She was a child, Prime Minister.'

'She doesn't look like a child.'

'He has an extremely beautiful wife, and two teenage sons.'

'And I refuse to stand in judgment on the man,' the Prime Minister repeated, then his voice lowered as he went on,

'Nevertheless, he won't be going to Moscow, and he may not be in office much longer. But that's strictly between us.' He passed the photographs over the table. Loretta returned them to her briefcase.

'Have they tried to contact one another since she went missing?'

'They appear to use dedicated mobile phones to arrange their little trysts. We've monitored the activity, round the clock, but no calls have been made since she disappeared.' Loretta rose to her feet. 'When you tell him he's not going to Moscow, will you tell him why?'

'I'll have to.'

'I'd rather you didn't reveal the source of your information?'

'I won't, but he's no fool. He'll have a good idea where it's come from.'

'I'll take my leave of you, Prime Minister.'

'You'll liaise with Dillon?'

Smiling broadly, she said, 'We'll give him every possible assistance,' then muttered under her breath, 'short of any actual help.'

CHAPTER NINE

SAMANTHA TOOK HER EYES off the fast-moving traffic and glanced at the girl in the passenger seat. 'You're unusually quiet this morning.'

Annushka bristled. 'You never have very much to say.'

'I enjoy listening to you.'

'No, you don't. You just sit there, watching me, letting me talk, hoping I'll tell you my secrets. How long will it be before you realize you already know all of my secrets? I don't have any more.'

Samantha smiled. The girl was very perceptive.

'And you've missed the turn-off,' Annushka added. 'Cheltenham's junction 15. You've driven past it.'

'We're being followed and the last thing I want to do is lead whoever it is to the place where the phones are being kept. I'll stay on the motorway for a few more miles.'

'Followed?' Annushka turned and peered between the seats. 'By that great big truck?'

'By a silver Vauxhall Vectra and a white Audi. The Vauxhall's behind the lorry; the Audi's a few cars ahead. They've been taking it in turns to tail us.'

Annushka hunched her shoulders and huddled lower in her seat. 'I simply can't bear any more of this,' she moaned. 'I'm scared. I'm really, really scared. *Everyone's* trying to kill me.'

Samantha risked another glance. The girl's face was pale, her body beneath the flowered silk dress rigid with fear. The last thing she needed right now was a hysterical girl. She had to distract her, to calm her. 'Don't worry,' she said softly. 'I won't let anyone harm you. Trust me.'

'Why should I trust you? Why should I trust anyone?'

Ignoring her questions, Samantha went on, 'You're very fragrant, and that's a beautiful dress.'

'Yves Saint Laurent, Rive Gauche; Alexander gave it to me. And this is the dress I was wearing when he kissed me for the very first time.'

'And where were you when he gave you that first kiss?'

'At a wedding reception. I was bored, so I began to wander around the house. I bumped into him in one of the sitting rooms. He was looking at some Russell Flint watercolours: nudes mostly. He turned, gave me a fabulous smile and said, "It's you! I couldn't take my eyes off you at the reception." So I said, "You seem to have found something else to focus your eyes on now." He laughed and said, "They're just daubs of colour, but you're here, in this room, and you're real and you're unbelievably lovely." Then he kissed me. It was the sweetest, tenderest kiss. Then he sat me on the edge of a table and kissed me again, and while he was kissing me I could feel his hand, caressing my leg. I didn't stop him because I really, really wanted him to.' She began to weep. 'And I miss him. I do miss him so very much. If he knew about the awful mess I'm in he'd do something about it. He's incredibly important. He'd stop all these people hunting me.' Prompted by a sudden thought, she sniffed back tears and frowned at Samantha. 'Did Alexander send you to protect me?'

Samantha reached out and squeezed her hand. 'It wasn't Alexander Fairchild. But try not to be afraid. Everything's going to be OK. I'm going to take the next turn off and lead them down country lanes.'

'And then what?'

'Then I'll deal with them.'

'Kill them, you mean?'

Samantha gave her a grim smile.

'I can't take any more of this,' Annushka moaned. 'They might kill you before you can kill them. And there could be lots of them.'

'There are four men, two in each car.' Samantha squeezed the girl's hand again. 'Trust me. Just do as I say and you'll be fine.' She slowed, flicked the indicators then turned up a slip road, took the exit for Malmesbury and followed a sign that listed Rodbourne, Corston, Little Somerford, Lea and Cleverton. It all sounded very rural and remote. She glanced in the mirrors. The silver Vauxhall was following at a discreet distance.

After half a mile the road narrowed as it wound up a hill. Bordered by overgrown verges and tangled hedges, it was deserted; so far the only traffic they'd encountered was a cattle truck and a tractor, both heading in the opposite direction. Samantha reached into the pocket in the door, lifted out the gun and laid it on her lap. She glanced at Annushka. 'Push your seat back as far as it will go, unfasten your safety belt and slide down into the footwell. Press your shoulders hard against the seat and your feet against the bulkhead. Crouch down as low as you can. Whatever you do, don't lift your head.'

Samantha braked and bounced the car on to the verge. When the silver Vauxhall had swept past, she lurched back on to the road, accelerated hard and lowered the passenger window. The buffeting of the slipstream, the whine of the revving engine, were loud in the car. With her left hand gripping the wheel, she steadied her gun hand in the crook of her arm and waited for the cars to draw level. Startled eyes glanced across at her, then flicked back to the road. She squeezed the trigger. The Vauxhall's side-light shattered, its driver jerked and slid out of sight, exposing the silhouette of his passenger. She loosed another two shots, then stood on the brakes. Tyres screamed. The silver car surged on, drifting, driverless, in a gentle curve that took it crashing through the hedge and into a field. Samantha glanced through the gap as they cruised past. The Vauxhall had come to rest at the end of a ribbon of flattened corn.

The men in the white Audi would probably turn back at the next junction and follow their friends. She had to check the car in the cornfield before they arrived, make sure the driver and his passenger were dead, then hide and wait. A place had to be found where Annushka could be concealed. She glanced down at the girl, crouching in the footwell. 'You can get back in your seat now. Everything's OK.'

Annushka scrambled up and groped for her seatbelt. 'What's happened?'

'I shot the driver. I think I hit the other man, too. The car crashed through the hedge.'

'Go faster,' Annushka urged. 'Let's get away from here before—'

'We can't, not yet. I have to find somewhere to hide you, then I'll go back, make sure they're dead and get their documents.'

The hedge merged with a copse of stunted trees that concealed the gateway into the field. There was no gate now, just a pair of massive stone posts. Samantha let the car roll to a stop, then reversed back along the road and down into the sunken opening. The long grass on the verge, the adjoining trees, made it an effective hiding place.

'I'm going to leave you here while I go back and check things.' Samantha was rummaging amongst the clutter in her bag, searching for ammunition. She picked out half a dozen rounds, ejected the clip from the gun, fed them in, then slammed the loaded magazine back with the flat of her hand.

'I'm scared,' Annushka moaned. 'You said there were two cars. 'What if the men in the other one come while you're gone?'

'Just sit here and keep your head down. No one can see you from the road.' Samantha slid the keys from the ignition, dropped them in her shoulder bag and pushed open the door.

'Don't leave me. Please don't leave me.' The words spilled out on a wail of panic.

'I have to. Just sit tight until I come back.'

Samantha made her way back along the field side of the hedge, the skirt of her cream linen dress brushing through ripening corn. As she neared the Vauxhall she could see the passenger slumped over the dash, his head pressed against the windscreen. When she rounded the car and wrenched open the driver's door, a blood-streaked head and shoulders rolled out and sightless eyes stared up at her. She searched the man's pockets, found a wallet, a passport in a tattered envelope, a mobile phone. As an afterthought, she rested her fingers on his throat. There was no pulse.

Blood was splattered over the passenger side-light and the glass was crazed around a bullet exit hole. Samantha heaved open the sticking door, then twitched the skirt of her dress clear of dripping blood. Torn flesh marked a massive wound above the man's ear. He was heavy, slumped forward, awkwardly placed. She grabbed his collar, pulled him across the seat and emptied his jacket pockets. A mobile phone began to jangle out a tune: probably one of his accomplices calling to check where they were. She switched it off, crammed it, along with the other items she'd taken, into her bag, then began to run back through the corn .

The sound of a car approaching up the hill was becoming louder. She ducked down behind the hedge until the Audi swept past, a white blur beyond the tangle of twigs and leaves. Seconds later she heard tyres screech, doors open, running feet and men shouting. She glanced over the hedge. A petrified Annushka was standing in the middle of the road, about twenty yards from where the white car had stopped. The girl suddenly turned and began to run back up the hill, the skirt of her dress billowing, her long hair streaming. The men began to chase her, calling her name, calling out to her to stop.

Samantha ran on behind the hedge until she found a gap, then clambered through and crossed over to the white Audi. The driver's door was hanging open, the engine was running. She slid behind the wheel, pushed the gear stick over and moved off up the rise. The men were middle-aged, overweight, out of condition.

One was trailing behind the other; both were so consumed by their efforts to capture the fleeing girl they hadn't heard the approaching car. She surged forward. The man in the rear glanced over his shoulder, his eyes widened, there was a sickening crunch and his body arched back over the bonnet before being dragged beneath the car.

Annushka was lissom, long-legged, young. She was drawing away from her remaining pursuer when she stumbled. She picked herself up and limped on, but the man caught her, slid an arm around her waist and held her, kicking and struggling.

Out of the car now, Samantha ran towards them, holding the gun. The man spun round, Annushka broke free, staggered on for a few paces then turned and looked on, gasping for breath.

'Put your hands behind your head and go through that gap in the hedge.'

The man stared back at her, his expression uncomprehending. When she repeated the command in Russian, he obeyed.

As she followed him across the verge, she glanced at Annushka. 'Stay here, watch the road. If you see anything coming, give me a shout.' The girl's hair was tousled, her face deathly pale. She was bending forward, gasping for breath, her hands pressed against her thighs.

The man eyed Samantha warily. His oatmeal-coloured linen suit was crumpled, his face red and beaded with perspiration.

'Don't look at me; turn and face the other way, then kneel down.'

He shuffled round and fell to his knees. She moved closer and stood behind him, staring down at his thinning grey hair. 'Who sent you? Why were you looking for the girl?'

'Milosovitch sent us.'

'Milosovitch?'

'Father of Tatiana, Vladimir Dvoskin's third wife. She told him she was worried about her stepdaughter, asked him to find her. That's what we were doing.'

'And what were you going to do when you'd found her?'

'Tell Milosovitch, then keep her safe until Tatiana arrived to take care of her.'

'You're lying.'

'It's the truth, I swear –'

Samantha swung the gun down on the side of his head. He howled and sagged forward. She leaned over him and put her mouth close to his bleeding ear. 'Your friends are dead. If you lie to me, I'll kill you too. Now, I'll ask you again, what were you ordered to do with the girl?'

'I've told you,' he moaned, 'to keep her safe until –'

She swung the gun down again. 'Don't lie to me.'

He drew in a shuddering breath. 'Bitch,' he moaned. 'You bloody bitch.'

'Milosovitch ordered you to kill her, didn't he?' She stabbed the muzzle of the gun into his temple. 'Tell me the truth or I'll kill you. I'm counting. One, two—'

'Yes, yes, he told us he wanted her dead.'

'And how were you to kill her.'

'An accident; it had to look like an accident. We were going to disable the passenger airbag on one of the cars, drive it at speed into a wall and make sure the passenger side took the impact. Kuzma was going to do the driving. He'd worked as a stuntman in Russian and Polish films. He—' The man stopped gabbling and began to beg. 'Please, have mercy on me. When you're hired by a man like Milosovitch, you can't refuse—'

Samantha squeezed the trigger. The sound of the exploding cartridge was loud in the summer-morning stillness and there was frantic beating of wings as birds took flight from the hedgerows. She knelt beside the man's body, emptied his pockets, then returned through the gap in the hedge. Annushka fixed her in a cold, unblinking stare. Her body was shaking, her mouth curved down in a display of disgust and loathing. Samantha didn't speak, just took her arm, led her back to their car and settled her in the passenger seat. The road was still deserted. She ran back up the hill, searched the body of the man lying on the tarmac, then returned to Annushka and slid behind the wheel. Minutes later they were driving down the slip road that fed into the motorway.

'Did you have to kill that man?'

Samantha studied the girl. Eyes bleak, she was staring through the windscreen towards the entrance to the street where her friend, Rebecca, had her home. After spending the afternoon in Cheltenham, they'd parked in front of a terrace of tall Regency houses that were separated from the main road by a broad area of grass. She said softly, 'Didn't you hear him admitting he'd been sent to kill you?'

Annushka nodded.

'If I'd spared his life he'd have contacted Milosovitch, more men would have been sent, and they'd have been even more vicious and determined because they had a score to settle. Killing him has kept us safe for a while.'

The girl's face was pale and still, almost mask-like. Over the course of the afternoon, resignation and despair seemed to have settled over her, displacing her fear. Presently she said, 'Babushka's mother, my great grandmother, was raped and beaten and left for dead during the Second Great War. She used to tell Babushka that it was a time when the souls of men were ruled by dark powers. I think that time is still with us.' Annushka turned and fixed Samantha in a chilling stare. 'I know I am going to die. Those men didn't kill me, but others that follow them will.'

'You're not going to die. I won't let it happen.'

'How will you prevent it? First they send Grigori, and you kill him. Then they send four more men for you to kill. Next time they will send a regiment of men, you will be overwhelmed and we will both die.'

'I promise you, no matter what it takes, I'm going to protect you. Stay close to me, and when I have to leave you, do as I say and you'll be safe. If you hadn't left the car back there the men would never have seen you.'

'You were gone a long time. I was frightened. As I waited I became more frightened, so I came looking for you.' She returned her gaze to the opening into Orchard Street. 'And why did we have to park over here? Why couldn't we just wait outside the house?'

'There may still be someone following us and watching us. We don't want to lead them to the mobile phones.' Samantha glanced up and down the service road that fronted the Regency terrace. There were only three other cars parked there. They were all empty. There was no one standing or loitering, just the steady flow of traffic along London Road, the occasional pedestrian heading home from work or walking into Cheltenham. She switched on the car's sat-nav and studied the network of nearby streets. The junction they were watching was the only way into Orchard Street.

'I think she's here,' Annushka announced.

Samantha glanced up.

'The dark-haired girl with the supermarket carrier bags: that's Rebecca.'

They watched her walk past the massive trunks of trees that took up most of the opposite pavement, suit jacket over her arm, her breasts filling a white silk blouse, her hips shaping a black skirt. She turned into Orchard Street.

'Shall we go?'

'Give her a couple of minutes; let her get inside the house and put her shopping down.' Samantha checked her reflection in the rear-view mirror, teased a few wayward strands of blonde hair back in place. Wearing the wig didn't irritate her quite so much now, especially in the air-conditioned coolness of the car. She took the tinted spectacles with the small round lenses from her bag and put them on. Annushka's friend, Rebecca, was going to get a good look at her. It was best that she should remember only blonde hair and quaint glasses.

'There's blood on your dress,' Annushka said. 'Just a speck, on the hem.'

Samantha glanced down. 'So there is. Nothing I can do about it now.' She pushed the door open. 'Let's go. The sooner we have the phones, the sooner I can bring this wretched business to an end.'

'When I introduce you, who shall I say you are?'

'Tell her I'm a friend from Moscow.'

There was a loud knock. Marcus Soames glanced up from his paper-strewn desk, watched the door open, saw Loretta Fallon enter and approach across drab brown carpet. She settled herself in the visitor's chair and dropped her briefcase by her feet. He smiled. 'How did the meeting go, ma'am?'

'Pretty much as I expected.' Loretta crossed her legs, arranged the hem of her navy-blue skirt around her knees. 'The PM's passed the search for the Dvoskin girl over to Dillon; told him to treat it as a terrorism problem. Home Secretary questioned the legality of what they were doing. He was quite agitated.'

'I thought they might bang on about the Belgravia fiasco.'

'PM mentioned it, but he wasn't over-critical. I think he was glad to have an excuse to pass the search for the girl over to the Met.' She frowned and her voice became urgent. 'Keep up the surveillance, Marcus: phone traffic, faxes, everything. We need to know what they're doing.'

One of three phones began to ring. He snatched it up, listened, then said, 'Thanks for keeping me informed. Call me as soon as you have more information.' He replaced the handset and looked at Loretta. 'Four men found dead along an isolated country road about ten miles from Malmesbury. Three of them had been shot through the head, the fourth run over by a car. They haven't been identified.'

They eyed one another across the untidy desk. He's beginning to look his age, Loretta reflected. The dark and curly hair was flecked with grey, the features had softened, become more than a little florid. But those wickedly blue eyes were still bright and alert, his posture erect; he was still very much the Guards Officer who used to ride with the Queen's Household Cavalry. She said, 'That list of mobile phone numbers they gave us; did the researchers check the owners' names?'

Marcus sifted through the papers on his desk, plucked out a sheet and passed it over.

Loretta glanced down at it. 'No princes or princesses of the House of Windsor, then?'

'Apparently not, ma'am. The Queen's secretary was being cautious when he asked her Lord Lieutenant to intervene; perhaps he thought there was just a chance Prince Harry might be there. Seems he was on a flight to New Zealand: goodwill visit, countering the threat of another referendum.'

'But Viscounts Farnbeck and Barksdale are listed,' Loretta went on, 'and the son of the fourth Baron Pelgrove, the granddaughter of one of the Queen's ladies-in-waiting, a nephew of the Prime Minister, a daughter of a High Court judge, the son of the chairman of a major bank. And the dead girl was an MP's daughter. There may have been no princes, but it was still a gathering of the children of the elite.' She handed the list back to Marcus. 'I told the PM about Fairchild's liaison with the Dvoskin girl.'

Blue eyes began to twinkle. 'And?'

'He was shocked; shocked and angry. I had to tell him. Would he want a man who's having an affair with the daughter of a murdered Russian oligarch to attend a meeting of foreign ministers in Moscow?'

'Hardly, ma'am, but the revelation could put the girl in even greater danger.'

'I had a duty to tell him, Marcus.'

'Indeed, ma'am. But having phones that hold incriminating images of the offspring of the great and the good is one thing; being the juvenile mistress of the Foreign Secretary is quite another. She could bring the government down. You said Dillon's been told to regard her as a terrorist?'

Loretta nodded.

'Then God help the girl.'

Rebecca Fenton gathered up magazines, wallpaper samples, a swatch of curtain fabrics, and dumped them on a coffee table. 'Sorry about the mess in here but there's nowhere else we can sit at the moment. The room at the front is still full of rugs and packing cases.' She glanced at Annushka. 'I heard about your father, on the television news. I'm so sorry.'

'Thanks,' Annushka said. 'It was quite a shock.'

'It's got to you,' Rebecca murmured gently. 'I can see that.' She picked up a mug and a plate. 'Can I get you anything? Tea, coffee?' She gave the woman with the pinned-up blonde hair and tinted spectacles a questioning look.

Annushka managed a smile. 'This is my friend, Georgina. When she heard what had happened, she flew over from Moscow to be with me.'

'Pleasure to meet you, Georgina.' Rebecca glanced from one to the other. 'A drink: can I get you anything?'

'We're OK,' Annushka said, 'and we don't have much time. I've really come for the mobile phones.'

Rebecca perched on the edge of an armchair and glanced at Samantha. 'Your friend, Georgina, she knows about the party?'

Annushka nodded. 'She's helping me sort things out.'

'You're lucky they're still here. I didn't like having them. I've been thinking about smashing them up with a hammer and throwing the bits in the bin. I'll get them for you. Won't be a sec.' She rose, crossed over to the door, then turned and gave Annushka a concerned look. 'You look absolutely shattered. Sure you won't have some tea? And it wouldn't take me long to rustle up a few salmon and cucumber sandwiches.'

'Thanks, but no.' Annushka gave her a tired smile.

Rebecca stepped into the passageway, then paused and looked back again. 'What are you going to do with the phones?'

Annushka glanced at Samantha.

'Have the memories wiped professionally,' Samantha said. 'Everything removed. Then parcel them up and send them to the boy who organized the party. If the owners get them back they'll be happy and we can all forget about it.'

She speaks flawless English, Rebecca mused, every bit as good as Annushka's. And what an incredibly husky voice; soft, not loud and actressy as husky voices sometimes are. She said: 'You'll make sure everything's erased before you hand them back? I daren't think what Mummy and Daddy would say if what's on them ever got out. And my grandparents!' She rolled her eyes. 'Grandfather's the Dean of Wetmarch. He'd have me exorcised or excommunicated or something.'

Samantha reassured her, then asked, 'Has anyone been in touch with you since the night of the party?'

'No one. I was quite jumpy about it for a while. Every time I heard a car driving down the street, every creak of the gate, I thought someone was coming for me. I'm only just beginning to calm down.'

Rebecca turned, pushed open a door in the panelling beneath the stairs, clicked on a light and disappeared down stone steps. Annushka settled back into the sofa and closed her eyes. Samantha heard a muffled exclamation, the sound of things being moved, feet hurrying on steps, then Rebecca appeared in the doorway.

'It's gone.'

Annushka opened her eyes and sat up. 'Gone?'

'The box, the biscuit tin I put the phones in. It's gone. I hid it under a stone shelf, on top of an old bucket.'

'Has it fallen—'

'I've pulled everything out from under the shelf. It's not there.' Rebecca moved back into the sunlit room and flopped down in an armchair.

Samantha was watching her closely. This wasn't an act: she was shocked all right. Concern was creeping, like a shadow, across her face as she grasped the implications.

'Has anyone visited the house?'

'Mummy and Daddy, when I was moving in. No one since then. If I want to socialize, I go out, and I haven't brought anyone back. I had a bad experience. That's why I moved here; why I've been wary of inviting anyone in.'

'Bad experience?'

'A boyfriend, at my old flat. He was helpful to me, doing jobs and things, and we lived together for a while. Eventually he became jealous and controlling and I had to tell him to leave.'

'He caused trouble?' Samantha asked.

Rebecca shook her head. 'I thought he would, but when he finally realized it was over, he went all silent on me and left. He never contacted me again. He was terribly upset, though.'

'Do you think he might have. . . ?'

'He probably doesn't know I've left the flat. He certainly won't know I'm living here.'

'And no one else could have got in?'

'I had the locks changed just after I did the move. All the spare keys are in the knife drawer in the kitchen.'

'And you've never seen signs of anyone having been inside?'

Rebecca looked down at her hands for a moment, then, in a faltering voice, began to recount events she seemed to find troubling. 'I thought I did, just a few days ago, but the doors and windows were secure, there were no signs of any tampering, but . . .' She frowned. 'Something made me feel a bit scared. It's an old house. I thought it might be haunted, by one of those poltergeist things.' She let out an embarrassed little laugh. 'It sounds crazy, and I feel so stupid.'

'What was it that made you think the house might be haunted?'

'Well, when I came home from the office one evening, I found crumbs, crumbs of brown bread, and seeds, like the ones they sometimes put in wholemeal loaves, and what looked like a dried-up splash of coffee on the drainer in the kitchen. This room's a mess but that's because I'm in the middle of decorating, and I'm fussy about worktops. I know I left it clean that morning, and I don't eat brown bread.'

'And the house was secure?'

'Completely. The doors were locked when I came home; the windows fastened. But that's not everything. When I went upstairs to change, the bed didn't seem to be quite the way I'd left it. I can't be sure about that; it's just a feeling I had. And a couple of days later, when I was emptying the washing basket in the bathroom, I found a pair of white satin knickers that were perfectly clean. They're things that come right up to my waist and I don't often wear them. The last time I saw them was when I put them in the drawer in the dressing table, just after I came here.'

'This man,' Samantha said, 'the one you told to go, did he like you to wear your big satin knickers?'

Rebecca's cheeks coloured. 'I really don't know. I suppose he must have seen me in them, but he wasn't the kind of man to make comments about things like that. He was a bit shy and withdrawn, easily embarrassed.'

'And you say he helped you with things?'

'That's right: mending kitchen cabinets, sorting out the electrics in the flat, getting my laptop working. He could fix anything. When I told him to go I think he felt I'd used him.' She shrugged. 'I suppose I had, a little.'

'What's his name?'

'Lionel. Lionel Blessed. He's with an IT company called Sungrove Solutions. That's how we met; his firm were installing a new system at the place where I work. It couldn't possibly have been him, though. He's a timid little conformer, always obeys the rules. He wouldn't dream of trying to get into anyone's home, and he's no idea where I'm living now.'

'Do you know where he lives?'

'He has a flat in Gloucester. I never went there and I don't have the address. I don't even have his phone number; it was on a scrap of paper I threw away when I moved here. We used to meet almost daily at the office, then he moved in with me. We didn't have much cause to phone one another.'

'What about meter readers? Presumably the gas and electric meters are in the cellars?'

'No one's read them since I moved in.' Worried brown eyes gazed across at Samantha. 'I simply can't believe the phones have gone,' she whispered, in a frightened little voice. 'How can they have just vanished like that?'

'It's not ghosts,' Samantha said wryly. 'Someone's been in the house and taken the things.'

CHAPTER TEN

G RACE FAIRCHILD STUDIED THE notes she'd scribbled on the programme. State reception, Bolshoi Ballet, two formal dinners, tour of Saint Basil's, visit to the Tretyakov Gallery: three days, three functions per day, so at least six different outfits, plus a spare, at least one spare, perhaps she should pack two. And something smart to travel in; something that wouldn't crease. She didn't want to look a crumpled mess when she stepped off the plane.

She was hungry. God, she was hungry. She'd starved herself for two months, lost more than twelve pounds, but she could get into her clothes again; no tight zips, no bulges. She could even get into that black Valentino cocktail dress she'd worn in Paris a couple of years ago. She took the hanger from the rail, held the garment in front of her skirt and jumper and studied her reflection in the mirror behind the wardrobe door. The flouncy hem was a bit frivolous, a bit too high above the knee, but it fitted like a glove, brought out the creamy paleness of her skin, made her look years younger.

Grace flicked a wave of auburn hair from her cheek and hung the dress amongst the items she'd selected for Tuesday. She'd wear it when they visited the Tretyakov Gallery, put a gleam in the Minister of Culture's eye, that heavy thick-set man – what was his name – Andrei Monya, or was it Malkin? She must brush up on names during the flight. She ticked off items on her wardrobe list. Monday was covered, so was Tuesday, but there was nothing on the programme for the morning of Wednesday. Better check with Alexander.

She left the bedroom and trotted down the creaking stairway. Everything seemed to creak and sag in their old farmhouse. Sometimes she wished they'd bought one of those big new places just outside the village: they'd been building them when they came, more than a decade ago. Don't start brooding about the house, you'll be enjoying yourself in Moscow next week, she admonished herself. Her spirits lifted. She was really looking forward to the trip. These little jollies were her reward for enduring the tedium and boredom, not to mention the loneliness, of life in Alexander's dreary rural constituency; what he called his safe seat.

Grace found her husband relaxing on the sofa, his unopened dispatch box by his side. He'd discarded his jacket, loosened his tie, but he hadn't changed into casual clothes. There was a glass in his hand and an almost empty bottle of Scotch stood on a small table near his elbow. A football match was playing on a television in a recess beside the inglenook fireplace. She nodded at the red box. 'Finished already?'

'Not even started.' He raised the glass, sipped whisky, swirled it around his mouth, then swallowed. 'I'll look through the papers later.'

'The Moscow conference; there's nothing scheduled for wives on Wednesday morning.'

He eyed her warily over the rim of his glass.

'I need to know what I'll be doing so I can pack appropriate clothes.'

'You don't need to bother about packing clothes.'

'It's a free morning? Nothing's been arranged?'

'We won't be going to Moscow.'

Stunned, she lowered herself on to the edge of an armchair. 'Won't be going? Why won't we be going?'

'Prime Minister wants me here. Emergency debate on the crisis in Somalia.'

'But I was really looking forward to it, and I've spent an absolute fortune on clothes.'

'Let me have the receipts. I can claim most of it back on expenses.'

'Who's he sending in your place?'

'Tavistock.'

'I thought Edward was your friend, Alex. He's behaving like a shit, humiliating you like this.'

Alexander shrugged, drained his glass, then returned his attention to the football match.

Grace sagged back in the chair and stared across at her husband. He had a morose, hangdog look about him, and she'd never known him ignore the contents of his box before. Something had happened. 'Why, Alex? Why is Edward Benson doing this?'

'I've told you. He wants me—'

'Rubbish. It's an emergency debate, nothing critical. Tavistock could handle it, or he could deal with it himself. He doesn't need you there, holding his hand. And *you're* the Foreign Minister. Sending an under secretary instead of you is going to raise eyebrows; it might even cause offence.'

Alexander shrugged, nuzzled his glass, continued to stare blankly at the moving images on the screen. He seemed unwilling to look at her. She noticed how grey and drawn his face was. His enthusiasm, his vitality, seemed to have drained away, leaving him tired and defeated. A sudden intuition chilled her. Steeling herself, she asked, 'What have you done wrong, Alex?'

'I haven't done anything wrong,' he retorted tetchily. 'It's just that Benson decided—'

'Edward wouldn't treat you like this, not after you've been so loyal and worked so hard for him and the party. We're old family friends, for heaven's sake.' She rose and turned towards the door. 'I'll phone Helen and ask her what's possessed her husband to do this to us.'

Alarmed, Alexander heaved himself out of the sofa, grabbed

147

her by the shoulders and pulled her back. 'That's simply not done, Grace.' He turned her towards him. 'You don't discuss Cabinet business with Edward's wife. He's the Prime Minister. He's made his decision. We've got to accept it.'

She tried to struggle free; he drew her close, crushed her against him and held her tightly, restraining her. She became still, gazed up at him for a moment, then said breathlessly, 'That's the first time you've put your arms around me in months, Alex. I think it's the first time you've even touched me. Pity it had to be in anger; love would have been nice, desire would have been better than nothing.' She looked into his face. His brow was furrowed, his cheeks gaunt, his parted lips downturned; she could see the worry in his eyes, smell the whisky on his breath. Frantic thoughts were racing through her mind, spawning notions that filled her with dread. 'You've done something wrong, haven't you, Alex? You're involved in some scandal. Is it a woman?' Her heart lurched. 'Who is she, Alex?'

'Don't be stupid.' He shoved her away, stepped back to the sofa and slumped down on the cushions. He retrieved his glass, drained it, then reached for the bottle.

'Who is she, Alex?' Grace demanded. An icy calm was settling over her. Her mind was suddenly alert, her memory clear. It really was more than a year since he'd treated her as anything other than a housekeeper, a dinner party hostess, someone to charm his colleagues and constituents. There'd been no intimacy of any kind. He'd spent more and more time in London, and when he was at home he was always shuffling through the papers in that wretched box. She'd assumed it was pressures of work, but perhaps she'd been wrong. She glared at him. He was still sipping whisky, still staring vacantly at that stupid football match. 'Tell me who it is,' she demanded. 'Is it one of your researchers? Is it someone I know? If there's trouble coming, you have to tell me.'

'You're being silly,' he snapped. 'You're imagining things. There isn't going to be any trouble.'

'Then why aren't we going to Moscow?' She sank back into the armchair. The summer evening was dissolving into twilight and the shadowy room with its low oak-beamed ceiling suddenly felt oppressive, almost menacing. His face was expressionless. He was deliberately ignoring her. 'Look at me, Alexander.' Her voice was shaking. 'And try to look at me as if I'm your wife, not a stranger.' He continued to ignore her. Something inside her snapped. Heaving herself forward in the chair, she screamed, 'Tell me who she is, you devious bastard!'

He stared down at the floor for a moment, then lifted his head and met her gaze. His hair was tousled, his hazel eyes dark, distant, unseeing. 'You really want to know?' he demanded angrily.

'Of course I want to know.'

'Annushka Dvoskin. The security people must have found out and informed Edward.'

'The girl who took Vincent's car and stole the mobile phones?'

He nodded, drained his glass, reached for the bottle on the table beside his arm and poured out the last of the whisky.

'I wondered why you were so unhappy about my phoning the police that night.' Grace's mind was racing. Snatching at a thought, she said, 'She's very young, Alex: she's still at school. I don't think she's in the sixth form yet. And Vincent's very sweet on her. He talks to me about her. She's just done her O levels. She's . . . she's barely sixteen.' Disgust shaped her features. Voice outraged, she hissed, 'You bastard, Alex. You unspeakable bastard. You've been fucking your son's girlfriend.'

'Must you be so foulmouthed?'

'Foulmouthed? How dare you call me foulmouthed when you've been so disgustingly vile and so utterly stupid, fucking some promiscuous little rich girl who's younger than your son!' She glared at him, her heart pounding, the blood beating in her ears. 'How long has it been going on?'

He was staring at the television again. A roar went up from the crowd. Someone must have scored a goal.

'Are you deaf? How long has it been going on?'

He sighed, sipped whisky, shrugged and said, 'A year, maybe a little more.'

Grace closed her eyes, tried to compose herself, tried to think. 'Then she probably hadn't reached the age of consent when it started?'

'She looked very mature,' he snapped back. 'And I wasn't the first.'

'Perhaps your son was the first.' Her breathing had become quick and shallow. She slid a hand across her chest, trying to ease a sudden pain. After a dozen thudding heartbeats, she asked, 'And when did you last see her? Today, yesterday?'

'I haven't seen or heard from her for a couple of weeks. She's missing. The police are trying to find her.' His voice softened, lost its harshness. 'Her father was assassinated, in Athens, about a week ago; you probably saw it on television.' Relief began to temper his feeling of angry defiance. It was out now. Grace knew. He looked across at her, seeing her as if for the first time in many months. Her auburn hair was long, luxuriant, gently waved, and she'd kept her sensational figure: full breasts, tight waist, broad hips, long legs. She was a mature woman of considerable beauty. Right now her dark eyes were closed and her pale skin had a waxy sheen. How long was it since they'd last made love? He'd no idea. All he could remember was that she'd been completely unresponsive, inert, still as a corpse. She'd merely accommodated him, not bothered to conceal, even for those few brief moments, her disinterest in him. He thought of Annushka, long limbed and slender; contemplated her hard pointed little breasts and pert buttocks. She was completely uninhibited – exhaustingly so – and, despite an irreverent cheekiness, a little in awe of him. He found that gratifying and rather touching. Dragging his thoughts back to the situation he found himself in, he asked, 'What do you propose to do?'

She didn't answer.

'Edward promised me faithfully he'd keep it under wraps.'

'Who else knows?'

'I'm guessing the security people, but they're sworn to secrecy.' He continued to gaze at his wife. She'd sagged back in the chair again. She was wearing her old tweed gardening skirt and her breasts looked heavy, a little droopy, beneath her shapeless green jumper. Her eyes were still closed. He said softly, 'It was nothing, Grace. She was just a diversion. She didn't mean anything to me. There's no need for this to affect us.' He paused, gave her a chance to speak. When she didn't respond, he went on, 'It would be best if you didn't make waves. If we stay calm and keep this to ourselves it'll soon blow over. Everything will be fine. We'll be back to where we were in no time.'

Soon blow over, everything going to be fine, back to where we were: how could he be so heartless and insensitive? He really was a loathsome little shit. Her father had been right to warn her. He'd advised her to give him a wide berth when he'd learned he was an aspiring politician. She'd taken no notice. Alex was charming, full of the smart patter politicians are so good at. And he was tall and handsome. Most of all, he was tall and handsome. He didn't give a damn about the girl, the child, he'd been abusing; didn't care about his wife and sons, never spared a thought for his constituents. After he'd gratified his own desires, his only concern was his parliamentary career. She'd often overheard him laughing and joking with colleagues after one of her intimate little dinners, talking about the things they were getting away with, sneering at the stupidity of the electorate. Politicians were power-seeking exhibitionists, charlatans, attracted to risk, lacking in prudence. What man with a scrap of sense and decency would risk everything for a fling with some pubescent little tart?

She opened her eyes, saw him frowning across at her, worry and fear etched into his face. In a voice made hoarse by screaming, she said quietly, 'I'm going to divorce you, Alex. If your involvement with the girl leaks out, I'll start proceedings immediately. If Edward manages to keep everything secret, I'll take my time, find somewhere to live, make plans, before I set the wheels in motion.'

'She meant nothing to me, absolutely nothing. There's no reason why you should—'

'You're a callous, selfish little shit, Alex. You couldn't even be bothered to keep on denying it. I utterly loathe and despise you. Don't you dare try to persuade me to stay.'

Sir Nigel Dillon reached behind his back, unfastened tapes and removed his lambskin apron. He folded it to protect the embroidered emblems, the tassels, the blue silk border, then laid it carefully in his attaché case before turning towards his companion. 'I must have a quiet word with you, Kelvin, before we leave the lodge.'

'I'm in no great hurry.' Sir Kelvin Makewood peeled off white gloves, tossed them in his case and dropped the lid.

'It concerns the Dvoskin girl. I was called to a meeting at number ten. Prime Minister's taken the search out of Fallon's hands and passed it to me. Told me to treat it as a terrorist problem.'

'Terrorism? Seems a bit over the top, Nigel.'

'Girl's on the loose with a Russian woman. One of them murdered a man in a flat in Belgravia. Her father's been shot, she's absconded from secure accommodation; PM thinks we should seize the opportunity and deal with her. The terrorism legislation gives me more freedom of action.'

'It makes sense, I suppose. Here, let me help you with that, old man.'

Sir Kelvin stepped behind his brother Mason and released a sticking clasp. Rainbow-coloured ribbons slid from around Nigel's neck and a gold pendant dropped into his hand: Euclid's forty-seventh proposition engraved on a small metal plate suspended from a mason's square: the jewel of a man who has held high office in the craft. Sir Nigel slid it into a pocket in his case and closed the lid before continuing. 'There have been developments. A couple of hours after the meeting, the PM contacted me, said he'd just been made aware that the girl posed an even greater threat. He wouldn't give me any details; just insisted that the job be given top priority. And, earlier today, four bodies were found in a remote country area not far from Malmesbury. All men, three of them killed by the gun that killed the man in the flat in Belgravia. Wallets, documents, all means of easy identification, had been taken, and their two cars were registered to a bogus hire firm we can't trace. We're working on it but, as yet, we don't know who they were.'

Sir Kelvin picked up his case. 'Intriguing, and I suppose it validates the PM's decision to use the terrorism legislation.'

They left the deserted robing room with its bench seats and rows of numbered pegs, its gleaming parquet floor, and headed down a broad, red-carpeted flight of stairs. A buzz of male voices was drifting up from the club room and the bar. The brothers were enjoying a convivial moment before departing the lodge.

Sir Kelvin smiled, gave Police Commissioner Dillon a searching look, then asked, 'What is it that you really wanted to talk to me about, Nigel?'

Sir Nigel passed his attaché case to his other hand. 'I understand there's a lodge in the city that has no name, that's never been assigned a number, that's not included on the register; all of its members Rose Croix Masons, all dedicated to the protection of the monarch?' Sir Kelvin was eyeing him warily now. Nigel cleared his throat, then added, 'I understand you're the Master of that lodge.'

'I'd be interested to know how you discovered that, old man. Your information's not quite correct. There is a lodge, just as you've described, and I am a member, but not the Master, Lord Gordmoncroft's currently the Master, and we're all sworn to resist any threat to the *actual institution* of monarchy and the aristocracy. As far as I'm aware, Her Majesty has no idea that we exist.'

'Quite so,' Nigel muttered, a little embarrassed, 'Quite so. Thing is, I'd like you to pass on what I've told you to the brothers there. And I need to know if you're trying to locate and silence the girl. We don't want your people caught in the crossfire.'

'Crossfire?'

'Two Russian women on the rampage, five men killed; I intend to move an armed unit in when they're found.'

'We're not taking any action. The brothers know I went to Darnel Hall that night and you joined me; know we did everything we could to ensure things were dealt with discreetly. No close members of the Royal Family attended the party, if we can call it a party, so the brothers are content to let it rest. But they'll be mightily relieved to hear the problem's been handed to you. One can't trust a woman; one certainly can't trust a woman like Loretta Fallon. Chief's job should have gone to Marcus Soames.'

'They said he didn't have the intellectual rigour.'

'Intellectual rigour! Balderdash. Organization's crawling with chaps with intellectual rigour. All the chief needs is an ability to lead, to identify the crucial issues, and above all a sense of tradition, a realization that the nation's standing, its destiny, resides in its greatest institution. I don't think Fallon has that. She takes an egalitarian view of things. When the elite aren't respected and protected, society descends into chaos.'

'Fallon's certainly not one of us,' Sir Nigel sighed.

'Precisely, old man.'

Ivory silk pyjamas pristine, black silk dressing gown falling open, Samantha reclined on the bed nearest the door, her shoulders propped up by pillows. She was drawing the beads of her mother's rosary through her fingers, slowly, like a caress, trying to recall the sweetness of her mother's face, the gentle murmuring of her voice at prayer. Samantha no longer recited the prayers, but the words still spoke to her out of the past, faint sounds whispering through the distant rooms of her lost childhood.

The light had faded in their hotel room; the sound of traffic along the Promenade was less intrusive. Annushka was curled up beneath a sheet on the other bed, her slender body completely still, her breathing slow and regular. Another few minutes, Samantha decided, then she'd go into the bathroom and make a call on the encrypted phone.

The events of the day had been traumatic for the girl. She'd heard the crash of the gun when she'd killed the man in the field; seen the mangled body of her other pursuer lying in the road. Discovering that the phones had been taken from her friend's house had reduced her to a state of trance-like despair. Only complete exhaustion could have enabled her to fall asleep so quickly.

Samantha glanced towards the window. A sudden movement of air through the opening beneath the sash had stirred the net curtains. In the street below, a car braked sharply and a horn sounded. Along the corridor, the lift hummed, its doors rattled open, then footsteps, padding over thick carpet, approached and moved on past the door. She swung her legs down from the bed, reached for her bag and crept into the bathroom. Once inside, she gently closed the door and tugged the light cord; mirrors and chrome sparkled, white tiles and porcelain gleamed. She took the phone from her bag and keyed in a number. Within seconds, out of the silence, came the rustling of the encryption, and a forceful voice demanded, 'Where are you?'

'In a hotel in Cheltenham.'

'Anything to report?'

'We were followed by four men when we drove here. I led them down a country lane and disposed of them. I questioned one before I killed him. Leonid Milosovitch, the stepmother's father, had hired them to find and kill Annushka: probably an inheritance thing. We went to a house where the phones were being kept; they'd been taken, a professional job, two locks picked. Has Marcus assigned someone to recover the phones, someone smart enough to get there first? Has the Met been searching?'

'Marcus has been kept busy with other things, and if the Met had found the phones I'm sure I'd know.'

'Perhaps some extreme monarchist group has organized a

search,' Samantha suggested. 'Makewood and Dillon might have questioned the partygoers again, got a little more information out of them and passed it on.'

'The phones were carried away by the Dvoskin girl. What more could they tell them?'

'Another girl helped her gather up the phones. They left the house together. When they parted, Annushka persuaded the girl to keep them. One of the revellers might have seen the girl leaving with Annushka.'

'From what I can gather, the guests were out of it, as they say: drugs, drink or both. They'd no clear idea who'd been at the party, or who they'd consorted with while they were there. It was more a gathering of kindred spirits than a meeting of mutual friends.'

Samantha listened to the faint rustling of the encryption for a while, then Loretta asked, 'Have you *any* idea where the phones might be now?'

'Just a very tenuous one. Could you have the researchers check someone out and call me back during the night?'

'Give me the name.'

'Lionel Blessed. Works for an IT company called Sungrove Solutions; he has a flat in Gloucester. If they could get me his home address and his work address, his mobile and landline numbers. And some idea of his working hours would be useful, but it's the home address I really want. Tell them not to delay the call back if they have difficulty finding the other information.'

'That shouldn't take them long. Before we finish, there's something I have to tell you: the search for the girl's been taken out of my hands and passed to the Met.' Loretta paused, then added, 'Dillon's been told to have recourse to counter terrorism legislation.' There was a long silence, then she asked, 'You there? You still there?'

Samantha let out a resigned sigh. 'I'm here. I'm just thinking about what you've told me. It could be ugly if they find us. Dillon's sure to deploy an armed squad.'

'You must stay hidden until the phones are recovered. I'll have the electronic search started up again. If the phones are in new hands, they might be switched on.'

'And if we don't retrieve the phones?'

'Then I'll have to decide how best to ensure the girl's safety and pull you out.'

'It won't be easy: five men have been killed.'

'She may have to be returned to Russia.'

'Where she'll be in peril from Leonid Milosovitch and his daughter.'

'There are other options. Just keep hidden for a few days while we do another trawl for the phones. And one final thing: if there's a confrontation, avoid killing at all costs. If members of the police are killed, I might not be able to sort out the mess.'

Annushka Dvoskin lay perfectly still, waiting for the woman who called herself Georgina to put down her beads, slide beneath the sheets and abandon herself to sleep. Never, in her entire life, had she felt so alone and afraid, so threatened by danger. Violence and death were her constant companions now. Only days ago, her father had been murdered. His security man, Grigori, had been shot when he tried to murder her. A man had been deliberately run down by a car, his face made featureless, the flesh scraped down to the bone; she'd listened to a man moaning as he was beaten about the head with a gun, heard the shocking explosion of the bullet that killed him.

And Georgina had begun to frighten her. She was always so calm and unruffled, always vigilant, forever listening and watching. And she killed without a second thought. When they'd gone down for dinner she'd insisted on a particular table so she could sit with her back to the wall and survey the entire room and its entrance, her gun in a clutch bag on her lap. When they'd returned to their bedroom, she'd wedged a chair under the handle of the door. Seeing her surprised look, she'd smiled and said, 'Hotel staff have pass keys. They can be bribed.'

But she had been kind to her. Today they'd visited a department store, bought suitcases for her clothes, a holdall for the cash and documents she'd taken from the flat. And in a smart little boutique she'd bought her a dress: dark smoky blue, scoop necked and clinging, the hem below the knee. She'd also bought her some Kurt Geiger shoes. When she'd tried to pay with money she'd taken from the flat, Georgina had told her not to use it, to deposit it in a new bank account, spend it with a card. When she'd protested that she'd plenty of clothes now, Georgina had laughed and said, 'Wearing something new, something you've never worn before, always lifts the spirits.' When they booked into the hotel she'd had coffee and brandy brought up to their room, made her take a bath, then she'd pinned up her hair for her, just like Babushka used to do. And all the time she'd talked to her in that soft husky voice about ordinary, everyday things, trying to calm her, to help her recover from the events of the day. She'd worn the new dress when they'd gone down for dinner. It made her look older. Alexander would have liked her in it. Her short dresses and skimpy skirts aroused him, but she knew he'd have been embarrassed to be seen with her in a restaurant dressed like that.

Annushka heard faint sounds of movement: silk sliding on silk, the creak of mattress springs, bare feet on carpet. A handle turned, then the bathroom door opened and clicked shut. She slid from the bed, darted over to the holdall beneath a desk-cum-dressing table and slowly, silently, drew back the zip. The phone charger she'd taken from the flat was hidden beneath the bundles of notes. She took it over to the bed and untangled the lead. Her phone, the phone she used for contacting Alexander, was in her Gucci bag. The special number he'd given her was the only one held in its memory. He'd been most particular when he'd made the arrangement: they would both have dedicated phones, to be used only for contacting one another. She peered into her bag, found the monogrammed case and inserted the tiny connector.

When she plugged the charger into the socket behind the bedside table, the screen remained dark. Her heart sank. She had to get out of this mess: the endless flight from danger, the violence, the killing. Alexander was powerful, he had great influence. How many times had he told her he loved her, how much she meant to him, that she made him feel alive again, that she was the most important person in his life? If she could contact him he'd come for her, protect her, take her away from danger while he sorted out the mess. But if she couldn't reach him . . . A faint image of a charging battery appeared on the screen. It was dim, barely visible, but it would seem the phone was still working. She slid it beneath the bed, tucked the wire behind the edge of the carpet and climbed back between the sheets. It would be charged by morning. The battery was a bit wonky, but if she kept the phone switched off it should stay charged until she had a chance to call Alexander. She closed her eyes. Thinking about Alexander had made her breathless. It would be wonderful to feel his arms around her again, feel his breath on her cheek when he murmured those silly-sweet things to her, feel the touch of his lips, the caress of his hands . . .

CHAPTER ELEVEN

Samantha parked the Mercedes at the head of the cul-de-sac and studied the houses. The open frontages were shallow, hardly a car depth; the dwellings were terraced and small. A meagre tiled canopy, supported on timber brackets, extended over a plastic front door and a metal garage door. It created an illusion of width, but it wouldn't afford much shelter. Above it, two windows looked into what was probably a sitting room, and two dormers, set in the steeply sloping roof, no doubt served bedrooms.

'Why have we come here?' Annushka asked.

'It's where Lionel Blessed lives, number fourteen, next to the house where the old man's watering his perennials.' Samantha glanced at her. This morning she seemed calmer, her demeanour happier. Two decent meals and a good night's sleep had done something to dispel the dark cloud of despair.

'Rebecca's ex?'

Samantha nodded. 'There's just a slender chance he could have the phones.'

'Rebecca said he'd no idea where she was living now. And you said the locks must have been picked.'

'It's not difficult to find out where someone lives,' Samantha murmured absently. She was studying the houses: no rear access, they overlooked one another, and an alarm box had been mounted above the front door to number fourteen. 'And perhaps Lionel Blessed can pick locks,' she went on. 'Didn't Rebecca say he could fix anything? Picking locks is a skill that can be acquired; all good locksmiths can pick locks.'

'But why Lionel Blessed?'

'He was obsessed with Rebecca: sexually obsessed. He probably still is. She said she thought the bed wasn't quite as she'd left it, said someone had taken a pair of knickers from a drawer and dumped them in the bathroom. Perhaps he'd been lying in her bed, fondling her underwear.'

Annushka wrinkled her nose and laughed. 'Sounds a bit pervy and far-fetched.'

'Men can be very pervy. And I don't have any other ideas.' Samantha took a notepad and her bag from between the seats and pushed open the door. 'Come on. Let's go over and see what we can find out.'

'What will you do if he's in?'

'Get inside, talk to him, and if I think he has the phones do whatever's necessary to get them back.'

Annushka grimaced. 'If you don't mind, I'd rather stay in the car.'

Samantha climbed out. 'You really ought to come with me. We may have been followed.'

'Let me stay in the car ... Please,' Annushka begged. 'We didn't see anyone; there's no one in the road.'

Samantha gazed at her across the seat for a moment, then decided to let it go. She didn't dare push the girl too hard. 'OK, but lock yourself in and if you want me, sound the horn.' She smoothed the skirt of her summer suit, then crossed over to number fourteen and thumbed the bell. Chimes ding-donged behind the door.

'He's away.'

She turned. The old man was looking at her over a clump of lavender, secateurs in hand. A faint breeze was ruffling his few remaining wisps of white hair; dampness darkened the knees of his brown corduroy trousers.

Samantha made a show of studying her notepad, then looked up at him. 'A Mr Lionel Blessed lives here?'

'Lionel, that's right.' The old man's breathing was wheezy and asthmatic. 'He's gone to Glasgow, on a job, back Friday. He told Ethel he'd be back no later than six in the evening.'

'Ethel?'

'The wife. She likes him. Reminds her of our boy. He helps her with her computer stuff and she cooks him a meal sometimes. We watch his house when he's away.' He gazed, beguiled, at Samantha's face, at her vivid crimson lipstick, the hair of her blonde wig drawn back and arranged in a chignon, her dark glasses: Emporio Armani, large and conventional, not the ones with tiny round lenses. In a barely audible voice, he added, 'Our boy was killed, serving in Iraq. He'd have been about the age Lionel is now.'

'How unspeakable. I'm so sorry,' Samantha murmured, then asked, 'Does Mr Blessed have a wife, a partner, I could talk to?'

'He lives alone.' Cloudy blue eyes glanced down at her black and white two-tone shoes, then wandered up over her tailored suit and came to rest on her dark glasses. 'Can I give him a message? Would you like me to give you his work number?'

'I'm from a recruitment agency. We're trying to put a team together to deal with a major project. His name's been suggested to us. I'd rather not phone him at work: people don't usually want their current employers to know they're being head-hunted.' She flicked her pad shut and gave him a dazzling smile. 'We're travelling north. We'll call again on the way back, but thanks for talking to me.'

Samantha returned to the car and slid behind the wheel. 'He's away on a job. Glasgow. Back Friday evening. We'll pay him another visit then.'

'Are we going to stay on at the hotel? The room was nice and the food was jolly good.' Annushka's tone was pleading.

'I daren't linger here any longer. Milosovitch probably knows by now that his men are missing. He's sure to make another attempt; and the police are searching for us. I'm going to take you to Wales, to a cottage a few miles from the sea.'

Grace Fairchild poured herself another cup of coffee and buttered her third slice of toast. No point starving herself to death anymore; she wasn't going to Moscow. Alexander had left early after spending the night in Vincent's room. The boys were staying at her mother's. She was alone in the house she'd come to loathe: sagging bedroom floors that shook when you crossed them, low-ceilinged rooms made gloomy by tiny windows, vaulted cellars that had a strange smell and were so creepy she never went down.

The shock of the night before had mutated into a cold, seething anger and a craving for revenge. How could he have had so little thought for her and the boys? And he'd displayed no remorse – the only thing that concerned him was his wretched career. And how dare the patronizing bastard accuse her of being foulmouthed? That was the last bloody straw. What the hell did he expect her to say: you've been rather naughty, darling, and I'm a teensy weensy bit upset?

She sipped coffee and munched toast. It had been wonderful in the beginning. She'd felt loved and cherished then. He'd been attentive and he'd confided in her; they'd been partners, setting out together on life's great adventure. His career in politics had coarsened him, made him slippery and devious. His mastery of the meaningless statement, the empty promise, had spilled over into his relationship with her. And politics was such a vicious, dog-eat-dog business. It had hardened his heart, just as honest toil hardens a labourer's hands.

Grace drained her cup, put it on her plate, then carried them over to the sink beneath the window. She glanced out over the lawn, towards the rose-covered trellis that hid a modest vegetable garden. Early-morning sunlight was sparkling on the dew-drenched grass. She turned on the tap and rinsed her cup and plate before stacking them in the dishwasher.

Money was what she needed, some ready cash. Without it she'd have no freedom of action. There was about £3,000 in their joint current account: household expenses would eat into that, but she could probably siphon off 1,000 or 1,500. Her own money, the money her father had settled on her, was invested in shares, and bonds that wouldn't mature for years. It wasn't a good time to sell shares, and if she cashed in the bonds she'd lose money. There had to be another way. She slammed the dishwasher door. Alexander's cars: she'd sell Alexander's cars. After all, they were matrimonial property; they half belonged to her.

She hurried across the hall – oak panelling, blackened by age and decorated with copper warming pans and a couple of nonde- script little oil paintings – and entered Alexander's study. Framed photographs of his majestic Bentley tourer and blue Bugatti sports car were hanging above the fireplace. She snatched a glossy maga- zine from a pile on the desk, lowered herself into his chair and flicked through to the back pages. A firm called Johnson and Mullbery had a full-page advertisement and an impressive London address. She picked up the phone and dialled the number. After some verbal tussling with the telephonist, she was put through to Mr Johnson.

'How may I help you, madam?' The voice was refined, its tone ingratiating.

'You hold classic car auctions?'

'Indeed we do, madam. It's what we're famous for. On the third Friday of every month. The next one is in about three weeks' time.'

'I want to dispose of—' She turned and read the captions beneath the photographs '—a 1926 Bentley 6.5 litre open tourer with a Vanden Plas Le Mans style body, and there's also a 1924 Bugatti Torpedo Type 30—' She screwed up her eyes, struggling to read the small print '—in the style of Lavocat et Marsaud.'

She heard a long intake of breath. 'And the condition, madam?'

'Immaculate. They've been fully restored by specialists, kept in a heated garage and seldom taken on the road.'

'You have two rare and very valuable cars. When were you thinking of having them auctioned?'

'At your next sale.'

'That's too soon. They have to be photographed, catalogued, presented to potential buyers. And it might be wise to stagger the sale. May I ask who's calling?'

'I gave your telephonist my name,' she said tetchily. 'Fairchild. Mrs Grace Fairchild.'

'Would that be the wife of Mr Alexander Fairchild, the Foreign Secretary?'

'It would.'

'I know the cars. They're very fine examples. Your husband inherited the Bentley from his father, I believe, and purchased the Bugatti from us, about ten years ago.'

'Sounds correct.' She cut to the chase. 'I want them in your next auction. They're garaged in an old stable block that's going to be converted into a granny flat. Work's starting in September, so the cars have to be sold as soon as possible.'

'If you insist, but that hardly gives us—'

'How much do you think they'll make at auction?'

'Mmm . . . Not easy to say. Market's rather volatile at the moment and wealthy Arab collectors keep pushing up prices. A Bentley tourer was sold last year, probably not of the same quality as yours, for £370,000. I'd expect the Bugatti to fetch at least £250,000. But selling them with such haste won't enable us to maximize the price for you.'

'Can't be helped. I have to get the garage cleared for the builders. Will you be sending someone to look at them?'

'Mr Mullbery will want to come himself. He'll bring a photographer and one of our engineers. When would be convenient?'

Grace closed her eyes and tried to think. This had to be kept secret until after the sale. Alexander would be in London until the end of the week, no doubt spending his days at Westminster and his nights with that nubile little schoolgirl. 'Tomorrow,' she said.

'Either morning or afternoon.'

'That's rather short notice. It's going to have to be in the afternoon. Shall we say around three?'

'Would it be possible to delay collection of the cars until the day before the sale?'

'They need to be available for viewing, Mrs Fairchild. A week before, at the very—'

'The day before the sale. That's my husband's wish.'

She heard an exasperated sigh. 'It can be arranged.'

'And my husband's under considerable pressure at the moment. He doesn't want to be bothered with the disposal, so would you send all correspondence to me at Larkspur Farm, Upper Bodding, Staffordshire.'

'Of course, Mrs Fairchild. I'm just noting that down. I'm not surprised your husband's under pressure, the state the world's in. Thank God he's at the Foreign Office. Thank God his party's in power.'

'I'll pass on your kind sentiments.'

'I'd be most grateful if you would. And thank you for contacting Johnson and Mullbery.'

Samantha turned off the A40 and headed up a steep rise, cruising past the mostly Georgian buildings that lined the high street of the old market town.

'So, this is Haverfordwest,' Annushka said. 'Quaint and crowded.'

'County town close to a National Park, in the holiday season; I suppose it's going to be crowded.'

'Are we staying here?'

Samantha shook her head. 'A cottage, in the countryside, not far from the sea. Before we go there, I have to find us another car. We've been driving around in this one for too long.' She took the left fork at the crown of the hill and motored along Dew Street. Up ahead, a painted signboard extended above an archway between two high and windowless stone buildings: *James Brangwyn. Car Repairs and Car Hire.* Samantha flicked the indicator, waited for a gap in the oncoming traffic, then swept through the opening into a rear yard enclosed by garages and workshops. She turned to Annushka. 'I'll ask them if we can leave the Mercedes here for a few days; hire one of their cars to use as a runabout while they service it. We can leave the big luggage here, just take a couple of overnight bags and the holdall with your cash and papers. OK?'

Annushka nodded.

A man of about twenty-five, with curly black hair and wearing blue overalls, appeared in the entrance to one of the servicing bays. He watched them for a moment, then began to amble over. Samantha glanced at Annushka. 'Talk to me in Russian while we're here,' she said, then stepped out of the car.

'What can I do for you?' The young man had a deep baritone voice and a lilting Welsh accent.

'I'd like you to give the car a thorough servicing, really check it over: oil change, new filters, brakes, steering, whatever.'

'Can't do it today. Too busy. Do it tomorrow, though.'

Annushka emerged from the car, blonde hair tumbling around her shoulders, eyes a vivid blue, the hem of her skimpy summer dress brushing her thighs. The man was captivated. Annushka smiled. He swallowed hard, began to blush, and his mouth curved in an inane grin.

Samantha glanced at Annushka. 'I think you've made a conquest. And he's very good-looking. He'd scrub up quite nicely.'

'He's cute, but I think he'd probably bore me to death.' Annushka flashed her a furtive smile. 'Let's hope he can't speak Russian.'

Samantha turned back to the man. 'Perhaps we can leave the car here for a couple of days . . .'

He hadn't heard her. He was still gazing at Annushka. '*The car*,' Samantha repeated.

He dragged his eyes away. 'Sorry, I didn't . . .'

'Perhaps we could leave it with you for two or three days, hire one of yours while you service it?'

'Why not. It would give us more time if we find anything wrong.'

'And you can let us have a car?'

He gestured towards a row of new-looking and mostly small cars at the end of the yard. 'Just take your pick. Keys are in the ignition; bring them over to the office when you've chosen one.'

'And we'd like to leave our luggage in the Mercedes. Would it be safe?'

'Safe as houses.' The lilt made the words musical. 'Yard gates are locked, garages are locked, and there's a guard dog.'

Samantha smiled at Annushka. 'Can you go over, choose one and put the holdalls in the boot?' She turned back to the man. He was watching Annushka walk towards the cars. 'We're heading across the Continent: Belgium, Frankfurt, Prague, Lublin then Kiev. I want the Mercedes really checking over, the tank filling, all ready for the journey when we collect it.'

He sucked air through his teeth. 'Won't be ready till late tomorrow then; probably after six. And that's if we don't find anything serious.'

'What time do you close?'

'Shut the workshops down about seven, but there's always someone in the house for the car hire. Just ring the bell on the small door next to the gates. Shall we go into the office? You'll have to sign for the car and we ask for a deposit. Cost of the petrol you use is deducted from it.'

Tatiana Dvoskin, attired in her widow's weeds, was sitting behind the desk in the large cabin her husband had used as his office. Weeds was hardly an appropriate word. The black dress was an Alessandro Dell'Acqua original: velvet bodice with long tight sleeves and a multi-layered chiffon skirt. She'd bought it on her shopping spree in the Kolonaki, together with black satin and suede shoes and handbag, and a long and misty lace-trimmed black veil that made her look ethereal and mysterious. She'd swept up her hair, clipped studs to her ears, and fastened a matching necklace of square-cut black gemstones, bordered with diamonds, around her throat.

There was a respectfully faint knock on the door. At her call, Cecil Trope, the secretary she'd inherited from Vladimir, entered the cabin. She fixed him in an aloof, imperious stare, a look she'd practised in her mirror. 'Come and sit down, Cecil.'

He crossed the room, taking short, brisk little strides, and perched his scrawny buttocks on the edge of the chair.

'The arrangements have been made?'

'They have, ma'am. Do you wish me to go through them?'

'Briefly.' Tatiana laid her forearms on the desk; he settled back in his chair, and began. 'Since yesterday evening, your husband's casket has been resting in the Metropolitan Cathedral of the Annunciation. It's been placed in a side chapel, before the shrine of Saint Philothei.'

Tatiana raised an eyebrow.

'Saint Philothei ransomed Greek women enslaved in the harems of the Ottoman Turks.'

Tatiana suppressed a smile. Hardly an appropriate waiting place for her godless and libidinous husband. 'You were able to obtain a new Russian flag?'

'Better than that, ma'am. The Embassy loaned a velvet drape for the casket, the Russian tricolour edged with gold braid.'

'And the flowers?'

'White roses, as you instructed. A wonderful display; they fill the chapel.' Cecil closed his eyes for a moment, gathered his thoughts, then went on, 'The funeral and burial services will be conducted by Father Andreas Papakostas; he speaks Russian fluently. This will be followed by the interment at the First Cemetery of Athens; quite an impressive burial ground located behind the Temple of Olympian Zeus.' He reached into a folder, drew out a slender black-leather bound book, and laid it on the desk. 'I thought you might wish to have this with you, ma'am: the Orthodox funeral and burial services, Greek and Russian texts.'

'Thank you, Cecil. That was most thoughtful.'

He flashed her a tight-lipped, prim little smile. 'During the proceedings a few crew members will remain on board the *Empress* to keep watch, and the chef and catering staff will be preparing the meal for the reception. The captain, the rest of the crew, and the cabin staff will be attending the funeral. The Russian ambassador is sending a representative. Both he and the priest have accepted invitations to the reception in the Grand Salon.'

'Please tell Captain Potamin I would like him to welcome people as they come on board the ship, and during the reception I want you by my side to translate for me, and to remind me of the names of the guests.' Mourners would, perhaps, have been a more appropriate word than guests, but she couldn't bear the hypocrisy.

'It will be my privilege, ma'am.'

'And you and Captain Potamin must ride with me in the funeral car. Vasila can sit beside the driver. What about the remaining security guards?'

'I understand Vasila's going to put them in the car that follows yours.'

'The priest and the ambassador's representative must also travel in my car. I take it there will be room?'

'The funeral directors are sending their finest and largest limousine. It comfortably seats six behind the driving compartment, so there will be a seat to spare. Do you wish to see the menu for the meal?'

Tatiana shook her head.

'One final thing, ma'am, and I hope you'll forgive any impertinence on my part, but I wondered if you would wish to be accompanied by a female companion; Oleska, perhaps, the maid who cares for your suite of rooms. Apart from yourself, all of the mourners are men.'

'That's a most kind thought, Cecil, but no. I just want you by my side, acting as my memory and translator.' She smiled at him. The slender, pale-faced English homosexual, with his pointed chin and lank hair, was more delicate and sensitive than any woman. She had no need of female company. And she felt she could trust him. Since her husband's death he seemed to have overcome his aversion to her sex and transferred his dog-like devotion to her.

When he returned her smile, his thin lips parted to reveal small and perfect teeth. 'The limousines are scheduled to arrive in –' he glanced at his watch '– twenty-three minutes. Captain Potamin will come to your suite and escort you to your car. One final thing, ma'am, Bogdan, your new radio operator, transcribed a message from your father a short while ago. He asked me to pass it on to you.' He laid an envelope on her desk and rose to his feet.

'Thank you, Cecil. As usual, you've been most efficient. I'm very grateful.'

When he'd left the cabin she tore open the envelope, took out the yellow slip and read:

Unable to fly in for Vladimir's funeral. Your mother is not in the best of health and I am overwhelmed by business affairs. The men I sent to find your missing stepdaughter have not made contact with me for more than forty-eight hours. I must assume they have failed, with all that that entails. I have dispatched another team, six men this time, and urged them to be diligent. My informant reports two sightings of the car she and her companion are using. Hopefully this will enable us to locate the girl and bring her to safety. I am also informed that she is still being hunted by the police. When the funeral is over, you must leave Piraeus and sail for Odessa. I will meet you there. Your mother and I send our love and condolences.

The bathroom was small, windowless, white tiled and expensively equipped; much better than the communal showers at Martha's.

Annushka tossed her hair forward, began to towel it dry, then paused and sat down on the rim of the bath. She'd suddenly realized how much she missed the school and her friends: the bustle, the chatter, the swimming pool and sports field, even the lessons. The Georgina woman wasn't a chatty companion; her eyes, her remoteness, her detachment, were a bit scary, her capacity for violence frightening, but she'd always been pleasant and kind to her. The problem was, they were always together during the day and they shared a bedroom at night. It made her feel like a prisoner. Annushka began to dry her hair again. She couldn't go on like this any longer.

They'd had some difficulty finding their new hiding place, wandering for ages down narrow, sunken lanes. Eventually they'd spotted the sign, *Clogwyn Farm*, and turned on to a stony track, no more than a single car wide and hidden behind high banks and hedgerows. After jolting along for a while they'd emerged into a grassy basin and found themselves looking at a farmhouse built against an old quarry face. Its tiny windows were set in walls of stone; blue slates covered the roof. A hundred yards away, on the crest of the enclosing hollow, a derelict cattle shed made a dark shape against the brightness of the sky. The place had seemed sunlit and peaceful when they'd stepped out of the car. Now, with the house surrounded by darkness, the silence was eerie, the sense of enclosure, of isolation, intense.

Suddenly feeling scared, she threw the towel down and trotted into the bedroom. Georgina was standing by the window, leaning into the embrasure. Moths, mesmerized by the light, were blundering against the glass. Annushka took a dryer from her bag, plugged it in, tilted her head, and directed the hot blast at her hair. She was sitting on the edge of a bed that had a white-painted metal frame. The mattress was hard, but the sheets they'd found in an airing cupboard were clean and dry and freshly laundered. Raising her voice above the drone of the dryer, she said, 'Anything out there?'

'A badger. It sniffed around the car, then wandered off across the grass. It's gone now.' Samantha stepped back and drew the curtains.

'Can we go to the coast tomorrow, visit one of those little fishing villages, have a meal somewhere?'

Samantha gave her an apologetic smile. 'Sorry about dinner. I'm not into cooking. We'll explore the coast and dine out for the next couple of days.'

'The meal was OK,' Annushka said, gallantly. 'I've had worse at Martha's.'

'And I know the farmhouse is pretty spartan,' Samantha went on, her tone still apologetic.

'I don't have any problems with it. It's clean and dry and it's only for a couple of days.' Annushka clicked off the dryer and glanced up. 'But it's a bit strange, no door or windows at the back, everything at the front.'

'Perhaps they built it against the old quarry face for warmth and shelter; it could be a bit wild here in the winter. Or maybe they just wanted to save the cost of a wall.'

'Who chose these places?'

'The people who sent me to keep you safe.'

'My father arranged it, didn't he? Arranged for someone to come and protect me if anything happened?'

Samantha smiled. 'I'll take a bath, then turn in. We'll make an early start tomorrow, go to the coast and have breakfast in a hotel.' She slid her gun from beneath the pillow of the bed nearest the door, picked up a white satin bag and headed for the bathroom.

Annushka heard the door click, waited a few minutes, then rose from the bed. Carrying her shoes, she crept out on to the tiny landing and headed down a steep and rather rickety flight of stairs. The front door was facing her. She stepped into her shoes, slid the bolts, then released the latch and went out into the night. She'd already tried to use her phone to call Alexander, but the house was isolated, hidden in a depression, and all she'd got was the *no signal* message on the screen. The failing battery wouldn't hold its charge much longer. If she didn't make the call tonight she'd have to risk charging it again tomorrow.

She needed Alexander so desperately. He was all she had now. She was sure that when he knew where she was he'd come to her, take her somewhere safe and clear up this dreadful mess she was in. Next to the Prime Minister, he was the most important man in England. The police would have to do exactly what he said.

She was running up the slope that enclosed the farm. The sky was overcast, no moon, no stars, and the darkness was almost complete. Hidden things were rustling in the grass. Suddenly apprehensive, she glanced back towards the house. Light was shining through the bedroom curtains and there was a faint gleam beyond the half-open door. She was almost at the top of the rise now, and the old cattle shed loomed above her. Not wanting to go near it, she stopped running, switched on the phone and keyed in the number. She listened to the purr-purr for what seemed like an age, then her spirits soared as that deep velvety voice said, 'Annushka? That you, Annushka?'

Relief overwhelmed her. Breathless after running, close to tears, she gasped, 'Alex, oh, Alex, it's so wonderful to hear your voice. I haven't got much time, the phone's on the blink and I'll be missed, so—'

'Missed?'

'By the woman my father hired to protect me. I'm in big trouble, Alex, and I want you to come for me; take me somewhere safe while you explain things to the police for me and sort everything out. I want you to come now.'

'Where are you?'

'Pembrokeshire, south Wales, a few miles from the coast. Nearest place is a fishing village, Broad Haven. The house is called Clogwyn Farm. It's very isolated, hidden in an old quarry at the end of a track.'

'That's rather vague, love. What's the number of the nearest road?'

'They're just tiny winding lanes. They don't have numbers. But the last town we went through was Haverfordwest; we're about three or four miles on from there. Can you come tonight?'

'Not tonight. I've got to be in the House tomorrow.'

'You have to stay at home?' Her voice was dismayed.

'Houses of Parliament. There's an emergency debate. But I'll come as soon as it finishes. Probably arrive in the late afternoon, early evening. Does this woman, your bodyguard, know you've phoned me?'

'God, no. She'd go crazy. She won't let me out of her sight. If I tell her I've phoned you she'll probably whisk me away to some other place. When you come, you'd better be careful until I've explained who you are . . . The phone's playing up now, Alex. I've got to go. Love you, love you, love . . .'

The frantic voice faded. Alexander Fairchild clicked off his mobile and closed his eyes while he recovered from the shock. Should he, or shouldn't he? He'd laboured a long time in the political vineyard, devoted his life to it. He'd climbed almost to the top. He was well liked by his parliamentary colleagues, popular with the electorate; another five or six years and he could be Prime Minister. Grace would simmer down. She wasn't stupid. She knew which side her bread was buttered. And if things remained a little frosty in the bedroom, so what? Things had never been more than lukewarm in that department for years. One phone call, one brief phone call, was all it would take to set things back on the path to normality.

He snatched up his desk phone and dialled. Presently he heard a click, the rattle of a handset being lifted, and a sleepy, rather irritated voice muttered, 'Dillon.'

'It's Fairchild. I've received information about the whereabouts of the Dvoskin girl.'

'Is it reliable?'

'Completely. Have you got a pad and pencil? There's not much of an address, but you'll probably want to note the details down.'

CHAPTER TWELVE

DETECTIVE INSPECTOR SLIGO LIFTED his tray from the counter and glanced around the canteen. Harsh, over-bright lighting glared off blue Formica table tops, exposed the drabness of the scuffed yellow tiles that covered the floor. The place was almost empty. It was still a bit early; maybe the team hadn't come out of the briefing meeting. A rumour was going around that they'd located the women. If they had, and if they were going to move in, he needed the details. He caught sight of Len Baxter, one of the Special Firearms Officers. Blue shirted, six-six tall, shaven head, massive shoulders, he was sitting in a far corner, devouring a fry, his newspaper propped up against sauce bottles. The briefing must have ended.

Sligo ambled across. 'Mind if I join you?'

'Why should I? Pull up a chair.' Baxter folded a slice of bread, dabbed it in the yolk of an egg, then leaned over his plate while he pushed it, dripping, into his mouth. He began to chew.

DI Sligo transferred his plate of eggs and bacon from tray to table, then sat down and gathered up his knife and fork. 'Still on standby?'

Baxter swallowed, belched, then muttered, 'Yeah. Have been for the last three nights. Wife's a bit peeved about it, taken her bat home, so I thought I'd have a fry before I knocked off.' He reached for his mug of tea.

Sligo asked, 'What is it this time?'

'Two Russian women, one's the daughter of that businessman who was murdered in Athens. They've killed five men so far.'

'Any sightings?'

'No reports, but the chief had a tip-off around midnight. They're holed up in a holiday let near the Pembrokeshire coast, a few miles from Haverfordwest; an old farmhouse called Clogwyn.' Baxter forked up the remains of his egg and chewed while he mumbled, 'Just got out of the briefing. After I've had this I'm going home to snatch some kip. We're travelling to Wales tonight, looking the place over, getting into position, then going in. It's a bit serious – more serious than two crazy tarts on the rampage – seems they're a threat to national security. Vernon Greenwood's leading the team. He's driving down with Dillon.'

Sligo glanced up. 'The Commissioner's attending?'

'Like I said, this one's serious. Politicians are shitting them-selves. We've been instructed to take body bags. We're going in hard.' Baxter tapped the side of his nose. 'That's strictly between you and me, old son.' He drained his mug of tea, belched, pushed his chair back, then picked up his paper. 'Better get home to the missus.' He glanced at his watch. 'She should still be in the sack. I might climb in and give her one before she remembers she hates me.'

Sligo watched the Special Firearms Officer make his way between the empty tables. When he'd disappeared through the swing doors, he rose and followed him out. He had to get to a public phone, make a call that couldn't be traced. Orlov might decide to let the police do the job. Then again, he might put his men in first so they'd be sure of getting paid. Either way, the information should earn him a winter break for the wife and kids. Florida, perhaps. The kids were always banging on about going to Disneyland.

Samantha turned towards the adjoining bed and whispered into the darkness, 'You OK?'

'I'm fine.'

'You don't sound fine. You've been sobbing away there for almost an hour. What's the matter? You were happier today; you seemed to enjoy being by the sea, and we had a couple of decent meals.'

'I know. It was very pleasant. And thank you for being so nice to me. It's just that –' the sobbing erupted '– it's just that I don't think Alexander loves me anymore; I don't think he's ever *really* loved me.'

Samantha sat up and clicked on her bedside lamp. 'What's made you think that?'

'I'm not sure.' Annushka contemplated telling her about the phone call, about his having broken his promise to come to her, but thought better of it. 'It's just that he was always telling me how much he loved me, that I was the single most important thing in his life, but he's not bothered to find me and get me out of this mess. And I did love him so. He made all those stupid boys seem like . . . well, like stupid boys.'

Keeping her voice gentle, Samantha said, 'He's married, love, to a beautiful woman by all accounts; he has teenage sons, he holds one of the highest offices in the land. He'll think twice before throwing that away. And not all boys are boorish and stupid. Some of them are sensitive and kind.' She decided she'd better stop there. She was beginning to sound like an agony aunt. Protecting the girl was enough; motherly advice wasn't part of her remit.

'What am I going to do?' Annushka moaned. She sniffed and snuffled, then began to cry again, a low keening sound, like a small child. 'My father's dead, Alexander doesn't want me anymore. I'm sure I'm going to die. Sooner or later, someone's going to kill me.' She turned her back towards Samantha, pressed her face into the pillow and abandoned herself to tears.

Samantha threw her sheets aside, crossed a lambswool rug and sat on Annushka's bed. She brushed the girl's hair away from her face and stroked her cheek as she whispered, 'He's married, love.

He's old enough to be your father. He belongs to someone else. His real life is with them. You were no more than a pleasant diversion. Walk away from it and charge it down to experience; that's the only thing you can do.'

'You have absolutely no idea how vile I feel,' Annushka sobbed angrily. 'And he did love me. He told me, over and over, that he really, really did love me.'

Lying toad, Samantha mused, then, deciding the girl needed comforting, not confronting with the truth, said, 'Let me make you a drink. There's some hot chocolate in a cupboard and plenty of milk in the fridge. And I'll put a splash of brandy in it. How about that?'

Annushka nodded and her sobbing subsided into sighs and sniffles.

Samantha heard a faint bleeping as she slid the gun from under her pillow. She reached for her shoulder bag, took out the encrypted phone and left the bedroom, closing the door behind her. She keyed it on.

A woman's voice demanded, 'Where are you?'

'The safe house in Wales.'

'Get out. Get out now. You have very little time.'

'Who's coming?'

'Police: an Armed Response Unit. God knows how they found out where you are. Don't talk. Just get out. And stay under cover; they may come with airborne surveillance.'

Samantha stepped back into the bedroom. 'Get up and get dressed, put on something warm if you can find it.'

'What's happening?'

'Police are coming, and they're heavily armed. If we don't get out they could kill us both.'

Samantha dressed in the black jeans and walking shoes she'd worn the day before, but pulled on a grey woollen jumper instead of her blouse. She hurriedly flattened her hair beneath the wig cap then arranged the wig as best she could. Annushka was hopping around, trying to slide a leg into her tights. 'You bring the bag with your money and papers. I'll take the bags with the clothes. We've got to get out before they drive on to the track that leads to the farm, or we'll be trapped.'

The night was still and clear. Stars glittered and a bloated moon bathed the countryside in a pale, cold light. They piled the bags on the back seat of the tiny Fiat, then climbed inside. Samantha keyed the ignition, the starter whirred, but the engine didn't fire. She tried again, pumped the accelerator, coaxing the engine to start. It didn't respond. On the third attempt the starter faltered, then groaned into silence.

Samantha climbed out of the car. 'Get the bags. We'll go up to that old cattle shed.'

They dragged the holdalls from the car and began to run up the grassy slope. 'Shouldn't we just get as far away as we can?' Annushka panted.

'They might bring a helicopter with heat-seeking cameras. Out in the open they'd find us just as easily in the dark as they would in daylight. We'll hide in the old building, under what's left of the roof. If there's no sign of a helicopter when they arrive, we'll slip away over the fields.'

'Listen,' Annushka hissed. They'd neared the rim of the hollow where the slope was steeper. 'I think I can hear a car.'

They paused for a moment. Above the sound of their heavy breathing they caught the wavering murmur of a car moving slowly over uneven ground. Annushka felt a rush of joy and relief. One car: Alexander was coming for her after all. She dropped her bags and began to run back down the slope.

Samantha grabbed her arm and hauled her back. 'Are you crazy?'

She struggled, tried to break free. 'Alexander's come. Everything's going to be all right. He said he'd come for me.'

'Said he'd come? When did he say he'd come?'

'Yesterday. I phoned him on the special mobile I use just for talking to him.'

'The one with diamonds on the case? It's dead; the batteries are flat. You couldn't have made—'

'I found a charger in the Belgravia flat. When we stayed at the hotel I plugged it in.'

Samantha shook her. 'You stupid little idiot. You could have got us murdered in our beds. It's not Alexander, it's a squad of armed police.' She began to drag the girl back up the slope. 'They'll have been instructed to kill us; solve his and a lot of other people's problems.'

'It's Alexander. I know it's Alexander,' Annushka wailed.

'Pick up your bag and run,' Samantha demanded. 'Let's get inside the cattle shed. We'll watch from there. If it is Alexander, I'll let you go to him. If it's not, you stay with me and do as you're told.'

They picked their way over fallen masonry, moved beneath the sagging roof and crouched amongst invading grass and weeds and abandoned farming things in one of the cattle stalls ranged along the far wall. Through the ragged gap in the stonework, they watched a car advance on to the patch of mown grass in front of the house. Doors opened, four men emerged, then, seconds later, a van appeared and slowed to a stop behind the car. More men climbed out, joined the others, then they crept towards the house. Two parted from the group, headed down the sides, then doubled back when they discovered there was no access at the rear.

'They're not wearing uniforms,' Annushka whispered. 'And the car's just an ordinary car, not a police car.'

'Whoever they are, they're not friendly.'

Men positioned themselves on either side of entrance, dark shapes against moonlit grey stone. Another approached the door, gun in hand, while the others stood back. The unlocked door yielded at the man's push. He paused, gestured, then they all followed him into the opening. Lights began to shine behind windows – in the kitchen, the tiny parlour, the bedroom – and they caught occasional glimpses of the men as they wandered around, searching the house.

'It's certainly not Alexander,' Samantha whispered.

'And they don't look like the police.'

'No, but I think the police have arrived. Look towards the end of the track.'

'I can't see any . . . Yes, men, lots of big men.'

'They've probably left their transport near the road and approached down the track on foot.'

Light, spilling from windows and the open door, reached out towards the new arrivals. Menacing in black uniforms and black balaclavas, their chests made massive by bulletproof jackets, they assembled behind the car and van, sub-machine guns cradled in their arms. Silver braid gleamed on the cap of a man in conversation with one of their number. After a few seconds, the man with the braid withdrew and climbed some distance up the enclosing slope. Lost in darkness, he turned to observe the action.

The beam of a powerful lamp cast a circle of dazzling light around the door of the house and a voice, made harsh and metallic by a loudhailer, announced, 'Police. This is the police. Come out with your hands above your heads.'

Lights went out in the kitchen and the hall, the door crashed shut, the bedrooms were plunged into darkness. There was a sound of breaking glass, then shots were fired from the house. A shouted command was followed by the deafening clatter of a dozen sub-machine guns. When the guns fell silent, the voice rang out again, 'Police. This is the police. Come out with your hands above your heads. You have one minute.'

Annushka and Samantha gazed down at the house. Its windows were shattered, its door ravaged by bullets. After what seemed like an age, the splintered door opened and two men emerged, one tall, the other stocky; both dressed in sweaters and baggy trousers. Hands clasped behind their heads, they stood there, shrinking from the blinding light.

A voice from behind the van called out, 'Watch it, he's got a gun.'

The tall man protested, 'No gun. We have no—'

They fell under a hail of bullets.

'They didn't have a gun,' Annushka whispered, her voice outraged. 'Even from up here, it was plain they didn't have a gun. Why did—'

'They've been instructed to kill,' Samantha muttered. 'The warning about a gun was a ploy, an excuse for the group to open fire. If we'd been in the house they'd have killed us.'

The men behind the car and van seemed to be conferring, then a voice through the loudhailer demanded, 'Come out, we know there are two women in there. Come out, all of you, with your hands above your heads.' Black-clad figures scurried across the grass and crouched against the farmhouse wall. Canisters were tossed through shattered windows. Seconds later, white smoke began to pour from the openings and drift in billowing clouds across the searchlight beam.

Samantha heard the swish of legs striding through long grass, the crunch of a shoe on a patch of paving. A tall, heavily built man, the braid on his cap gleaming in the moonlight, appeared in the opening. Annushka let out a frightened little gasp and clung to Samantha. The man clambered inside, sidled along until he was facing an intact stretch of wall then tugged down a zip. He bent his legs, knees outwards, and broke wind, the sound rising in pitch from a moist baritone rasp to a mosquito-like whine as he straightened up. Grunts and sighs of relief accompanied a copious splashing against the stones.

Mind racing, Samantha reviewed the situation. When the shoot-out at the farm was over and the police discovered there were no women, they'd come up here, searching. They might call for dogs, a helicopter with a heat-seeking camera. If they were caught, they'd be killed. They had to find a car, get away from the place while the police were busy laying siege. She slid her hand into her shoulder bag, drew out the gun, then rose to her feet and crept up behind the man.

He was tall. She had to reach up to press the muzzle of the gun against his bull-like neck. 'Don't speak, just put your hands behind your back.'

He let out a surprised grunt. The cascade stopped and he began to turn. She rammed the gun beneath his ear. 'I told you to put your hands behind your back. This thing's got a hair trigger and I'm as crazy as two cats in a sack. If you make any sudden moves, you're dead. Now, slowly, put your hands behind your back.'

She groped in her bag and drew out a pair of handcuffs. When his hands appeared, she stabbed the muzzle of the gun under the hem of his bulletproof jacket, hooked gleaming metal over one huge wrist, squeezed the bracelet tight, then secured the other.

Gunfire and shouting were erupting from the farmhouse. The men, having seen the fate of their friends, had decided to fight on.

Samantha glanced over her shoulder. Annushka was still crouching in the shadows. 'Speak Russian,' she cautioned, then said, 'Bring the bags. I have to watch our friend here, so you'll have to carry all three.' She grabbed the Commissioner's arm, took a radio from his belt, his gun from its canvas holster, and tossed them amongst the grass and weeds before propelling him, flies still undone, through a doorway in the gable end of the building.

'Do you know who I am, you wretched woman?' he snarled. 'Do you realize what's going to happen to you? How dare you abuse me like this.'

She stabbed him hard with the gun. 'I know who you are, Dillon. You're the Metropolitan Police Commissioner. And I know what you are: you're a corrupt lying bastard. You don't uphold the law, you defile it. You don't serve it, you use it to favour your friends. Start walking. We're going to cross the fields to the place where the track meets the road. I presume that's where you left your cars?'

'What's it to you where we left the cars?'

'It means a lot to all of us, because we're going to take a ride in yours, and if there isn't a car to ride in, you're dead.'

The sound of gunfire faded behind them as they half ran, half walked, over rough pasture. On their left, a moonlit hedge marked the sunken track that led to the farm; up ahead, no more than a dark line beneath a sky filled with stars, a low stone wall defined the distant country road.

Breathless with running, Annushka gasped, 'Are you going to kill him? Please let me go away if you are. I don't want to see. I simply couldn't bear it.'

'I'm not going to kill him, but after I've done what I'm going to do, he'll probably wish I had.'

The police had driven their two vans a short way down the track to block any escape from the farm. Dillon had reversed his car into the opening, just far enough to conceal it. They'd posted no guard over the vehicles, set up no road blocks; this had been a covert operation, one they hadn't wanted to advertise.

Sir Nigel Dillon was sitting, in some discomfort, in the back of the car, arms secured behind his back, his mouth gagged with the crotch of Annushka's tights: the legs had been wound round his head and securely tied. He was still snorting, still making gargling sounds, as they cruised through Haverfordwest along Perrots Road. Samantha turned right on to the A40, then right again into Cartlett Road. The Riverside twenty-four-hour car park, its four floors dimly lit, rose up ahead. Samantha turned into the entrance, tugged a ticket from the machine and the barrier rose. The late-night scattering of cars became sparser as they ascended; the third and fourth floors were deserted.

Samantha parked in an unlit corner, distant from the lift and ramps, then turned to Annushka. 'Get the bags while I deal with Dillon.' She stepped out of the car, tugged open a rear door and smiled down at her captive. Face brick-red, eyes wild with fury, he began to kick and thrash around. She pressed the muzzle of the gun against his throat. 'Keep still, Nigel. If you move, I'll kill you.' She pulled off his shoes, tossed them in the front, then unbuckled his belt and tugged his trousers and underpants down to his knees. Shocked and outraged, he didn't resist when she used the belt to bind his ankle to tubing beneath the driver's seat. She rounded the car, opened the door, unbuckled tapes, dragged off his bullet-proof jacket and took a mobile phone from his shirt pocket. She removed his tie; used it to secure his other ankle to the nearside seat support. Bloodshot eyes blazed up at her. He was sprawling across the back seat, legs spread wide, trousers down, his hairy genitalia exposed.

Glancing at Annushka, she said, 'Get me a bra and a pair of knickers from one of the bags.'

Annushka groped around inside a holdall, found the items and handed them over.

Samantha displayed the garments on the front seat, alongside Dillon's braided cap, then took a lipstick from her bag and smeared his collar and neck and cheeks. As an afterthought, she tore open his shirt and smudged his vest.

'Got to leave you now, Nigel, but I'll make a call and ask someone to come and set you free.' Smiling down at the apoplectic face, she slammed doors, picked up a couple of bags and led Annushka across the expanse of concrete to the lift. While they waited for it to ascend, she clicked on Dillon's mobile and dialled. When the operator came on the line she named a red-top tabloid and asked her to put her through. After a couple of conversations she was passed to the man she wanted, and a surprisingly wide-awake voice announced, 'City desk, night editor speaking.'

'I've got a story for you.'

'Who is this?'

'One of your readers.'

'What kind of story?'

'Sir Nigel Dillon, Metropolitan Police Commissioner, tied up and almost naked in the back of a limo at the top of the Riverside car park in Haverfordwest. He's been enjoying a bit of bondage.'

The man laughed. 'You're having me on, sweetheart.'

'It's true. We've just left him. He was getting a bit too kinky, turning nasty, if you know what I mean.'

'Who's left him?'

'Me and my friend. He picked us up in the town.'

'Give me your name, love, and a number where I can contact you. If it's true, we'll pay. If you let us take your pictures and give us a story we're talking serious money.'

'We just do a bit on the side. Our husbands don't know, so no names and no pictures. I've told you where he is. He needs to be unfastened and let out, so you'd better send someone quick if you're coming. If you're not, tell me and I'll phone another paper.'

'Just hang on a minute, love.' The line went dead. After a few seconds she heard office sounds again and he was saying, 'We've got someone covering the strike at the Milford Haven oil terminal. We're phoning him now. He should be there, with a photographer, in about half an hour. Wait for him and give us a story, love. We can blur your faces in the photos. I'm talking big money here, at least ten grand.'

Lift doors rumbled open. Samantha dropped the phone in a litter bin and followed Annushka inside.

The girl let out a shocked little laugh before asking, 'Where are we heading for now?' The lift began to descend.

'Brangwyn's garage, collect the car, then on to Cheltenham. We'll spend a couple of nights at that hotel you liked, then drive to Gloucester and see if Rebecca's ex has those mobile phones.'

CHAPTER THIRTEEN

THE QUEEN BEAMED WITH pleasure. Benders had replenished her Tupperware boxes. She selected an apricot, a couple of prunes, considered the figs for a moment, then thought better of it. As if reading her mind, the butler poured coffee into her cup and the under butler placed a jug of hot milk beside it. She reached for her spoon. Philip was unusually silent this morning, never a grouse nor a grumble; no reminiscences about sausages, no talk about scrambled eggs. His aged but still handsome face was hidden behind that vulgar little newspaper he borrowed from one of the footmen. She spooned Duchy natural yoghurt on to her fruit. 'You're very quiet, dear. I hope you've not forgotten we're going to Stevenage?'

He peered at her over the paper. 'Stevenage?'

'Civic reception, then we're opening a new children's wing at the Lister Hospital.'

'Thought William and Kate were doing that?'

'He's visiting his charity for young offenders; she's visiting a primary school in Lewisham.'

The Duke's head disappeared behind his newspaper and a clipped voice muttered, 'I can't believe it. I simply can't believe it.'

'What can't you believe, dear?'

'Dillon, caught with his pants down in the back of a car in Haverfordwest. There's a great big photograph of him, clear as day, dishevelled, almost naked, private parts blurred out, women's underwear next to his peaked cap on the seat.' He read the head-line again, savouring every word: *Hullo, hullo, hullo! Pants-down Policeman, Dillon of the Met, Enjoying a Bit of Back Street Bondage in Haverfordwest.*

The Queen gazed, disbelievingly, at her husband. 'Sir Nigel Dillon, the Metropolitan Police Commissioner?'

The Duke began to chuckle. 'Pompous beggar. He could bore for England. Sat near him a few times at civic functions, droned on and on. Bored everyone to sobs.'

'Should one laugh, dear?' The Queen's tone was reproachful. 'I thought him quite charming, and he was so dignified. Very much the man for the job. And his wife was most knowledgeable; she was a vet before they married. She gave me some very good advice about worming Holly.'

'She ought to have neutered old Nigel,' the Duke muttered inaudibly. The newspaper began to shake and the sound of wheezy laughter drifted across the table.

'Your eggs are getting cold, Philip,' the Queen said sharply. 'I think you should stop reading that awful nonsense and finish your breakfast. The car will be coming soon.'

Grace Fairchild opened her dressing gown and studied her reflec-tion in the cheval glass. Losing all that weight had certainly worked wonders. Her stomach was flat again – well, almost flat; perfectly flat if she held it in a little – her waist was slender, her hips not too broad. There was the merest hint of cellulite on her upper thighs, but there wasn't much she could do about that. She turned, flicked up her dressing gown, and contemplated her pos-terior. After her eyes, and possibly her breasts, it was, perhaps, her most striking feature. And her legs were long and still quite shapely. There was a certain chorus-girl heaviness about the thighs, but most men would consider that attractive. What man would want to look at a woman with scrawny thighs?

She allowed her gown to fall back. She could hardly believe she was thinking what she was thinking, but the more she thought about it, the more plausible it seemed. And she wouldn't be the first: a while ago she'd read about some American businessman's wife doing it. She'd thought it utterly outrageous at the time, but it didn't seem so outrageous now. Losing his cars would only make Alexander angry. She wanted to make him squirm; make him so embarrassed, so humiliated, he'd never dare show his face in public again.

A feeling of excitement began to ripple through her. She'd do it. Why not? A couple of days in a spa – massage, manicure, pedicure, skin-toning, hair removal, hair stylist, make-up – then she'd be ready. She opened the wardrobe and lifted out her fur coat: Barguzin Russian sable, silky darkness relieved by bands of smoky grey. Almost ankle length and with a huge collar, it had cost Alexander a fortune. He'd bought it for her just after Vincent was born, but it still looked incredibly stylish. Things had been wonderful then. What had gone wrong? Fucking politics, that's what had gone wrong. He no longer liked her wearing it; he was worried about the animal rights people, about it losing him votes. All the more reason to put it on. Seeing her in it, remembering how much it had cost him, would be a sackful of salt in his sore and bleeding wounds. And she'd wear those Christian Louboutin shoes with the red soles and killer heels. They really embarrassed him: tart's shoes, he called them. Anything to make the bastard squirm. It really did seem so very doable, now. She must telephone the spa, book herself in, then contact his secretary and check his diary.

Annushka touched her hair. 'Do I look very different?'

'Casual glance, from a distance, yes, very different.'

'You look heaps better without that blonde wig.'

Samantha smiled. 'We've been blondes long enough. Now they've got two blondes fixed in their minds and written in their notebooks, it's time we changed.'

They'd spent the morning in a hairdressers. Annushka's hair

was brown now, shorter, not much more than shoulder length. Samantha's was black and stylish again, the hairdresser having done her best to match Crispin's more talented efforts. They were sitting outside a café that looked over the gardens at the Montpellier end of Cheltenham's Promenade, Annushka cool and demure in a cream shantung dress, Samantha more business-like in a grey suit with a red pinstripe. They were both wearing sunglasses.

'A man's taking a good look at the car.' Annushka inclined her head towards the Mercedes, parked about twenty yards away.

'A man leaning against the park railings has been watching it for quite a while,' Samantha added, 'and so has a man standing outside the bank. They probably know a couple of blonde women have been driving around in a black Mercedes coupé. They'll be waiting for us to go back to it.'

'Who are they? Are they the police, or are they some more people sent by my stepmother? You get rid of one lot then another comes looking for us. Is it ever going to end?' Annushka's lips and chin were trembling.

Samantha reached over the table and laid her hand on hers. 'Try to hold on; everything's going to be OK. We'll abandon the car, go and have a lazy lunch somewhere, then hire another, something decent. When we've done that, we'll go back to the hotel, collect the luggage and motor over to Gloucester and confront Rebecca's ex.' She squeezed Annushka's hand and rose to her feet. 'Come on. I know a very decent little Italian restaurant, tucked away behind the Promenade.'

They stepped out from beneath the shade of the awning, into the sweltering brightness of the summer day. Annushka slid her arm through Samantha's and they began to stroll past elegant little shops, heading down the hill, towards the town. When they reached the last of the Grecian figures that decorated the frontage, Samantha glanced back. The man who'd been walking around the car had joined his friend by the bank; the man leaning against the railings was still watching.

Engine purring, air conditioning wafting out coolness, they closed on Gloucester, comfortable in the sleek silver car they'd hired a couple of hours earlier. Annushka pointed, 'Over there, on your right: Melton Avenue.'

The name plate was almost hidden beneath a swathe of crimson fuchsia. Samantha slowed, then turned into a tree-lined road. They cruised up a shallow rise, moving past big, bay-windowed 1930s semis, then made a left and began to meander through an estate of smaller, meaner houses: unadorned brick boxes with plain, uncomplicated roofs. After a couple of wrong turnings, Samantha found the narrow cul-de-sac where Lionel Blessed had his home. The dormer windows and long tiled porches relieved the drabness of the dwellings, but with the garage taking up most of the ground floor, they probably offered even less space for living.

A metallic-blue hatchback stood on brick pavings outside number fourteen, its front bumper almost touching the garage doors, its rear projecting over the pavement. Samantha parked across the frontage, deliberately blocking it in. A curtain twitched in the adjoining house and the old man who'd spoken to her when they'd first called peered out. When Samantha emerged from the car, the net curtain fell back.

'Can I wait here?' Annushka pleaded. She was looking up at Samantha with frightened eyes.

'You're going to have to come with me. Things have got worse, not better. I daren't let you out of my sight.' Samantha reached inside the car, took her bag from between the seats, her notebook from the pocket in the door.

'You won't hurt him, you won't kill him?' Annushka unfastened her seatbelt. 'Please don't do anything to him while I'm there.'

'Depends how he reacts. If I think he's got the phones and he's holding out on us, I'll have to persuade him to talk. Just go into another room, but don't leave the house. OK?'

Annushka joined Samantha on the pavement. They squeezed

past the blue car and rang the bell. Chimes ding-donged beyond the white plastic door. Seconds later it opened and a tallish man with straight dark hair and wearing a blue-striped butcher's apron frowned out at them.

'Mr Blessed?' Samantha smiled up at him. 'Mr Lionel Blessed?'

'That's right.'

'We're from a leading recruitment agency. We called a few days ago, but you were away. We have a proposal we'd like to put to you.'

'Mathew told me you'd be calling.' His voice carried a lingering trace of a Birmingham accent; his tone was brusque and unwelcoming.

'Mathew?'

'My next-door neighbour. Look, I'm really not interested in a move. I'm happy with my present contract, the work's interesting, I don't do too much travelling, and I've just bought the house. I'm settled here. I'm afraid you've wasted your time.' He managed to meet Samantha's gaze for a moment, then his eyes left her face and wandered, in a somewhat covert way, first over her pinstripe suit, then over Annushka's filmy summer dress. What he saw seemed to overwhelm and embarrass him, make him less sure of himself.

Samantha sensed he was a shy, withdrawn sort of man. His shirt collar was unbuttoned, exposing a pronounced Adam's apple. His pale cheeks and chin were dark with evening stubble, his hands clean and carefully manicured; his arms, bare to the elbow, frosted with black hair. A large and complicated-looking watch was strapped around his wrist. Samantha made her voice coaxing. 'I'm sure you'd be interested in what we have to say. It's a big project, you'd be a member of an impressive team; a great thing to have on your CV.'

His frown deepened. Discomfort was burgeoning into irritation. 'I've told you, I'm really not interested. Like I said, I'm perfectly happy with—'

'Just let us come in and give you the details,' Annushka begged.

There was desperation in her voice. She wanted to get this over with. 'Five minutes, that's all it would take, then we'd be able to say we'd spoken to everyone on the list. They won't like it if we go back to the office and we haven't contacted everyone. If you're not interested after five minutes, we'll go.' Blue eyes wide, her beautiful young face appealing, she gave him a ravishing smile.

Lionel blushed. He sighed, his body relaxed and he gave a resigned shrug as he muttered grudgingly, 'OK, come on in.' He opened the door wider and stood back. 'But no more than five minutes. My dinner's in the oven and it's almost ready.'

Samantha glanced at Annushka, inclined her head in a you-go-first gesture, then followed her into the narrow hall. Lionel closed the door. Flustered by their nearness, their fragrance, he flattened himself against the wall as he moved past them. Immediately on their right was a door to what Samantha took to be a downstairs toilet. On their left, and a few paces along the narrow beige-coloured hallway, bright light was escaping around the edge of the not-quite-closed connecting door to the garage.

He led them, their high heels tap-tapping on imitation wood strip, down the side of a flight of stairs and through a door at the end of the hall. It opened into a dining kitchen at the back of the house. Annushka perched on a spindly chair, he leaned against the worktops, Samantha remained by the door, inhaling the pleasant aroma of cooking food. Smiling across at Blessed, she said, 'This isn't about jobs, Lionel. It's about Rebecca Fenton. I understand you knew her; that you were more than friendly.'

Alarm then anger flared on his face. 'What is this? You can't just trick your way in here and—'

'We can and we have.'

'And what's my relationship with Rebecca got to do with you?'

'We're not interested in relationships, Lionel. We're trying to locate a box of mobile phones that's been take from her home.' She watched him intently as she said that. Bushy eyebrows had lowered; he'd begun to glower.

'What would I know about a box of phones,' he muttered defensively. 'I've not seen her for ages, not since we split up, and that was about six months ago.' A bleeping sounded. 'That's my dinner. It's ready. I'd like you both to leave. I'd like you to leave now.' He crossed over to the cooker, picked up a towel to protect his hands, opened the oven door and lifted out a casserole dish. When he'd balanced it on the hob, he closed the oven door and turned to face them again. 'I don't know anything about phones, and I don't want to know anything about her. She made a complete fool of me. I fixed up her flat, helped her decorate it, sorted her computer, and when I'd done every job she could think of, she told me to leave, just like that. And if I'd known what she was really like, how vile she was, I'd never have got involved with her in the first place.'

Known how vile she was. Samantha gave him a searching look. Had he seen the images on the phones? 'I understand you were more than fond of her, Lionel. What made your feelings towards her change?'

He opened his mouth to say something, then thought better of it. There was a wariness in his eyes now. He swallowed, his Adam's apple bobbed, then he said, 'A while before we split up she started going out by herself; said she was meeting girlfriends, colleagues from the office. I believed her at the time, but now I'm sure she was lying. She was seeing other men.' He scowled. 'I can't think why I'm talking to you like this. I want you to leave. Get out; get out, the pair of you.' He pushed himself away from the cooker and lurched towards her. There was a crash. He turned. The casserole dish had toppled off the gas burner, its heavy iron lid had slipped and stew was oozing over the white enamel. He tried to lift the dish, burned his fingers and muttered curses as he groped for the towel. He glanced over his shoulder. 'Go!' he yelled. 'You and your friend. I don't want to talk about Rebecca Fenton. I don't even want to hear her name. She uses people, makes them think she's something she's not: so refined, so pleasant when she wants something, but deep down she's not what I'd call a decent person.'

They watched him struggling with the casserole dish, spilling more of the stew, burning his fingers. Samantha pressed on. 'You more than liked her once, Lionel, you loved her. What's made you hate her so?'

He spun round, tossed the towel down, yelled, 'Get out of my house, get out now!', then advanced towards her. She backed out of the room, bumped into Annushka who was already heading for the front door. When they were halfway down the hall, he lunged at her. Samantha side-stepped, tripped him, sent him tumbling into the brightness beyond the partly open door to the garage. He fell, sprawling, and his head thudded against the leg of a workbench. Samantha slid her gun from her bag and followed him.

Chimes ding-donged, then ding-donged again. She glanced at Annushka, whispered, 'Answer it. Whoever it is, get rid of them,' then knelt beside Lionel Blessed and pressed the gun against the side of his head. She heard the front door opening and the wavering voice of an alarmed old man asking, 'Is everything all right? We heard things falling, Lionel shouting. I thought I'd better come round.'

'I'm so sorry,' Annushka said. 'He's arguing with my sister; she's his wife. They're always like this.'

'Sister, wife?' He frowned. The girl looked familiar, but there was something different about her. 'Haven't I seen you before?' His voice suddenly became accusing: 'You're one of those recruitment people who called earlier in the week. I saw you sitting in the car.'

'We had to tell you that. If Lionel had found out we were coming he'd have kept away. He's left her and the children, you see. She has to talk to him about things, but he won't meet her, won't answer solicitors' letters. She's desperate.'

'Children? I didn't know he had children. I didn't even know he was—'

'Three,' she said. 'They have three. All small. He's just walked out and left them and he's not sending her a penny piece.'

Samantha smiled to herself. Annushka was a mistress of mendacity. Lionel touched a gash on his forehead and groaned. She jabbed him with the gun and hissed, 'Don't make a sound.'

'Always thought there was something a bit funny about him. Wife was taken in, but he didn't fool me.' The old man's voice was bolder now, more assertive. He was responding to a pretty girl in distress. 'Is there anything I. . .?' He let the question hang in the air.

'We're fine. My sister's used to it. I'm just so sorry you've been disturbed.'

'If you're sure . . .'

'You're very sweet,' Annushka said. 'I'd better get back now. Bye.' Seconds later the door closed, heels pattered on the fake wood-strip and she stepped down into the garage. 'Man next door, bothered about the noise. He's gone.' She glanced around the brightly lit space. A partition had been erected close behind the up-and-over door, turning the garage into a cosy workshop. Small hand tools were clipped to a rack above the bench, an Anglepoise lamp was casting a circle of even brighter light around a slim metal box clamped in a vice. Suddenly realizing what it was, Annushka said, 'Have you seen this?'

Samantha rose to her feet. Keeping the gun trained on Lionel Blessed, she risked a glance along the workbench. 'It's a lock. He was probably working on it when we arrived.' She noticed an information sheet in a binder that lay open on the bench and stepped closer. Large red print spelled out *Pickcraft*. Wrapped around it, forming a kind of logo, were the words *Stay Within the Law*. The sheet was headed *The Orion Five-lever Curtained Mortise Lock*, and there was a crude drawing of the mechanism, followed by guidance on picking it.

Samantha slid open a drawer beneath the bench top, found a set of two-piece picks in clear plastic cases, some smaller picks in a wallet. She turned to Annushka. 'The door across the hall; I think it's a toilet. See if there's a towel in there. If there is, wet it and bring it back.' Annushka swirled off. Samantha grabbed Lionel's arm and snapped, 'Stand up.'

He tried, but his heels wouldn't grip on the painted concrete floor and he slid back down the wall.

She heaved on his arm. 'Come on, get up.'

Heels slithering, struggling harder, he managed to rise to his feet. She waved the gun towards a chair beside the bench. He limped over to it and flopped down. Annushka returned with the towel and began to dab his wound and wipe the blood from his face. He glowered at her.

Samantha said, 'The phones, Lionel. We know you have them. You picked the locks on Rebecca's front door, went inside, had a pervy look through her underwear, found the phones in the cellar, viewed images of her with other men. That's when you began to hate her.'

He laid his head in his hands and his shoulders began to heave. 'I loved her,' he sobbed. 'I didn't realize how much until she told me to go. I couldn't get her out of my mind. I thought that if I could just get inside her house, touch her things, see the place where she lived, I'd somehow share in her life again.' He glanced up, his tear-streaked face ugly with anguish. 'I didn't join the Pickcraft club to learn how to get inside her house. I needed a new hobby, a distraction, something to stop me going mad thinking about her. It was only after I'd found I could do it that I had the idea to go in and take a look around.' His head sagged again; lank hair fell over his face. The sobbing was making him incoherent.

Samantha prodded him with the gun. 'The phones, Lionel, you looked at the images on the phones. You decided to take them away.'

'I wish to God I'd never seen the things. I loved her so much and now I can't get those pictures of her out of my mind. I opened the box, took one out, switched it on. I didn't think it would work. I thought they'd been thrown away. And then I saw her, with a man, doing things, intimate things. I couldn't bear it. I was going out of my mind, but somehow I felt I had to see what else was recorded on the phone. I'd been in the house a long time by then, so I just grabbed the box and came away.' He raised his head again and looked towards a shelf. 'It's up there. Red and gold; Marks and Spencer's Christmas biscuits.'

Annushka threw the bloodstained towel on the bench, lifted down the box and tugged off the lid. She stared down at the phones.

'Is yours there?' Samantha asked. 'The one that matters.'

Annushka moved the phones around, then selected one and examined it more closely. 'This one's mine.'

'You're sure?'

'Absolutely. It's the only one with a red case, and there's nail varnish on some of the keys.' She counted the phones. '. . . eight, nine, ten. One's missing. There should be eleven.'

Samantha prodded Blessed with the gun. 'Where is it, Lionel?'

'My bedroom. The door faces the top of the stairs; phone's in a drawer under the bedside table.'

'I'll get it.' Annushka returned to the hall and the sound of thudding feet faded as she climbed the two flights of stairs to the rooms in the roof.

'That the one with pictures of Rebecca?'

Lionel nodded. 'That's why I kept it out of the box. I suppose pictures of her could be on some of the others, but there was plenty of stuff on that one; the batteries went dead before I could see it all.'

Samantha reached into the box, took out the phone Annushka had said was hers, and slid it into her bag. Seconds later, Annushka thudded back down and bustled into the workshop. 'It's here.' She dropped it in the box.

'Look at me, Lionel.' Samantha touched his ear with the muzzle of the gun. He slowly raised his face. Tears of loss and humiliation were running down his cheeks. 'You've waded into some very deep shit, Lionel. Powerful people are searching for those phones. You must tell me the truth, or you could end up dead. Have you looked at any images other than the ones on the phone that was in your room?'

He shook his head. 'The one I switched on was more than enough.'

'We're going to leave you now, Lionel. We're going to forget you broke into Rebecca's house, had a pervy look through her underwear and stole the phones.' She moved her face closer to his and lowered her voice. 'And you're going to forget you ever saw them. You're going to forget us. We never came here. You're not going to remember a thing, are you, Lionel?'

He shook his head, buried his face in his hands and began to sob again.

Annushka replaced the lid on the box and picked it up. Samantha said, 'Try to find a bag or something to cover it in the kitchen. We don't want the neighbours to see what we're taking away.'

When she'd gone, Samantha leaned over him again. 'Rebecca was doing you a favour when she told you to leave. If you'd listened, if you'd called it a day, you'd have spared yourself all this heartbreak.' She heard heels tapping down the hall and backed out of the workshop. Lionel Blessed was still slumped in the chair, head in hands, sobbing. She closed the workshop door, slid the gun into her bag and followed Annushka out.

They circled Gloucester, then headed east along a dual carriage-way. The sky had clouded over, bringing a welcome relief from the brightness and the stifling heat.

'I felt sorry for him,' Annushka said presently.

'Lionel Blessed?'

Annushka nodded. 'So eaten up by jealousy. He'd fallen in love with the wrong sort of girl. Where are we heading?'

'Back to the mews flat in Chelsea. We'll stay there for a couple of days; lie low and catch our breath while things are sorted out.'

'I can't go on running like this,' Annushka muttered. 'I want to get my life back. And you're heading for Swindon; you should be heading for Oxford.'

'I think we're being followed.' Samantha checked the mirrors.

'God, not again.'

'I could be wrong. It's not much more than a feeling at the moment. After Swindon I'm going to head for Chertsey. We'll pull in at the Connaught Hotel, see if anyone follows us into the car park, perhaps have some tea.'

Warm summer rain was falling when they arrived at the hotel. They parked near the entrance doors and dashed inside. Samantha approached the man behind the reception desk. 'Would it be possible to have tea and cakes –' she glanced at Annushka '– and some scones, perhaps?' Annushka nodded.

'Of course, madam.'

'And could we have it served in a room that overlooks the car park at the front? We're expecting a friend and we don't want to miss her.'

'First door on your left along the corridor. I'll have it brought through.' He reached for the telephone.

The room was empty. Having settled Annushka in a seat by the window, Samantha said, 'I need the powder room. I won't be long.'

Annushka gave her a frightened look. 'I'd rather you didn't leave me.'

'Someone must stay and watch. Keep a note of the cars that come in and where they park. I won't be long.'

Samantha returned to the corridor and followed the signs, climbed a broad flight of stairs that led to a small vestibule lit by wall lights and decorated with Tamara de Lempicka prints in chrome frames. She pushed through a door, into a room lined with mirrors, where porcelain gleamed, starkly white, against black imitation marble.

After making sure the cubicles were empty, she began to search for a hiding place. There were no exposed cisterns, no pipe ducts, no niches or cupboards. Glancing up, she saw the strip lighting was hidden in a recess beneath a reflecting cornice. She went into the cubicle furthest from the door, lowered the lid over the WC and stood on it. When she reached up she could put her hand in the lighting trough, feel the warm fluorescent tube. She searched in her bag, found the mobile phone Annushka had used to video events at Darnel Hall, wrapped it in toilet paper, then hid it in the narrow, dusty space. She stepped down, took out her encrypted mobile and dialled.

After a brief wait, the cold commanding voice asked the usual opening question: 'Where are you?'

'The hotel just outside Chertsey, where you briefed me. I'm in the women's toilets, the ones up a short flight of stairs off the foyer.'

'Do you have the phones?'

'I've just hidden the one that holds the video of the killing in a ceiling-level lighting trough where it passes above the last WC cubicle. You can reach into it if you stand on the seat. It's wrapped in toilet paper.'

'Are you afraid of something?'

Samantha laughed softly. 'When I'm in your employ, I'm per-petually afraid of something.'

'I mean why are you getting rid of the phone?'

'Someone could be following us. I can't risk them getting hold of it.'

'That makes sense. I'll collect it tonight. Do you have the rest?'

'I've recovered them all. There may be images of intimate stuff on some of the others. I'll get them to you when I can.'

'Where are you heading now?'

'Back to the mews flat in Chelsea. I thought it best to get closer to you. And I'm hoping you're going to act quickly now you have the phone. The girl's had enough. She's constantly terrified. And the threat from Milosovitch and the girl's stepmother has to be addressed.'

'Action's already being taken on that. Keep the girl and the other phones safe. I'll be in touch within the next forty-eight hours.'

Samantha emerged from the cubicle and glanced around. The powder room was still deserted. After refreshing her lipstick and washing her hands, she headed back to Annushka.

The girl was looking out over the car park, a well-filled cake stand and a tray of tea things on a low table beside her. She turned and glanced up as Samantha approached.

'Anyone driven in?'

'No one's come in; no one's gone out.' Annushka's gaze became accusing. 'Please don't leave me alone like that again. I was so scared, and you were gone for ages.'

'Someone had to watch the car park.'

'All the same . . .' Her reproach evaporated and relief allowed her to smile. 'Let's have some tea, then we can go back to that little flat and lock ourselves in. I felt safe there.'

Sir Kelvin Makewood strode through the apple orchard, ducking his balding head as he passed beneath low branches laden with ripening fruit. He could see the gables of the house above the trees: white stucco and black timbering, stockbroker's Tudor. Worth a packet now, a place like this in Surrey. Nigel had been careful in the management of his personal affairs, shrewd and ambitious in the pursuit of his career, wise in his choice of a wife. How on earth had he got himself into this unspeakable mess?

The back door opened. Evelyn Dillon stood on the step and watched him emerge from the orchard and cross the lawn. Her short fair hair was gently waved, and she was shapely in her flowered summer dress. As Sir Kelvin drew near he could see that her expression was troubled; see the fear lurking in her dark eyes.

'You managed to avoid them?' she asked.

He nodded. 'Parked in the back lane, came through the orchard.'

She held up her face. He kissed her on the cheek; the gesture of greeting one gives the wife of a dear friend. He'd have very much liked to kiss her in an altogether different manner, and the impulse caused him a twinge of shame.

'Newspaper reporters and television people are almost blocking the road at the front. There's even a van with a big aerial dish on the roof. The neighbours must be absolutely sick of it. Where is it all going to end?' Her voice had become tearful.

Sir Kelvin grasped her hand and squeezed it. 'Try not to worry, Evelyn. It's all going to be sorted out.'

She tugged her hand free, then turned and led him through a large kitchen into the front hall. 'I don't see how it can be, I really don't.'

Sunlight suddenly burst through the stained-glass upper panel of an impressive front door and the air was pierced by shafts of coloured light. 'He's in here,' Evelyn whispered. 'He'll be glad to see you.' She opened a door, stood aside and the Queen's Lord Lieutenant strode into the sitting room. She called after him, 'I'll bring you both some tea,' then closed the door.

Sir Kelvin gave his friend a concerned look. 'How are you, old man?'

'Awful,' Nigel Dillon said, in a throaty whisper, then added, 'Absolutely terrible. I'm finished. I can't see any way out of it.'

Sir Kelvin lowered himself into an overstuffed sofa, at the end nearest Nigel's armchair. 'What happened, exactly?'

Nigel sighed, reflected for a moment, then said: 'I went with an armed unit to an isolated farmhouse in Wales. Man leading the team was a first-rate fellow, chap called Greenwood – you were with me at the lodge when he was raised to Master Mason. We'd had a reliable tip-off that the women were there, we'd never have got another opportunity like that again, so I thought I'd better go along and watch over the proceedings.

'Shots were exchanged, a couple of men came out of the house, then things turned nasty and the squad opened fire. There was a derelict old building on a rise above the farm. I walked up the slope to check it out and get a better view of the action. When I stepped inside, one of the women stabbed a gun in my back and handcuffed me, then they took me across fields to where we'd left the cars. It was utterly humiliating, Kelvin: me, being overpowered by a woman. And it was no use shouting, the guns were making such a racket no one would have heard. She was a vicious little bitch with nightmare eyes. When she threatened to kill me, I knew she meant it.

'They gagged me with a pair of tights, yanked the crotch into my mouth like a bit on a bridle and tied the legs so tight I could hardly breathe, let alone swallow. Then they put me in the back of my own car and drove to Haverfordwest. They went to the top of a multi-storey car park, tied my ankles to the seat supports, then pulled my pants down, tore my shirt open and daubed lipstick all over me. The bitches even took underwear from one of their bags and draped it over the seat.

'Press arrived not long after, a reporter and a photographer. They didn't untie me, didn't even speak to me, they just opened the car doors and took photographs of me: hands tied, gagged with a pair of tights, legs spread, pants down, covered in lipstick. Reporter called the local force before they left, asked them to come round and release me, said they hadn't touched anything because they didn't want to disturb evidence. You know the rest.'

Sir Kelvin eyed his friend for a moment, then asked, 'The women, do we know where—'

'Bitches!' Nigel interrupted angrily. 'Absolute bloody bitches. Spoke to one another in Russian. Older one had the gun; I think she was minding the girl. She was very calm, very professional, utterly ruthless. She'd have murdered me without a second thought.'

'How's Evelyn taken it?'

'Badly. I think she's having difficulty believing me.' Sir Nigel sighed, rested his huge hands on his knees and stared down at the floor. He was casually dressed, blue check shirt, open at the neck, khaki sweater, brown corduroys, brown suede shoes as big as boats. His usually rather florid face was grey, his blue eyes vague, his expression one of dazed stupefaction. He sniffed. 'I'm going to have to resign, Kelvin. Even if I manage to convince the PM and the committee I'm telling the truth, I've lost all credibility.'

Filled with a profound compassion, Sir Kelvin Makewood remained silent. He knew that what his friend said was true. The women had destroyed him. Presently he asked, 'Do we know where they are now?'

Nigel Dillon nodded. 'Car they'd been using was found parked in Cheltenham. One of the men assigned to watch it saw a woman and a girl sitting outside a coffee place nearby, both smartly dressed, both very attractive. Hair colour was wrong, but he was suspicious, so he followed them, on foot, to a restaurant, then to a car hire place. He put out a call for transport and a driver, and they tailed the hire car to a hotel, watched porters load it with luggage, then followed it to a house in Gloucester. The women went inside for about thirty minutes. When they left he tailed them while his partner called at the house. Occupier was a man of about thirty, said he'd been threatened by one of the women who'd pulled a gun on him; said she'd taken away a box of old mobile phones he'd found in a builder's skip in Cheltenham. The officers were sure then that they were on to something, and passed the details up the line.

'I've been at home since that business in the car park – letting the dust settle, talking to my lawyers, trying to calm Evelyn down – so Ingrams, my deputy, dealt with it. Officer in the car was told to continue tailing the women, keep them under surveillance, but on no account to approach them. I understand the instruction came from the PM himself. After that cock-up in Belgravia and the hiatus in Wales, the politicians are probably getting cold feet. The women were followed to a hotel near Chertsey, then to a mews flat in London. That's where they are now.'

'And they're ruthless and anarchic and they have the phones,' Sir Kelvin muttered. 'Just think of the people they could ruin; our sort of people, members of the aristocracy even.'

'There could be more to this than selling pictures to the media, Kelvin. They could be deliberately having a go at the establishment; perhaps they're trying to bring the government down. Trouble is, we don't know what's recorded on those phones.'

'What's your next move?'

'Probably be taken out of my hands tomorrow. Prime Minister's summoned me to number ten. I think I'll be told to resign.' He drew breath and let it out in a defeated sigh. 'The flat's under surveillance, the politicians have been asked for guidance; until we have it nothing more can be done. Arrest is out of the question. We'd be opening a very messy can of worms if they were put on trial.'

'Is there any chance they'll authorize a discreet killing?'

Sir Nigel shrugged. 'It's the only sure and certain way to deal with the situation. Home Secretary would never go along with it though, and the PM's probably listening to him now. That could be why we've not had a decision.'

'But the women have the phones, dammit. We can't dither any longer. If the politicians are tying your hands, my group will have to act.'

Sir Nigel gave him a questioning look.

'Put someone in we've used before. He's good, the very best; a former SAS operative, discharged on medical grounds.'

'Discharged on medical grounds?'

'His wife left him for a bookmaker, took the children with her. When he confronted her, she wasn't contrite; just mocked him, said he was stupid and useless, taunted him about his lack of sexual prowess. He went for her, had his hands round her throat, then broke down, thank God. Dashed out into the street, shouting and raving; hit by a truck, suffered multiple fractures and severe concussion. He was in hospital for quite a while; came out with his hatred for his wife transferred to all women. He's very disturbed and has to be carefully medicated, but he's lost none of his skills. He might be mentally crippled, but he's still a splendid physical specimen: incredibly fit, highly trained, knows all the tricks. One could almost call him a killing machine. They wouldn't stand a chance.' He gave his friend a grim smile. 'Wouldn't you say they deserved it after what they've done to you?'

Sir Nigel Dillon's eyes glittered. 'And if it went wrong, we could say it was a random attack by a psychopath under medication.'

'It won't go wrong, old man. He's never let me down. Do you have the address of the place?'

'Better than that, I've got the plans.' Nigel reached down the side of his chair, lifted an attaché case on to his knees and took out a grimy manila envelope. He handed it over. 'Only entry is at the front and it's protected by security cameras. Small enclosed yard at the rear reached through a door at the back of the garage. The living area's on the first floor: a typical stable and coach house conversion. Address is written on the envelope.'

Kelvin rose to his feet. 'I'm going to have to leave you, Nigel. I'd hoped to stay longer but we must act quickly.' They shook hands. 'Remember, you're surrounded by friends. Whatever happens, we're always there for you.'

CHAPTER FOURTEEN

B ARSTOW SEATED HIMSELF ASTRIDE the ridge and leaned against a chimney stack while he recovered his breath. Simple jobs sometimes presented difficult problems. Security cameras at the front, security cameras at the back; he'd had to climb above them, but finding a place where he could get on to the roof hadn't been easy. The front was exposed to the view of passers-by, and the rear was completely enclosed by yards and houses. He'd had to approach down an alleyway that served another street, traverse the high garden walls of adjoining properties, then clamber over outhouses before he could heave himself up on to the roof of the terrace. He adjusted the straps on his harness, made himself more comfortable, then counted the fire stop walls protruding through the slates. The flat where the women were hiding was some way along the terrace.

He allowed his head to fall back against the brickwork, closed his eyes and breathed in the cool night air, trying to calm himself. Above the deep and constant rumble of the city he could hear the barking of a dog, the drone of a plane, the murmur of a car passing along the nearby road. He felt tense and edgy. It wasn't the job – that was going to be easy – it was because he hadn't taken his medication. The tablets he'd been prescribed were the only things that brought him relief, that kept him calm and prevented the explosions of rage. The shock treatment hadn't worked, the therapy hadn't worked, only the tablets with the unpronounceable name calmed him. The problem was, they took away his edge and dulled his responses. When he was out on a mission for the Major, he didn't dare take them. Right now he could feel his heart-rate increasing, the tension building up. Worst of all, when he didn't take the tablets, he began to dwell on the past and think about Wendy. The thoughts went round and round inside his head, faster and faster, making the rage and anger boil up. It was boiling up now. He had to get a grip.

He pushed himself off the chimney and rose to his feet: tall, hard muscled, his face blackened; dressed in a black body suit, black boots, gloves and balaclava. Teeth bared in a smile of anticipation, he began to stride along the ridge, agile and confident, a dark shape moving across a night sky stained by the lights of the city.

This would be the third job he'd done for the Major. The first had been the blackmailing call-girl and her smarmy pimp, then that cheating bitch of a wife, trying to rob her husband blind in the divorce courts. Women! It wasn't just ordinary blokes like him who suffered: rich and powerful men got worked over, too. He'd been glad to do the jobs. It had been a means of repaying the Major for his kindness, for the way he'd called the brothers to his aid. They'd stood by him, got him the very best medical treatment, watched over him until he was well again, helped him recover his self-respect. Major Makewood – Sir Kelvin – had been more like a father to him than a superior officer.

When he reached the roof above the women's flat, he leaned back on his spongy rubber heels, walked down the slope and peered over the edge. A light was shining behind a window just beneath him; a window with two tall panes, one with a fanlight at the top. Obscure glazed, it probably served a bathroom.

A sound startled him. Someone was fumbling with the catch on the fanlight. It clattered open and fragrant, moisture-laden air began to waft out into the night. Treacherous bitches: full of lies, seductive wiles and trickery, powdering and scenting themselves, tarting themselves up. His heart was really pounding now. Stay calm, he cautioned himself, it's an easy job. And he mustn't forget he had to retrieve some mobile phones. He had to keep at least one of the women alive until he'd done that.

He stepped back from the eaves, climbed up to the ridge and tied one end of a length of nylon rope around the chimney stack. He clipped the other end to his harness, then paid it out as he walked backwards, down the slates. He leaned over the edge. There was no longer a light behind the window; the room was empty now. He pushed himself off, let the rope run through his gloved hands as he fell, then gripped it and swung back towards the wall. The soft rubber soles of his boots, his bending knees, absorbed the impact. With his arm through the open fanlight, he reached down, lifted the handle on the other pane and swung it open. The tiled sill was covered with jars and bottles. He laid them in the wash basin, then swung his legs inside. When his feet found the floor, he unclipped the rope, pushed it clear and closed the window.

Their fragrance was all around him now, reviving memories that still tormented him, that still caused him such excruciating pain. In a wedge of light spreading out from the gap beneath the door he could see discarded tights, underwear, scattered towels. Slovenly cows. No order, no discipline, flouncing around doing just as they pleased, making a mess of the place, messing with people's minds, fucking up their lives. His heart was pounding again. 'Control yourself,' he breathed. 'Get a grip; just do the job, find the phones, kill the dirty whores, then scarper.'

He opened the door and peered out, the whites of his eyes gleaming in his blackened face as he glanced this way and that. Faint sounds of movement were coming from a room. He crossed a tiny landing and peered around the edge of the open door. A naked girl, her buttocks high and firm, was standing with her back to him, spraying deodorant under her arm.

'Fancy a cup of something?' The husky voice had drifted

through another doorway.

The girl half turned and raised her other arm; the spray hissed. 'That would be nice.'

'Tea, coffee, cocoa; I think we have some cocoa.'

'Cocoa would be good.'

Barstow heard a stirring, darted to the top of an enclosed flight of stairs, descended into the darkness, then turned and, with his eyes at carpet level, looked back down the landing. A woman wearing a black silk dressing gown and red slippers emerged from one doorway and stepped through another. Fluorescent lights flickered on in a tiny kitchen. Water poured into a kettle.

Steamy vapour still hung in the air, perfuming it, filling it with that cloying female stink. It disgusted and enraged him. Stay calm, stay calm, he kept reminding himself. He had to get those phones. When that was done he could let go, give way to the mounting frenzy, kill the dirty bitches: slash and stab, slash and stab, cut and hack their . . . His heart was pounding wildly, every beat a reminder of what that dirty slag, Wendy, had done to him, how cruelly she'd mocked him. He climbed back to landing level, tall, black clad, menacing, then drew a long knife from its sheath and moved, soundlessly, into the kitchen.

The black-haired woman was trying to light a gas ring. The igniter was clicking but the hissing gas refused to burst into flames. He crept up behind her, wrapped an arm around her throat, another across her breasts, jerked back her head and lifted her off the floor. She began to writhe and choke.

Not too tight, take it easy, don't snap the bitch's neck; that was for later. He reached out, turned off the gas, then relaxed the pressure on her throat and grabbed a breast. Squeezing hard, he growled, 'Stop kicking and struggling or I'll—'

Samantha raised her legs until her knees were under her chin, her thighs pressing against her chest. His grip tightened, constricting her throat, stopping her breath. She pressed her heels against the edge of the worktop, jerked her legs straight and sent him staggering back, his arms still wrapped around her.

She heard a crash as the table collapsed and crockery scattered across the floor, then he slipped and fell, his head and shoulders smashed against the wall and his grip slackened. She turned and faced him. He grabbed her hair, tore at her pyjamas. She plunged her thumb into his eye until her nail scraped on bone, then tried to gouge out the slippery ball. He screamed, his body convulsed, and strong arms hurled her across the room.

She scrambled to her feet; turned to see him retrieve the knife and push himself up from the wreckage on the floor. Rage and pain were twisting his craggy features. Blood, oozing from the socket of his ruptured eye, was carving a crimson track through black face paint and dripping from his chin.

'Bitch!' He spat out the word. 'You're going to regret doing that.' Making wild slashing movements with the knife, he hunched his shoulders and moved towards her.

A mind-numbing fear had gripped Samantha. Her terrified gaze was locked on his blackened face, his bloody eye socket, his grimacing gash of a mouth, as she groped behind her on the worktop, frantically searching for something she could use as a weapon.

'Scared now, are yer?' He let out a gruff, gloating laugh and brandished the knife. 'You'd better be scared because you're going to pay for what you just did. And you're going to pay for what that dirty bitch, Wendy, did to me. She was a whore, not a wife; mocking me, laughing at me, taking my kids to live with her lover in his fancy house, sleeping in his bed.' He was close to Samantha now and she could feel his acrid breath in her face, smell his sweat. His voice lowered, became menacing. 'But you won't be laughing at me, you won't be mocking me anymore, because you'll be—'

The crash of the gun was deafening. Tiles above a worktop shattered and fragments flew. He ducked and spun round to face the door, his body tensed and ready to spring. The gun roared again and he staggered back against the cupboards.

Annushka stepped through the doorway, the black automatic clutched awkwardly in her shaking hands. The man sprang at her; she screamed, closed her eyes, squeezed the trigger. The gun roared and he jerked back and fell amongst the crockery fragments that littered the floor. He was moaning now, trying to push himself to his feet, groping blindly for the knife.

Keeping her back to the wall, Samantha circled him, joined Annushka in the doorway and took the gun. Pointing it at him, she demanded, 'Who are you? Who sent you?'

'You filthy slag, Wendy,' he moaned. 'Have there been so many you can't remember your own husband?' He coughed. Small eruptions of blood escaped from the side of his mouth and trickled across his cheek. 'You're just a cheating bitch, Wendy, that's all you are. And you're . . .'

His breathing had become laboured, his voice faint. Samantha knelt beside him and pressed the muzzle of the gun against his throat. 'I'm not your wife. I'm not Wendy. I'm the bitch they sent you to kill. Who sent you? Did Milosovitch send you?'

'Major,' he moaned. 'The Major sent me.'

'The Major?'

'Makewood . . . Kelvin . . . special duties . . . got to recover phones, got to kill the lousy traitors. Committing treason, threatening security, putting the country in danger.' His good eye suddenly opened and glared up at her; bloodstained teeth parted in a grimace of hate and pain. He made a grab for her wrist. She squeezed the trigger, winced when the cartridge exploded, saw his body shudder and blood spread out over the tiles.

Samantha rose to her feet, slid the gun on to a worktop and folded Annushka in her arms. The shaking girl began to sob. 'I heard a dreadful noise. I thought someone was hurting you, so I took the gun from under your pillow and I came and . . . and I killed him.'

'You wounded him,' Samantha insisted. 'You didn't kill him. I killed him. You just watched me do it.'

'I shut my eyes. I didn't see.'

The girl couldn't be allowed to carry so heavy a burden of guilt. 'You wounded him, in the shoulder. And the way you were waving the gun around it was a miracle you hit him at all. I killed him, just now, that last shot.' Samantha's gown was streaked with the dead man's blood. She shrugged it off, drew her torn pyjama jacket over her shoulders, then led Annushka to the bedroom and wrapped her in a duvet. 'You need something to steady your nerves. There's some brandy somewhere. I'll find a glass and—'

A bleeping sounded, faint but persistent. Samantha reached for her bag, took out the encrypted phone and keyed it on.

'Where are you?'

'Chelsea. In the mews flat.'

'Are you OK? You sound tense.'

'I'm fine,' Samantha said. 'Absolutely fine.'

'Everything's been resolved. The girl can be taken back to her home, the place called Underhill Grange. Her grandmother's waiting for her there. Marcus sorted out a visa and arranged the flight, had her met at Heathrow.' Loretta fleshed out the details, answered the occasional question, then asked, 'The box of phones. You still have it?'

'Of course.'

'Leave it in the flat. I'll have it collected.'

'The place is in a bit of a mess. And there's a body.'

'A body?'

'A man; he seemed a little crazy. I shot him and his voice was becoming faint, but I think he was trying to tell me the Major sent him.'

'Could have been Sir Kelvin Makewood, one of the Queen's Lord Lieutenants, the one who went to Darnel Hall the night the girl died. Perhaps he decided to act when Dillon lost control of things. I'll send a team in to clean the place up and dispose of the body. Where will you leave the phones?'

Samantha tried to gather her thoughts. 'I'll . . . I'll put them in the fridge. They're in a red and gold biscuit tin.'

Annushka's slender body was hunched and shaking violently beneath the duvet. Samantha sat beside her on the bed and slid an arm around her shoulders. 'It's all over,' she murmured. 'You're no longer in any danger. You can go home.'

'Home?'

'To Underhill Grange.'

The girl drew in a shocked little breath, then turned and gazed at Samantha, scarcely able to believe what she was being told. 'Would you stay there with me? For a while, at least, until I can be sure I'm safe. I couldn't bear to be on my own. I'd be too—'

'Your grandmother's waiting for you.'

'Babushka's at Underhill?'

Samantha nodded. 'Do you want to drive there tonight, or shall we—'

Annushka burst into tears. 'Tonight. Please take me tonight. I want to go to Babushka.'

CHAPTER FIFTEEN

Samantha paused beside the reception desk of the Connaught Hotel and glanced into the cocktail lounge. The red-carpeted room was deserted, save for a solitary woman, sitting in a far corner, gazing out over sunlit gardens.

Loretta Fallon glanced up as she approached and gave her one of her rare smiles. Samantha lowered herself into a chair. 'Would you care for some tea?' Loretta gestured towards a tray on the low table. 'It's still drinkable.'

Samantha shook her head, tugged off crimson gloves and laid them on her crimson bag. Loretta's cool grey eyes were appraising her. This had better not be another job, Samantha fumed. If it was, she'd refuse.

'That's a beautiful suit,' Loretta said. 'Such a perfect fit, and the red's quite stunning. Matches your car: I presume the Ferrari in the car park's yours?'

Samantha nodded. 'Car's fairly new but the suit's ancient. I bought it in Milan, three or four years ago. Versace: they have a boutique along the Via Monte Napoleone. Their seamstress took it in for me here and there.'

'Took it in? One finds one usually needs things letting out.' Loretta glanced down. 'And the red shoes are simply gorgeous: such heels.' She laughed. 'Talking about high heels, I don't suppose you've heard about Grace Fairchild's performance?'

Samantha shook her head and relaxed back in her chair,

thinking she'd never seen Loretta quite so animated.

Loretta laughed again. 'I'd have been surprised if you had. They've kept it all very quiet. It seems she visited her husband at the Foreign Office: the one built to intimidate and impress in Whitehall, not the Old Admiralty Building. He was chairing a meeting of European Foreign Ministers in the Locarno Suite. She managed to get past attendants and secretaries, burst through the doors, pulled out a chair and climbed up on the table.' Loretta pressed the tips of her fingers together and let out another delighted little laugh. Recounting the tale was giving her considerable pleasure.

'The table in there's yards long and the men were all sitting at the far end. Grace sashayed towards them like a model on a catwalk, stiletto heels gouging away at the polish. She was wearing a rather splendid ankle-length fur coat – one of the secretaries said she was sure it was Barguzin sable. When she came close, she said, "I'd greatly appreciate the thoughts of the wise men of Europe on a matter that's been perplexing me," then threw it open. She was stark naked underneath, not a stitch on. She just stood there, smiling down at her husband, hands behind her back, holding the coat open, lifting it off her backside, and said, "What I want you to tell me, gentlemen, is why my husband would cast me aside for a skinny little schoolgirl?" Then she began to strut up and down, asking each one in turn which they'd prefer: pubescent girl or mature woman.

Loretta laughed again. 'The German Foreign Minister blushed crimson, snatched up his papers and scurried out but the others sat back and enjoyed the display; I gather the Italian was very complimentary. Fairchild started screaming at her to get out, asked her if she'd gone mad, said he'd call the attendants and have her thrown out. She just kicked his glass of water over him and went on flaunting herself. When she'd had enough, she said, "Wise men of Europe? You're just a bunch of leering imbeciles, no better than my husband," then closed her coat and strutted off down the table. When she reached the end she looked back and said, "By the way, Alexander, Johnson and Mullbery auctioned your car collection this morning. It made a record price. I'm just going to collect the cheque," then climbed down and swept out. Fairchild resigned the next day, from his ministerial post and his parliamentary seat.'

'Hell hath no fury,' Samantha murmured.

'She destroyed him, just as you destroyed Dillon.' Loretta laughed and gave her a naughty-naughty look. 'That was a wicked thing to do.'

'He deserved it. If you hadn't warned me, we'd have been butchered in our beds.'

'Dillon's wife's left him. She refused to believe him when he said he'd been set up.'

Samantha steered the conversation onto different tracks. 'I didn't get a chance to check the video on the phone. I presume it gave you enough leverage to resolve the situation?'

Loretta nodded. 'It was quite dreadful. A gang of naked, drug-crazed louts, laughing and shouting while they manhandled a screaming girl. They just threw her off the landing. We were able to identify them all: list read like pages from *Who's Who* and *Burke's Peerage*. I took it to the Prime Minister in the early hours. After he'd viewed it he asked me to destroy it. I reminded him the treatment of the Russian girl had been high-handed and contrary to law. He blamed Dillon, said he'd failed to keep him properly informed, that he'd exceeded his remit; then he asked me to arrange the girl's protection and make it clear to her that her safety depended on her silence. I moved Marcus in. He dealt with the details.'

'And you destroyed the phone?'

Loretta's lips curved in a smile. 'Downloaded the video on to a disk, then had its memories professionally erased. It's been given back to the girl. And we identified the owners of the other phones that were in the box, recorded their names, stored all the images.'

Loretta lifted a briefcase onto her lap. 'Where are you heading now?'

'Paris. Resume the holiday, enjoy what's left of the summer.'

'Crispin going with you?'

'He's meeting me in Folkestone. We're crossing over from there.'

'He seems to be taking great care of you,' Loretta said enviously. 'You can send him to me when you get tired.' She took two envelopes from her case. 'A statement of the payment we agreed. It's been transferred into your Swiss account. And I also have this for you. It was sent care of Marcus Soames. I think it's from Annushka Dvoskin.' She fastened the briefcase and rose to her feet, a tall and somewhat angular figure. 'I'd better get back. I just wanted to hand these things to you personally, and to say thanks.' She began to head off, then turned, let out an embarrassed little laugh and said, 'I almost forgot. You might be interested to know I'm mentioned in the New Year Honours list. I'm to be made a dame.'

'Dame Loretta Fallon?' Samantha gave her a quizzical smile. 'Are you going to accept?'

'I have to, for the sake of the Department. I daren't show disdain for the very institutions I'm sworn to defend.'

Loretta strode off between the tables. She didn't look back. Samantha waited a while after she'd gone, then gathered up her bag and gloves and followed her out into the car park. She slid behind the wheel of the Ferrari Fiorano, slammed the door, then tore open Annushka's letter. It was brief and penned in handwriting that was spiky and bold. She read:

Dearest Georgina,

I was dismayed when you just disappeared after driving me to Underhill. Did you have to leave me like that? There was so much I wanted to say.

I'm recovering. There are days now when I don't keep looking over my shoulder; days when I forget to be afraid. A man called Marcus Soames has been so kind and helpful to me, so charming to Babushka. He has told me that the past must be forgotten: that any mention of it will expose me to danger. I could not bear that again.

I shall be in Moscow for the rest of the summer, living with Babushka and attending meetings with my Russian trustees. I may have to give evidence at the trial of my stepmother and her father; they were arrested by the authorities when the Ocean Empress *docked at Odessa. Marcus Soames has advised me to be circumspect, cautioned me to be discreet. I think he has also whispered words in high places so that I will not be much troubled by it all.*

Next year I shall go to America and read business studies at Harvard. What better place to learn than in that cradle of unfettered capitalism? I shall gradually assume control of my father's many enterprises; become one of the entrepreneurs I once so despised.

I constantly think about the time we spent together. I have come to realize how shallow my life was, how vain and superficial my attitude to things. You were endlessly patient with me, always kind, constantly vigilant. I was often arrogant and rude. I am deeply sorry.

I know now that my father didn't send you, that you came to me from some organization of the State. As Babushka says, we are all at the mercy of dark powers. I am also profoundly aware that I owe you my life, and for this, and so many other things, I shall be eternally grateful. Thank you.

With great affection,
Annushka Dvoskin

Samantha relaxed back into the soft leather, closed her eyes and reflected on the events of recent days. Fairchild had been destroyed by his lust for a girl who was little more than a child; Dillon by perverted loyalties. Power and its attainment had blunted the moral sensitivities of both men. And the establishment, the elite, the great and the good, had managed to draw a veil of secrecy over the shaming circumstances of a young girl's death.

A feeling of having been used, of being tarnished by it all, was growing in her. Perhaps she should have taken matters into her own hands, released the incriminating video to the media so that what passes for justice could have run its course. Samantha slid Annushka's letter into her bag and keyed the ignition; the Ferrari snarled into life. Still, she reflected, she'd done what she'd been hired to do: she'd protected the girl and recovered the phones. What was it that the soon-to-be-honoured Loretta had said when she'd given her the job? 'We're all whores, Miss Quest. We all have to sell some part of ourselves for food and clothes and shelter.'